The Anthology

By

Milton J. Davis &
Balogun Ojetade

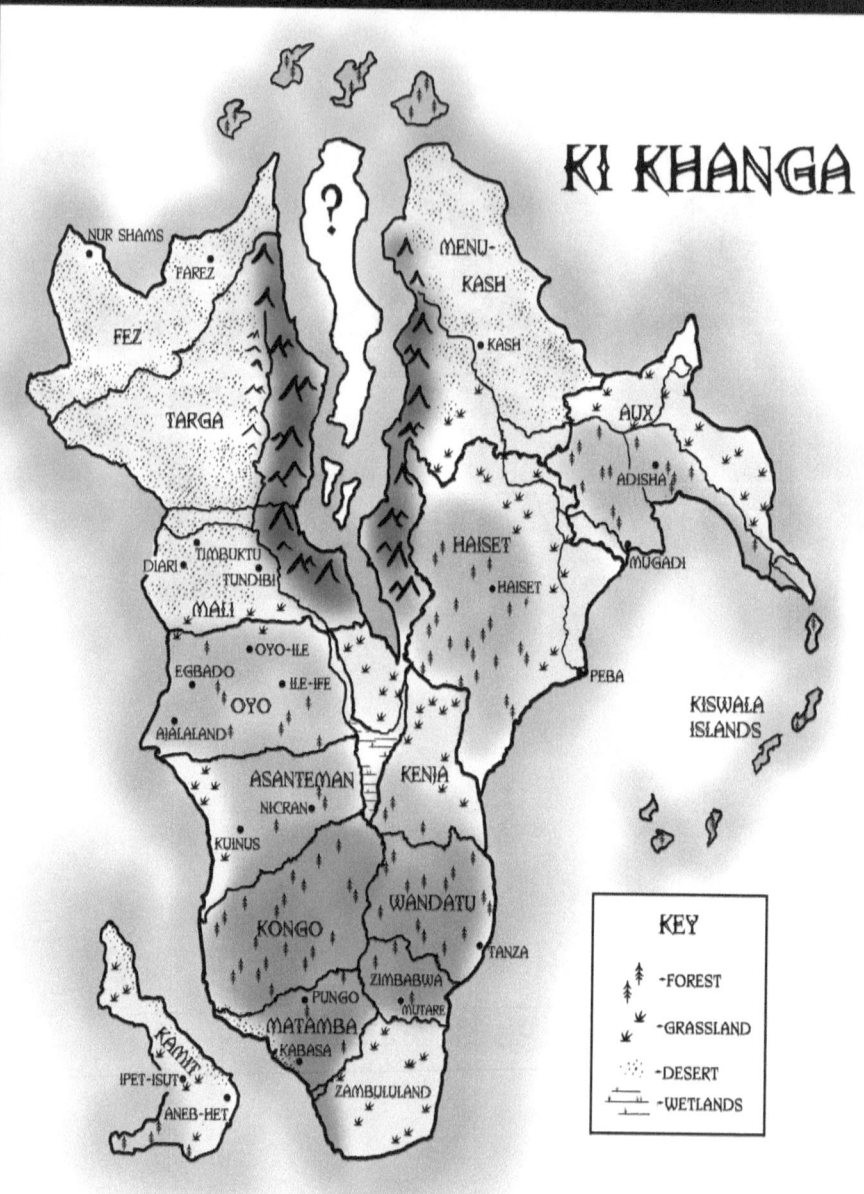

The Anthology

Cover Art by Mshindo Kuumba I
Cover Design by URAEUS

Manufactured in the United States of America

First Edition

ISBN 978-0-9960167-6-6

Table of Contents

KI-KHANGA:

ALWAYS SOMETHING NEW OUT OF AFRICA

By Charles R. Saunders

Diversity is the watchword for the Africa of the world we know. In terms of differences in climate, culture and creativity, the continent that gave birth to humanity is beyond compare. Language alone is one example: more than 700 distinct tongues are spoken in Africa. And there is more genetic variation among the African people than there is anywhere else in the world.

It is no wonder, then, that such a place can serve as a nexus for the literature of the imagination – a foundation upon which new additions to the already vast history and mythology that thrived in Africa during pre-colonial times can be built.

Ki-Khanga is one of those additions. Ki-Khanga is an Africa that could have been, located in a world that might have been. Sprung from the fertile minds of Milton J. Davis and Balogun Ojetade, Ki-Khanga is a place of magic and mystery, heroism and horror, spears and seduction. It is a place roiled by the long-reaching repercussions of an ancient feud between pre-human races and the subsequent wrath of an affronted deity. Not only does magic work in Ki-Khanga – magic *defines* Ki-Khanga, in more ways than one.

Conceived originally as the setting for a forthcoming role-playing game, Ki-Khanga provides fertile ground for Sword and

Soul fiction as well. Together, Milton and Balogun have spun a series of fantasy tales for this book that do full justice to the alternate Africa they've created. The stories take place in a wide range of cultural backgrounds that both mirror and diverge from those in the Africa of our world's past, from Khem (Egypt) to Oyo to Zimbabwe. Creatures from both African folklore and the authors' fertile imaginations abound.

The human characters populating Ki-Khanga are memorable as well. In the stories in this book, you will meet the likes of Nubia, a vengeful warrior-woman; Adjoa and Kwadjo, a pair of royal twins who vie for their father's throne; the Old Hunter, who protects his homeland from arcane threats; Kiro, a fisherman who is more than he appears to be; Shaigu and Pandare, a team of reluctant assassins; Timneet, a sorceress and patient mentor; Akhu, an inventor and animal-trainer extraordinaire; Edfu, a foppish noble who must defend a fortress against a mystical threat; Anju, a prince who lives in the shadow of a dire prophecy; Akinah, a king's daughter who is also a sorceress; Omolewa, a resourceful young woman with a ferret and a secret; Zaakah, a tattooed woman who is a potent user of magic; Omari Ket, a mercenary warrior who squeezes out of scrapes he just can't seem to avoid getting into …

This anthology is more than just an introduction to the wonders of Ki-Khanga; it's an immersion. With the breadth and depth of their new and different Africa and its inhabitants, Milton and Balogun have accomplished a significant feat of world-building and character-creation. It is a milestone in the continuing evolution of Sword and Soul.

Read on, and enjoy.

The Cleave

The Womb of it All

By Balogun Ojetade

The original inhabitants of the area now known as "The Cleave" were the Utuchekulu – a race of dwarves – and their mortal enemies, the Rom – a race of stone giants.

The eons old war between the Utuchekulu and the Rom was one of the bloodiest in the history of Duniyaa ("the World / Earth") and both sides even stormed heaven in an attempt to murder each other's ancestors.

Daarila – the Creator of Laarees and Duniyaa ("the Heavens and the Earth") – in his fury at the two warring races (and humanoids in general) for their assault on Laarees – decided to destroy all of Ki-Khanga.

Daarila's wife – Eda (also called "Odu" in some parts of Ki-Khanga; considered to be Daarila in mortal flesh) – pleaded and bargained for Ki-Khanga and its inhabitants. Daarila complied, but demanded that the Utuchekulu and the Rom be destroyed. Daarila struck the homeland of the two doomed races with His powerful spirit-axe, causing a devastating earthquake that destroyed the Utuchekulu and the Rom and carved out the island mass known as The Cleave.

The raw anger and wrath of Daarila, which coursed through His spirit-axe, possessed the flora, fauna – and even corpses of the two destroyed races – creating many of the monstrosities that inhabit Ki-Khanga today.

The most powerful and miscreant of these malevolent creatures are kept bound in The Cleave by the Tyrak [TY-rahk] – a powerful race of were-orca (killer whales), were-dolphins and were-octopi.

The were-dolphins rule the four islands above The Cleave (also called Tyrak). They are skilled diviners and wise administrators. The were-dolphins are also capable fighters when necessary.

The were-orca are the powerful warrior class of the Tyrak. Their immense strength, incredible speed and amazing resilience augment their fearsome and brutal combat skills.

The were-octopi are the psionic class. They possess great control of oceanic animals and water elementals; they also cast illusions that fool all the senses.

The Tyrak inhabit all four islands above The Cleave. They patrol the island lands in their human or human-animal hybrid forms; underwater in their animal forms; and on the surface of the water with their dreaded "Black Armada" – war galleys forged from the nigh-indestructible bones and flesh of the now extinct indigo dragons, which once roamed the farthest depths of the ocean.

The Black Armada ships are propelled by magic means, moving up to 20mph (incredible speed for a ship of that era).

Each Galley is armed with ten onagers (a siege engine similar to the catapult) per side, which fire flaming stones – and a huge ram made from the spiked skull of an indigo dragon. These ships are feared throughout Ki-Khanga.

The Tyrak keep the creatures from The Cleave *in* and would-be explorers of The Cleave *out*.

Charged with their mission by Eda – their Creator – the Tyrak take their duties seriously and execute them with a loyalty and zeal unmatched by anyone – or anything – on the planet.

Ki-Khanga is a world of heroes…a world of champions…a world of gods, monsters, magic and magnificent places of wonder… and the mysterious Cleave is the womb of it all.

Within this book are stories that the Cleave – and its offspring – have given birth to. Open it – if you dare – and experience the triumphs and terrors that are…Ki-Khanga!

Nubia's Revenge

By Milton Davis

She waited for them atop the steep hill, a battleground of her choosing. All her life she'd prepared for them. All her life she pursued them. Now she stood alone, the hooves of their mounts shaking the ground beneath her feet. They killed her parents. They slaughtered her people. Hatred rose in her mouth like a foul liquid and she forced it down. This was no time for emotion. It was a time for concentration, a time to release all she had learned. An undulating line of conical helmets broke the jagged horizon and she raised her bow. They would all die by her hand. Every last one of them.

The closest rider's brow appeared and she released her arrow. It struck him between the eyes and he tumbled backwards from his horse. Her second arrow struck another rider in his mouth, stifling the battle cry he intended to yell. Her third arrow passed through the jowls of the third man attempting to turn away. He remained on his mount, his hands attempting to stop the blood flowing from his cheeks. He was alive, but the poison would kill him eventually. The other riders milled before her, circling the one who led them. He was a man almost too big for his mount, a hard face brute covered in the shaggy coat of some animal she did not recognize. A golden helmet bordered with precious stones rested on his bearded head. He stared at her intensely, as if seeking some recognition. He would find none. She was a babe when he last saw her, if he saw her at all. Her village was one among many his horde raided and razed, a settlement whose memory was washed away long ago in blood. But she remembered. She would never forget.

She stood before the temple walls with the others, each seeking entrance for their own reasons. The Dogon held knowledge beyond all others; it was said that the came from another world and they hid their knowledge within their simplicity. Those surrounding her sought what the Dogon possessed for various reasons, but she was sure her reason was the most ominous of all. Acolytes emerged and a clamor rose among the applicants. She said nothing. The servants of the teachers approached each person asking them one questions: What do you seek? When the acolyte reached her she answered simply. Revenge.

The riders charged in unison, their leader lagging behind the wall of horseflesh and steel. She ran toward them, loading her bow as she ran. She shot the horses one by one, bringing down three before they were upon her. The first man was the first to die. She leaped on his horse, stabbing him in the neck with an arrow then pushing him from his mount. His cohorts swarmed her, and then discovered her prowess with a scimitar. Two more died, tumbling to the grass with slit throats. A blade stabbed her thigh and she ignored it. Pain was temporary, vengeance complete. She tired of the mounted duels quickly. With a sudden effort she leaped from the horse to land on her feet.

They were outmatched. It was obvious with the first arrow loosed that she would eventually kill them all. Yet they persisted. If men as vile as these could have a positive trait it would be their relentlessness. It was the reason for their conquests. It would also be the reason for their deaths.

When the others left, she remained. She made no attempt to feed or bath herself. She sat before the temple, moving only to relieve herself. Even that necessary function ceased as she began to starve. But she would not leave. The acolytes peered over the walls and shouted at her. Their masters had made their choices.

There would be no more selections. She was wasting her time.

When she could no longer sit up, she lay in the mud, staring at the walls. The doors finally opened and a robed man approached her. He knelt before her dying form, curiosity in his eyes.

"Why do you persist?" he asked. "You are dying."

"Everyone I love is dead," she replied.

"Then join them," he replied.

She forced herself up to stare at him.

"I will not die until they die," she said.

"Revenge serves no purpose," the man said.

"Revenge keeps me alive," she retorted.

The man clapped his hands and acolytes appeared. They lifted her to her feet.

"We will accept you, only to prove that you are wrong."

She managed to smile. They would fail.

The riders realized their mounts were more a hindrance than help against her. They dismounted, their swords held before them as they encircled her. Their leader remained on his mount, and expectant smile on his face. His ignorance sparked her anger again. This man, this stupid, petty man was the cause of her family's death. With only brutality and strength they destroyed her life. Now they approached her with the same weapons, expecting to vanquish her despite their dead cohorts littering the grass around them. What drove such men to still imagine there would be a good outcome for them? She pushed the emotions aside once again. Reason did not prevail here. Instinct was at work, primal destructive urges. At least in this case, they would cease.

They bathed her, fed her and gave her robes. She joined the other students recently accepted and learned the ways of the Dogon. They taught of the world from which they came and of their wish to one day return. They taught them of healing herbs and medicines. They taught them the ways of wrestling and weapons, because only a mind free of fear can reach the highest levels of thought. She learned and she excelled. Six years after entering the walls of the temple she stood before the high priest, the best among an elite class, and the first among the most skilled. The priest stepped down from his simple chair and carried the robe of priest to her, the first step toward priesthood. He extended to her.

"Have you taught me all there is to know?" she asked.

The priest was startled by her question. "Yes. We hold nothing back. Truth cannot be owned."

"Then I will go," she said. "I have men to kill."

She turned and walked away. No one attempted to stop her.

"Revenge will leave you with nothing!" the high priest shouted.

"We will see," she whispered.

They circled her and she circled with them, bow in her left hand, dagger in her right. One darted in and she danced away, fast enough to avoid his grasp but slow enough to allow him to grab her skirt. He ripped it away, revealing her near nakedness. The anger of their comrades' deaths gave way to unbridled lust. She looked at them with a sensuous smirk. Let them lust. Lust would break their focus. Lust would make them careless. Use all your weapons, her teachers instructed her. Death comes in many forms. The man held the skirt up like a trophy then pressed it to his face, inhaling deeply. When he removed it he leered at her then pounced. Her dagger flew from her hand as he jumped, finding its place in his neck. His scimitar was in her hand before the others could attack. She spun among them, her movements both sensuous and deadly. When she ceased her dance they all lay dead. She sauntered to her skirt then slowly tied it around her waist as the last man looked on. She took a stance as he finally approached, patting his palm with the flat of his blade. His confidence sickened her.

"Very good," he said. "I'm impressed. I take it the Dogon were saddened by your departure, as they were when I left their pitiful temple."

His words startled her but she did not flinch.

"The Dogon think they can pacify us by teaching us their

ways. They think by teaching us the secrets of the world we will immerse ourselves in more cerebral pursuits. But there is one flaw in their logic."

He raised his sword to guard position, as did she.

"Our bodies are only vessels to them," he said. "They fill them, but they do not *feel* them. They don't understand our need for emotions. They don't share our desire for pleasure and power...or revenge. With their knowledge a man or woman can achieve all their desires."

Their swords clashed. He was powerful, much more powerful than she expected. She quickly adjusted, parrying his pounding blows and dodging his quick kicks. She suspected he left the temple once he gained his martial skills, thinking it was all he needed to fulfill his dreams. She watched his eyes as they fought, the fatigue and frustration growing with every blow deflected. Tension filled his face, his teeth gritted. She smiled and he roared. Speed accompanied his thrust and it slipped by her guard. The edge of his blade creased her stomach as she pivoted away. It was a cut that should have disemboweled her. Instead a thin red line appeared.

His eyes bulged. "You should be..."

She drove her blade into his stomach. "Dead?"

She twisted her blade then ripped it from his body. He wavered then fell. She stood over him.

"You left the temple too soon," she said. "There are herbs that toughen the skin and muscles until they are almost like iron."

She spat on his face and stabbed him again and again. She stabbed him for her mother and father, her sisters and brothers. She stabbed him for every person in her village. She stabbed him long after life left his body. When she ceased her arm quaked and her legs went limp. She fell to her knees beside him, her body overcome by deep sobs. She fell forward, her face in her hands. When her sobbing ceased, she came to her feet empty. She dropped the sword then took off her wrist protectors. She removed the quiver from her back and placed it beside her bow. The stench of death had summoned its followers; vultures and crows circled overhead as jackals lurked on the horizon. The high priest's wisdom appeared in her mind and a melancholy smile came to her. Revenge did not heal. Death did not cleanse. She was still alone.

She stood before the temple as she had years ago, filthy and starving. This time the high priest emerged, shuffling to her prone form. She looked into his eyes and he frowned.

"Why have you come back?" he asked.

"Revenge was not enough," she said.

"What do you want from us now?" he asked.

"I wish to learn. I wish to heal. I wish to live."

He reached down to her and helped her stand. As they walked together to the temple entrance she knew she would leave again. But this time she would leave for the right reasons. She would teach. She would heal. She would live.

How Adjoa Became King

By Balogun Ojetade

Adjoa seemed to glow as the noonday sun reflected off of the flecks of glittering gold on her ebony skin. She wiped the single tear, which rolled down her cheeks, with the back of her hand as she swallowed her sobs.

For the first time in eleven years, she knelt at the feet of her father, which were wrapped in strips of white, cotton cloth.

For the first time in eleven years, she held her father's hands, which were now ice-cold.

For the first time in eleven years, she stared into her father's eyes, but his eyes were now dull and devoid of life.

Kwame Opare – the great Asantehene of the mighty nation of Asanteman – had war-danced out of this earthly plane and was now attending court with other ancestral kings.

As his daughter – and as an Okomfo of great skill – Adjoa had been given the honor of washing her father in the proper medicines and wrapping him in the traditional white cloth to ensure a smooth journey to Soro – the domain of Spirit.

Someone knelt beside her. The person smelled pleasantly of coconut and honey with a hint of cinnamon. Adjoa turned her head toward the person and stared into a face much like hers. "Kwadjo?"

"The Nananom be praised, I thought it was you!" the man replied, embracing her. "Yes, it is I – Kwadjo – son of Asantehene Kwame Opare! You have grown into a beautiful woman, dear sister!"

"You only say that because we're twins," Adjoa chuckled. "If *I* am beautiful, then you – by default – must be also."

Kwadjo leaped to his feet and turned slowly. His crimson and gold kente cloth lapa, accessorized with a gold necklace and headband, accentuated Kwadjo's flawless, burnt sienna skin.

"Well…aren't I?"

"Yes, brother," Adjoa giggled. "You will make a fine husband for one – or more – of the mighty sisters of Asanteman."

"No, Adjoa," Kwadjo said, shaking his smooth, bald head. "Eleven years in Fez has turned my tastes toward…*fairer* things."

"Fairer?" Adjoa said confused. "Please, explain."

"There will be plenty time for that," Kwadjo said, dismissing Adjoa's inquiry with a wave of his hand. "Tell me about *you*, how have your priesthood studies progressed?"

"I was fully initiated as an Okomfo two years after we left the palace," Adjoa replied. Recently, I was enstooled as a Chief Priest.

"Chief Priest? Congratulations!" Kwadjo said. "Nana Yaa really pushed you. That old woman can be brutal."

"Our *grandmother* is actually kind to a fault," Adjoa replied. "She did push me, though."

"Well, as for me," Kwadjo said. "I was recently promoted to Master Sorcerer, Third Grade."

"Congratulations!" Adjoa said. "Third Grade…I assume that is really good."

"Ah, I forget how uninformed the Asante are," Kwadjo said smugly. "Master Sorcerer, Third Grade is the fifth highest rank in the Sorcerer's Guild of Fez!"

"Good, then." Adjoa replied.

Kwadjo placed a hand on Adjoa's shoulder. He inhaled deeply and shook his head. "You know, at first, I was taken aback when grandmother chose *you* for the Afa priesthood and not me." Kwadjo slid his hand from Adjoa's shoulder and turned his palms toward each other. A bolt of electricity zigzagged back and forth between his hands.

"Now, however, I realize how stifling the priesthood can

be. True expression of Yao lies in the Arcane – not the Divine."

Adjoa frowned. "Nonsense! How can you…"

A firm hand on her shoulder haled Adjoa in mid-sentence.

"Children…children; enough chat. We have work to do!"

Adjoa and her brother turned to face a petite, elderly woman with tightly braided white hair.

"Greetings, Nana Adjoa…Kwadjo," the woman said jovially. "I am Senior Obirempon, Akosua Boateng."

Adjoa knelt before the Senior Obirempon. Kwadjo nodded his head, but did not kneel. Akosua raised Adjoa gently. She then, shot a glance at Kwadjo and shook her head. Kwadjo shrugged apathetically.

"You have come to announce the candidate for Asantehene, no doubt." Adjoa said.

"Yes…and no," Akosua replied. "Come with me."

The little woman took each twin by a wrist and walked them briskly toward the drummers, who were beating a war rhythm in honor of Asantehene Opare. Akosua stood before the drummers and raised both hands above her head. The drumming immediately ceased.

"Agoh!" Akosua shouted.

"Ameh!" The dense crowd of citizens replied in unison as they gave the Senior Obirempon their full attention.

Akosua gestured toward a pair of ivory stools, which flanked the Sika'dja – the sacred golden stool of Asanteman which gave the Asantehene the combined power of all the souls of the mighty Asante, past and present. Adjoa sat on the stool to the right of the Sika'dja. Kwadjo sat on the left.

"Mighty Asante," the Senior Obirempon began. "Today, we celebrate the transition of our brother…our king…Asantehene Kwame Opare!"

The Asante cheered passionately – their powerful voices in harmony with the bell like jingling of their gold necklaces, bracelets, anklets and belts.

"To add to this momentous occasion, we present you with not one, but *two* candidates for kingship!"

The crowd cheered louder.

"While two candidates are rare, rarer still are the fact that both candidates are siblings – twins at that – and are the children of our beloved former Asantehene!" Akosua said.

The old woman placed a hand under the arm of each twin and helped them to their feet. "As the Nananom – our venerable ancestors – have decreed, the twins will prove their merit in a contest of will and skill. The winner shall be appointed our next Asantehene of Asanteman!"

Adjoa exchanged a quick glance with Kwadjo as the Asante cheered them on.

"A contest?" She whispered.

Kwadjo replied with a broad smile. "Exciting, isn't it?"

****

Eda forest was abuzz with activity. Children chased each other around groups of women who were selling well-crafted gold jewelry and kente cloth sewn in bright colors and intricate patterns. Drummers and wrestlers entertained the teeming throng of citizens who had come to witness the contest between the twins. Adjoa and Kwadjo walked to the center of the gathering, led by Senior Obirempon Akosua. The drumming, chatter and wrestling came to a sudden halt.

"Mighty Asante," Akosua began. "Turn your gaze toward the flora to the north."

Adjoa followed the Senior Obirempon's finger, which pointed at a pair of massive trees in the distance.

"Follow me," Akosua commanded. "But I warn you – keep your children close."

The crowd marched behind Akosua. Adjoa felt more and more nervous with each brisk step.

Kwadjo – on the other hand – seemed to take everything in stride, tossing ginger candy to the children and flirting with the young women – who all competed for his attention.

Akosua raised her fists skyward and everyone stopped in their tracks. Fearful gasps and inquisitive whispers echoed throughout the forest. Adjoa was sickened by what she saw – the twin trees were massive monstrosities, each standing ninety feet tall and forty feet in circumference. Their branches looked like the gnarled legs of a spider and etched into their coarse, black trunks were immense faces with fiendish, human-like expressions.

"Witness the Bagya Dua – the grotesque and wicked Blood Trees," Akosua said. "Our beloved Asantehene was riding through this forest, giving chase to a gazelle he had been hunting for three days."

Adjoa listened intently. She knew her father had been strangely exsanguinated after falling from his horse, but she had not been given any details.

"The Asantehene would often hunt alone – he found peace in the solitude," Akosua continued. "

"But he was tired and did not realize that he had stumbled into the abode of the Bagya Dua until it was too late. One of the creatures snatched the Asantehene out of his saddle; the other creature captured his steed. The wicked visages of the trees then drained every drop of the Asantehene's blood and the blood of his poor horse. The trees then hurled the carcasses of their prey to this very spot where we stand. A search party found them here."

"I say we kill the damnable things!" Kwadjo spat.

"You have the right idea, son," Akosua said. "However, *we* aren't going to kill them; *you* and your sister are."

"Come again?" Adjoa inquired.

"This is the contest," the Senior Obirempon replied. "You both must destroy one of those monsters each. If one of you fails, the other will be named Asantehene. If you both succeed, or you both fail, the winner will be decided by a fight to the death."

"Come *again*?" Adjoa repeated.

"Such is the decree of the ancestors!" Akosua replied.

Well-trained in the ways of the ancestors, Adjoa knew Akosua's words rang true. The Asante were warriors and the king of the Asante had to be a warrior without peer.

"Either contest is fine with me," Kwadjo said smugly.

Adjoa rolled her eyes.

"Let the contest begin!" Akosua shouted.

A thunderous applause rose from the crowd.

"Adjoa, as the elder twin, you decide who goes first," Akosua said.

Adjoa gestured toward her brother with a thrust of her fingertips, which made the sleeve of her blue kente dress sound off with a crisp pop. "Since he is so eager, let my brother go first."

"It is an elder who insults a youth that a youth insults," Kwadjo said, quoting a proverb from the venerable ancestors.

"Do not lay hands on a load you cannot lift," Adjoa shot back.

Kwadjo pounded his left palm with his right fist as he glared menacingly at Adjoa. "Do not conduct a feud with an animal in a halfhearted manner; if you find a *snail*, hit it with a cutlass!"

Adjoa dismissed Kwadjo with a wave of her hand. "A man with crossbows in his *eyes* cannot kill even a one-legged duck!"

The crowd burst into laughter.

Kwadjo lunged toward his sister, but Akosua leapt between the twins, halting Kwadjo's advance with a stiff palm to his chest.

"Enough!" Akosua ordered. "Direct your yao toward the destruction of that accursed tree!"

Kwadjo nodded and approached the Bagya Dua, stopping several yards from the creature in order to avoid its deadly grasp. He stood with his feet slightly wider than the width of his narrow shoulders; he raised his hands until they were in line with his sternum and then he turned his palms outward, toward the Blood Tree.

The young sorcerer began to speak in an arcane tongue unfamiliar to Adjoa's ears. A moment later, a swirling, blue and gold ball of light appeared out of the ether in front of Kwadjo's palms.

Kwadjo thrust his hands forward and the ball of light torpedoed toward the Bagya Dua that consumed Asantehene Opare's horse. The ball of light flew into the open maw of the tree's "face". A moment later, the trunk of the tree corkscrewed violently. Its branches braided themselves together and then wrapped themselves around its warped trunk. The citizens watched the spectacle in stunned silence. Suddenly, the tree flew into the air, its blood-red roots pulling a large chunk of earth with it. The tree landed – with a loud thud – an acre away.

The crowd erupted in cheers and rousing applause. Kwadjo smiled broadly and blew kisses at the women as he strutted back toward the Senior Obirempon and Adjoa.

"Your turn, dear sister," Kwadjo crooned.

"Adjoa looked down at the indigo, leather pouch dangling at the middle of her chest. She removed it and then poured its contents – a dull, yellow powder – into her left palm. Adjoa etched ancient sigils into the powder with her fingertips and then chanted a prayer over her palm. She formed a tight fist around the powder, took a deep breath and then exploded forward into a full sprint toward the remaining Blood Tree. The branches of the tree lashed out, attempting to seize her in their terrible grasp. Adjoa leapt, ducked and somersaulted, lithely avoiding the branches.

The crowd cheered her on. Adjoa reached the trunk of the Bagya Dua. She opened her fist and then blew the powder onto the tree.

Adjoa spun on her heels and took off – again dodging the vicious branches of the monstrosity. Returning to Akosua's side, Adjoa nodded as the crowd cheered. The cheering diminished to silence as several minutes passed with nothing happening.

"So, how long will it be before your Bagya Dua is destroyed?" Akosua asked.

Adjoa lowered her gaze. "Twenty-eight days," she whispered.

The Senior Obirempon slipped the tip of her index finger into her ear and wiggled it around as if she was trying to remove an obstruction. "I'm sorry…I must have misheard you. How long did you say?"

"Twenty-eight days," Adjoa shouted.

The forest shook with the crowd's laughter. Adjoa noticed that even the Blood Tree's expression had changed from a vicious snarl into an amused grin.

Akosua raised her fist and everyone fell silent. "Are you making mockery of this contest and of the memory of your father?"

"No, I am not," Adjoa replied. "Spirit does not submit to man's time."

"Alright then, we will return in twenty-eight days," Akosua said. "If the tree still stands during that time, Kwadjo will be enstooled as Asantehene...and *you* will be executed!"

"Fair enough," Adjoa replied.

"And I promise you, sister, running will do you no good," Kwadjo said. "For I will hunt you down myself!"

"People chase only those who flee," Adjoa replied.

Kwadjo smiled broadly. "Then in twenty-eight days, you will die by the executioner's sword...or by mine!"

****

Twenty-eight days later, the citizens of Asanteman followed Adjoa, Kwadjo and Akosua back to Eda forest. Upon reaching the site of the competition, they were greeted by a young Bagya Dua growing out of the remains of the Blood Tree that Kwadjo had seemingly destroyed.

"It would appear that you didn't quite accomplish your task, Kwadjo, Akosua said.

"Wait," Kwadjo cried, pointing toward Adjoa's tree. "Let's not forget why we came here today, which is to determine the efficacy of Adjoa's Divine expression of Yao. As you all can attest, her Blood Tree still stands."

Adjoa smiled slyly. "Please, follow me...if you aren't afraid."

She turned from the crowd and briskly walked toward her Bagya Dua. The crowd reluctantly followed. To everyone's amazement, Adjoa walked right up to the tree without a single branch reaching out to grab her.

"Look at the creature's face," Adjoa said. "What do you see?"

"Its expression can only be described as…agony," Akosua gasped.

Adjoa kicked the trunk of the Blood Tree. The creature collapsed upon itself, shattering into small, dry chunks of wood. "Agony, indeed!"

The crowd gathered around Adjoa and cheered – "Afa yeh ebio tumfo so sene bayi!" – "*The wisdom of Afa is more potent than magic!*"

Akosua grabbed Adjoa's wrist and raised the young woman's hand above their heads. "So, have we found our king?"

"Ain! Ain! Ain!" The crowd cheered in affirmation.

"Then it is agreed," Akosua said.

Adjoa sat upon the Sika'dja. "Thank you, mighty Asante! I promise to serve you well!"

"May I suggest your first act as Asantehene?" Akosua asked as she placed the golden crown upon Adjoa's head.

"Certainly," Adjoa replied. Her smile widened as she watched her twin brother scurry away into the shadows of the forest.

"Please kill that damned Bagya Dua your brother failed to destroy!"

Adjoa rose from the stool. "It would be an honor!"

With that, Adjoa poured the yellow powder from her pouch into the palm of her left hand. She then etched the divine sigils into the powder and began to pray…

Old Hunter

By Milton Davis

He knew long before the drums warned him. The nauseous pang in his belly was his sign as it had been since his initiation rites. Each Namaqua had his or her special tell, their own physical alarm warning them of a Breach. As Old Hunter, his was the most sensitive. He rose from his cot in darkness, the sun yet to climb the misty eastern horizon. As he stood the drums sounded, their rapid cadence vibrating against the bottom of his bare feet. The lodge came alive with the sound of urgent voices, rattling wood and shrill whistles as each warrior dressed, armed themselves and called their mounts. There was a Breach of the Cleave, and the Namaqua would seal it.

He strapped on his armor then retrieved his ax from its plain wooden case. As he lifted the long handled weapon to his shoulder the door to his room opened. His daughters entered.

"Are you ready, baba?" Nabunya asked. She smiled nervously, displaying the dimples for which she was named. Her bow rested across her back, a quiver of arrows strapped tight to her left leg. She worried about him too much, especially when they were summoned. The years had been kind to him and the spirits of those gone before surrounded him but he could not deny time. Every fight could be his last, but it was the same for the younger hunters as well.

"Of course he is," Citalala answered for him. She stared at her sister as if her question was uncalled for. His oldest daughter leaned on her lance, scolding her younger sister with her eyes. He kept his head low so they could not see him grin. Citalala admired him. She thought he would live forever. He wished she was right.

Old Hunter walked passed his daughters into the large living area. The room was sparse; a central fireplace occupied the room with a low table and three low stools. The only other piece of furniture in the small room was a low altar holding an incense holder. Five weapons hung on the wall behind the incense holder; two swords, a bow, a long spear, and an ax similar to his own. Old Hunter's daughters knelt before the altar as Old Hunter inserted five incense sticks into the holder the lit each one with a candle. He joined his daughters before the altar then the three lowered their foreheads to the wooden floor.

"We pay respect to those that have gone before us, those that now rest in the Creator's bosom. Join us as we ride to protect those blind to that which threatens them. Guide our blows as we strike. Give us your blessing and your strength."

They stood in unison. Old Hunter hugged each of his daughters then led them outside. The others gathered before the house armed and ready. They bowed; Old Hunter and his daughters nodded in unison. Old Hunter walked among them, inspecting each of their weapons. There could be no weakness among them for creatures from the Cleave gave no quarter. Madness knew nothing of surrender; evil claimed no respite. Each warrior lowered his or her head in respect as Old Hunter came before them, handling weapons that had many owners before the ones that now held them, weapons that owed their strength not to the metal and wood that made them, but to the spirits of the wielders within them.

Citalala touched his shoulder. "They are coming."

The dumas appeared quickly over the horizon, covering the distance in moments. The lean felines separated quickly, each going instinctively to its rider then lying calmly like an obedient pet. They were far from it. The dumas shared a bond with the Namaqua, a bond that hinged on the death of creatures from the Cleave. When the Namaqua gave homage that another beast was vanquished, the duma fed.

The largest duma strode to Old Hunter. It brushed against him before sitting and allowing itself to be saddled. Old Hunter strapped the saddle in place as he'd done hundreds of times, wondering as always if this would be his last hunt. He wondered who would inherit his axe, a weapon passed on to him at the death of his father, who received it from his father. The thoughts did not linger long. Focus was required to deal with any minion from beyond the grey peaks forming the border of the Cleave.

The dumas ran to that border, undeterred by their human riders. There was no beast faster than a duma, not even the creatures of the Cleave could match them in speed. Old Hunter lay flat against his duma's back, gripping the leather strap encircling the cat's neck. There was no need to guide it; the dumas had the scent before they reached the Namaqua. Old Hunter searched the rapidly approaching horizon to see what type creature the Cleave had unleashed. When he finally saw it his eyes went wide. He hit the duma hard on the side, the signal for it to stop. It howled in protest but slowed until it trotted. Old Hunter struck it again and it stopped, turning its head quickly to snap at his hand.

The others guided their reluctant dumas to him. Old Hunter sat up, his eyes still locked on the distance.

"Can you see it?"

The others nodded.

Citalala dismounted and came to him. "It's very tall."

Old Hunter nodded. "Nabunya, take the archers and form a perimeter. You will fire on it until the others can move in closer."

Nabunya nodded. "Yes, baba." She rode off to rally the other archers around her.

"You will stay behind?" Citalala's words were more statement than question.

"No," Old Hunter answered. "The final blow must be struck."

Citalala raised her thick lance. "I will do it."

Old Hunter looked at the lance with sadness. Mumbeja, his wife, once wielded it with a skill unsurpassed. When she died it was passed on to Citalala, but not without some difficulty. Citalala was not ready for such a powerful weapon when it was first given to her and the sprits possessing it rejected her. It was passed on to her cousin, Hareena, who wielded it proudly until only a few seasons ago. When it was presented to Citalala the second time the spirits did not protest. She had proven her worth with it many times since.

"It is my duty," he said. "You will ride beside me."

Citalala nodded.

They rode towards the beast. It stood at least 100 spears, its skin black and slick like a beetle's carapace. Large spikes protruded backwards from the sides of its thick neck then ran along the crest of the back before trailing down its spin to its trashing tail. Its proportions were man-like; it walked on two legs, its muscled arms punctuated with large clawed hands. As they neared it seemed to be running away from them. Old Hunter hoped this was all this would be, a cautious following of a beast that had lost its way.

The creature turned toward them and his hopes disappeared. It roared, brandishing a mouth of dagger-like teeth as is shook its primate like head from side to side. The archers quickly slowed to take their positions while Old Hunter and the others kept riding closer. Old Hunter concentrated on the beast's movements, watching its gestures and stance. A realization took hold and he brought his signal flute to his lips. Three sharp whistles brought the dumas to a halt. There was nothing aggressive about the beast. It seemed to be defending itself, turning toward them only to keep from being attack from behind. He surmised that if they kept their distance and advanced slowly, this beast would find its own way back over the mountains and back into the Cleave.

Citalala apparently did not agree with him. She rode on alone, her duma quickly closing the gap. Her rash action forced his hand.

He blew two sharp chirps and the archers loaded and fired. The arrows reached the beast before his daughter, most bouncing off its tough hide while a few barely lodged in it. Old Hunter kicked his duma but the beast refused to move. He leaned close to its ear.

"I know this is foolish, old one, but I cannot let my daughter die. Either you will take me or I will go alone."

The duma growled then sprang forward. Old Hunter stayed close to its body watching as Citalala drew closer and the beast staggered back, swatting away the arrows like swarming summer flies. Then it saw Citalala and her duma. It swung its claws at them and the duma dodge, Citalala ducking as the hand passed over them.

Then it swung the same hand back, knocking Citalala and the duma into the air. They landed apart, both sprawling into the low grass and neither moving.

Old Hunter sat up on the duma and snatched the ax from his back.

"Spirits guide me," he whispered. He heaved the long handled weapon with both hands. It spun end over end, the blade finally biting into the beast's shoulder.

"Take me, spirits," he yelled. He held out his hands and the spirits of his fathers answered. Old Hunter rose from the duma and streaked to his ax. His hands wrapped around the handles as his feet touched the creature's shoulder. He yanked his ax free just as the beast began to turn his head. Old Hunter spun the ax to its flat side and struck the beast's jaw hard before leaping free. He rolled and came up to his feet, holding his ax before him and thanking the spirits within for their strength. The beast stumbled away, grasping at its jaw. Then it turned and ran.

Old Hunter ran to Citalala. She was up on her hands and knees shaking her head. Her duma limped to her, its left hind leg lifted from the ground as it walked.

Old Hunter knelt beside his daughter.

"It was a foolish thing you did," he scolded.

"Yes, baba, a foolish thing," she answered. She extended her hand towards her lance and it slid across the grass to her.

"Your spirits still favor you despite that," Old Hunter said. "Stay here and tend your duma. We must drive this beast back home. It seems it no more wants to be here than we want it to."

The others seemed to finally see what Old Hunter had sensed. They rode after the fleeing beast, driving it to the mountains with shouts and waving weapons. Suddenly the beast crouched and leaped, soaring over the grassland as if in flight then landing at the base of the grey peaks. It scrambled up the sheer granite slopes emitting a series of sharp, urgent barks. It was answered by a bellow that shook Old Hunter's innards. Boulders tumbled from the clouds like rain, some striking the beast so hard it lost its grip. But before it could fall a massive hand emerged from above, a clawed appendage similar to the beast but many times larger. It caught the beast, which wrapped its arms around that of the much larger creature. The arm lifted, taking the beast into the clouds.

A huge face appeared in the clouds. It opened its maw and bellowed again with a force that made the riders scramble back. Old Hunter stood, his sweating hands working his ax hilt. Citalala stood beside him.

"What do we do baba?" she asked.

Old Hunter gave her a grim smile. "We pray that our deaths will be swift."

The face hung over them for what seem like an eternity, then it slowly withdrew into the mists. It bellowed one last time, its departure marked by ground shaking steps and more boulders tumbling down the mountainside. The dumas and Namaqua gathered around Old Hunter and his daughter their faces displaying their dread.

"The Goddess has spared us this day," he said. "Let us hope She remains generous."

The others nodded and their fears seemed to dissipate. Old Hunter mounted his duma then lifted Citalala on as well. The old duma walked slowly, staying by its wounded companion. Old Hunter glanced over his shoulder to the mountains. Never had he seen such a large beast.

"Will it come again?" Citalala asked.

"We will pray that it doesn't," he said.

He smiled at his daughter. "It seems you still have much to learn."

Citalala dropped her head. "It seems I do baba."

Nabunya and her duma joined them.

"The ancestors were expecting us," she joked.

"They will have our company soon enough," Old Hunter replied. "But not today."

Citalala climbed onto her sister's duma and they rode back to the village. Old Hunter looked back over his shoulder to the grey clouds obscuring the mountain peaks. One day they would not be strong enough. But for now, they were enough.

A Name Long Forgotten

By Balogun Ojetade

A chill settled over Sati-Baa – the "Shining Jewel at the Center of the World", folks called it. But I called it, simply, 'home'. Been calling it home ever since I came, kicking and screaming, into this cruel world of the haves and the have-nots. If I was one of the *haves*, I might have come into the world laughing and dancing. I don't know, because since I could walk, I've worked hard for all that I have ever gotten.

I started working the river with my father in my ninth sun cycle, hauling in fish for my mother's restaurant. This was my eighth sun cycle in that occupation and, perhaps, my last, as I had seriously contemplated joining the Sati-Baa Constabulary in the next sun cycle, when I was old enough. Chief Constable Boun needed more men and women to help keep order in this bustling burg. Besides, the Chief Constable was my favorite uncle and a pleasure to be around.

Anyhow, I had just finished hauling in my last catch of the day, a spin-fin – nasty creatures, but damn, they taste good – and handed the frightful thing off to my father.

"Good catch, Kiro," he said. "I'll make sure this spin-fin is reserved for *our* dinner table."

"Hopefully, mother will cook it with some hooligan-peppers," I said, stepping into my small rowboat.

"I'm sure she will," my father replied. "The Koku clan loves their food with a lot of kick."

I nodded and rowed off, heading for home and a few

minutes of rest before dinner.

I quickened the pace of my rowing as I neared Saato Pass and the lone house that sat there – a small cabin of twisted and pocked wood, whose sole inhabitant was an old woman, with eyes as dark and piercing as a raven's and skin like the murky waters of the wetlands in summer. Her name had long been forgotten, but the fear she instilled in the people of Sati-Baa had not.

Screams of agony...screams of utter terror and despair tore across the bitter, evening air.

I docked my boat and crept toward the house, struggling to keep my balance on the moist, red earth. Upon reaching the house, I gingerly pressed my back against the side of it and then shuffled toward its single window. I peered inside. Two men lay on the floor, their bodies twisted at sickening angles; their expressions, masks of suffering. Around them danced a gaunt, squat old woman...the woman whose name had long been forgotten.

I ducked beneath the window and scurried, on all fours, to my boat. I hopped into it, shoved off and rowed furiously. Soon, I neared the bay that led to the Main Constabulary Station, which lay just at the edge of town proper. I docked, leapt from my boat and sprinted up the path leading to the stone double doors of the Main Station.

I placed my palm against the cold stone door to my left and shouted "Koku Kiro!" The enchanted doors, recognizing me as a citizen of Sati-Baa in good standing, slid inward, allowing me entrance.

Uncle Boun met me in the foyer. He reached out his massive arms and embraced me. "Greetings, Kiro! Come to give me your acceptance of a position?"

"No, uncle," I replied. "I have come to report two murders."

"Murders! I *knew* your father would lose it one day," my uncle spat. "Eating too much spin-fin will do it every time!"

"It wasn't my father, uncle Boun," I said. "It was that hag who lives out in Saato Pass. Two men lie dead in her house as she dances around them."

"Stay here," uncle Boun ordered. "I'll take the Elephant

Unit out to investigate!"

What followed, I can only go by the accounts of my uncle and the trio of elephant-mounted constables who patrolled the wetlands. They rode out to Saato Pass, their elephants beating craters into the earth as they galloped across the wetlands. Upon arrival at the hag's house, they found the pair of her victims hanging from a tree like morbid fruit. A shuffling din caught their attention and caused them to look in the direction of the hag, who was sprinting into the shadowy marsh.

The Elephant Unit gave chase, but soon lost sight of her. After a few moments, they heard a low splash in the distance. They followed the noise to a sink hole in the soft earth. Within it was the hag, fighting to keep her head above the surface.

"Help me!" she screamed. "My foot...it is entangled in seaweed!"

"Don't move," my uncle commanded. "Let the wetlands have her. It'll save us the papyrus."

The hag sank beneath the dark water. A moment later, she wrestled back to the surface.

"I am Onisako Mojiji!" She hissed. This is not the last time you shall see me. In twenty sun cycles to the day, I will arise to take vengeance upon you and your precious Sati Baa, with great malice and cruelty!"

She then sank into the murky depths, never to rise again.

Today is twenty years to the day and already, I have received several reports of what can only be described as monstrous frogs...twice the size of our unit's bull-elephants and able to swallow a small rowboat whole. A few of those reports also tell of a gaunt and hideous woman, rising out of the marsh with the frogs and watching their carnage from the shore, dancing and cackling wickedly with glee before vanishing into the shadows of the marsh.

Timneet

By Milton Davis

The white haze enveloping Shaigu seeped into his nostrils and cleansed his mind. He lounged in Paradise again, surrounded by swaying date trees and grinning servants carrying silver platters filled with foods of every delicious description. Below the dais dancers cavorted; voluptuous women whose dress, movement, and manner hinted the pleasures to come. Above it all sat the Teacher on his gilded stool, his body hidden by layers of elaborate tobes, his smiling countenance overseeing every activity in his walled sanctuary. Shaigu had been blessed to be chosen. He was smiling when Pandare's firm hand gripped his shoulder and shook him hard.

"That's enough," his blood brother said. "We must go."

Shaigu's first instinct was to slap Pandare's hand away but his brother was right. He inhaled one last time then crawled out of the vision tent. Pandare stood over him wrapped in robes to protect him from the desert sun.

"I hope you are renewed," he said, disapproval heavy in his voice.

Shaigu stood then knocked the dust from his clothes. It was a futile gesture but it came instinctively. He was a man of the forest and was not used to the constant sand of this vast emptiness. The dry air killed the haze effect quickly, leaving Shaigu with only his will and his camel.

Pandare looked into the horizon, his hand shielding his eyes. Green mountains signaled the end of the desert and the beginning of a more temperate environment.

"Another day's travel at least, maybe two," he judged.

Shaigu broke down the tent and folded it neatly. He stuffed it into its canvas case then secured it to his back.

"I hope it's one," he said. "We don't have much food left."

"It's your fault," Pandare chided him. "You eat like we're still in Paradise. You must discipline yourself. We have to make the right impression when we enter Sala. We must be starving acolytes, not well fed merchants."

Shaigu said nothing. It was easy for Pandare to make such statements. He was eating just as much if not more. But he was right. This was not a trip to a market or a search for potent herbs. They journeyed to Sala to kill a man, a dangerous man whose very existence threatened not only the school but the life of Teacher.

As always Pandare was correct. The green hills beckoning them took three days to reach, three long hunger filled days. By the time they reached Sala's gates there was no need to pretend; they were starving. Sala perched on the edge of the desert, her grey walls in contrast to the pale tan sands and the verdant mountains rising behind her. The walls were like nothing he'd ever seen, circular tower-like sections connected by straight walls.

"Clever design," Pandare commented. Shaigu nodded his head despite his hunger and fatigue. He didn't know much about Pandare's life before the Temple but he did know that he had been a warrior of some kind. Some whispered he was a fallen general forced to choose between entering the temple or death. But there were always rumors floating within the Temple. Shaigu's story was not so glamorous but resembled most of his brothers. He'd lived in the streets of Sala before being captured by men who combed the alleys for those like him, hoping to sell them to anyone willing to pay their price. Those who couldn't be sold were given to the Teacher for his blessings. Shaigu was one of the gifts. But instead of being sent to the fields he was chosen for Training. The Teacher saw promise in him and Shaigu worked hard not to disappoint him. Despite his hard work he was still the weaker of the two. There was no jealousy however; Pandare was his brother. The only thing that mattered was the will of Teacher.

"What do you mean?" he asked.

"See how the turrets are built into the wall?" he asked. "Any army attacking the city would not be able to form a uniform line. Some would be trapped between the turrets and massacred."

Shaigu had no idea what Pandare was talking about but he nodded his head anyway. He didn't want to appear stupid.

"Look," Pandare said.

The city gate squealed open, the sound annoying despite the distance. Pandare frowned.

"The Teacher said they rarely opened the northern gate," Shaigu said.

"The key word is rarely." Pandare answered. "Try to look destitute. Maybe whoever is coming won't kill us."

"That will be easy. We are destitute."

Four riders emerged, taking their time approaching the duo. They rode the finest horses Shaigu had ever seen. Colorful robes covered their lean bodies; their heads crowned with turbans. Only their ebony faces were exposed. Sabers hung from finely crafted baldrics draped over their shoulders; a quiver of arrows bounced against their horses rumps beside their bows. Pandare and Shaigu stopped as the riders circled them, inspecting them with their intense brown eyes.

"Who are you?" one of them asked. A gold ingot inscribed with symbols hung from his neck, probably a symbol of rank. He spoke Ngar, to Shaigu's relief. He had not done well mastering the native tongue of this land.

"We are unfortunate travelers," Pandare replied. "Our caravan was attacked by raiders and only the two of us survived."

The man looked at them skeptically. "You are from the North. We never receive caravans from the North for the Kashites do not trade. You're lying."

Pandare looked away from the soldier. "Yes, you are right, master. We are not merchants. We have come from the south in hopes that Amadou the Learned will take us on as disciples."

The rider smirked as his companions laughed. "I thought so. You wouldn't be the first fools to perish in these sands seeking the conjurer. "

The leader turned to one of his men. "Kai, give them your provision bag."

Kai guided his horse to them then tossed them a leather bag. Shaigu caught the bag and began to open it. Pandare grabbed his wrist then led him down into a bow.

"We thank you for your generosity," he said.

"Thank you," Shaigu repeated.

"You may not be so thankful once you see Amadou. Our business is done. We'll ride back to the city and inform Amadou of your presence. He may send someone for you but he may not. I would go lightly on the provisions. It's a long way back across the desert."

The sentinels rode away. Shaigu scrambled to his feet then quickly opened the provision bag. There was a water gourd, two red round fruit of which he was not familiar and a flat cylindrical object that resembled bread. He forced himself from gorging on the tempting fare. Instead he extended the bag to Pandare. Pandare peered inside the bag and frowned.

"It's not much," he commented.

"What are you talking about?" Shaigu argued. "There's more than enough to get us through the night if need be. We've lived off less."

"The rider said Amadou may not come," Pandare reminded Shaigu. "If he doesn't we'll have to go back. I don't think they have any intentions of letting us into Sala without him."

Shaigu shrugged and took one of the red fruit out of the bag. He bit into it and closed his eyes in ecstasy. The sweet flesh culled his hunger and the rich juice seemed made to quench his thirst.

"This is truly food of the Maker!" he exclaimed.

Pandare frowned at him as he gobbled the fruit. "I hoped you're enjoying it. When the time comes I won't share mine."

Pandare's words were prophetic. For seven days they waited, their food and strength dwindling away. Pandare, despite his warning, shared his fruit with Shaigu after the water gourd was empty. They nibbled on the moist bread on the fifth day, their desperate eyes locked on the city gates. By the morning of the seventh day their food was exhausted as were they.

Shaigu lay on his back beside Pandare, staring into the afternoon sky. The bright sun did not affect him; he was too fatigued to care. They had failed the Teacher. Maybe their bones would be of some help to the next assassins, a sign that their quest would be futile. As he closed his eyes for what he hoped wouldn't be the last time a shadow intruded on his light.

"Are you alive?" a voice asked.

Shaigu nodded his head.

"You're tough ones. That could be useful."

Coarse hands wrapped around his wrists and ankles then lifted him from the hot sand. They carried him for a short distance then placed him gently on a wooden board.

"Is the other one alive?" the voice called out.

"Yes," someone replied. "He's talking!"

Moments later Shaigu felt a body touch his.

"Where are you taking us?" he heard Pandare croak.

"To Sala," the now familiar voice replied.

Shaigu turned his head toward Pandare. His brother looked at him as well, a weak smile on his face.

"See?" Pandare said. "This was a test."

They lurched then rocked slowly. They were in a wagon of some kind, but the details didn't matter. They were on their way into Sala. Their mission was still intact. Shaigu managed to sit up. They rode in a two wheeled cart drawn by a donkey. Two tall men walked on either side of the beast, both draped in white shirts that fell to their knees. Flat conical caps covered their heads.

"Here," a voice said. He turned to his right to see the third man. He was young, probably barely past his initiation rites. Two ritual scars adorned his cheeks, a sign of his successful passage into manhood. He was dressed similar to the other men, the only exception a red beaded belt riding low on his waist. He extended a water gourd to Shaigu.

"I am Kakou," he said. "Who are you?"

Shaigu took a long drink from the gourd before answering. "I am Shaigu."

Kakou gestured past Shaigu. He turned to see Pandare frowning at him, his hand extended.

"Oh, I'm sorry, my brother!" He handed the gourd over quickly.

"You are a selfish man, Shaigu," Kakou said.

"How do you know this?" Shaigu challenged him.

"A man reveals himself in his action, not his words," Kakou said.

"Wise word from such a young mouth," Pandare said.

Kakou grinned. "They are not my words. They are Amadou's."

"We have travelled far to see him," Pandare said. "It is our hope that he will take us on as students."

Kakou's smile faded. "That is not possible. Amadou rarely takes students, especially those who are not buSala. His skills are unique and essential to the defense of our city."

"We are simple folks," Pandare said. "All we wish is to sit at the feet of your master and learn enough of his wisdom to help our people. It is all we ask."

"You're wasting your pretty talk on me," Kakou replied. "My teacher has arranged lodging and food for you. You can stay until you are fit to go home. "

Kakou moved closer to both men. "Do not take advantage of my teacher's benevolence. It would not go well for you if you tried."

Shaigu gave Pandare a worried glance. Pandare shook his head angrily and Shaigu dropped his head in shame. He was giving in too easy. There was still a chance they could see Amadou. At least they were entering the city. It was better than starving to death in the desert.

The Sala's gates opened wide for the small entourage. Shaigu expected the musky odor of a populated city but instead his senses were greeted by an intoxicating blend of herbs and incense. The two men sat up to see the sights of Sala and were taken aback.

Shaigu pinched his lips together to keep from uttering words of praise. The city was the closest the two had come to experiencing Paradise since they left its gilded walls. Colorfully painted family compound walls bordered the brick paved streets, each compound separated by narrow alleys where fruit trees and other succulent vegetation flourished. The people traversed the wide avenues on oxen drawn wagons, camels, donkeys and horses while others walked leisurely along the mud packed sidewalks. Their garments were as gaily colors as their buildings, the men covers in large shirts that draped to their knees, the women garbed in dazzling dresses that bunched tight at their waists and emphasized their comely figures. Before them was the first market place, but Kakou guided their wagon onto a narrow road that bypassed the bustling bazaar. The street they followed was quieter but no less colorful, the vegetation a bit more unruly. They travelled a few moments longer before stopping in front of a tall building adorned with the most beautifully carved doors Shaigu had ever seen.

Kakou knocked and the door immediately opened.

"Good blessings to you," Kakou said.

"And to you, Kakou," a soft male voice answered. "What does your teacher wish of me today?"

"I have two men from the desert that need lodging until they are fit to go home," he said.

"I will see to it," the man replied.

Kakou stepped away and the man emerged from the building. He was a giant, towering over Kakou like an acacia over grass. He strode to the wagon and bent closer, his eyes squinting.

"Welcome to my hostel," he said gently. "I am Ogbe. I am honored to have you as guest. Come, we will see to your needs."

Shaigu and Pandare climbed from the wagon. Pandare approached Kakou and bowed.

"Please thank your teacher for us," he said humbly. "Though we are saddened he will not see us, we wish him well."

Kakou bowed in returned. "Take care, both of you. Your determination will not go unrewarded."

Shaigu bowed as well, watching Kakou as he climbed into

the wagon and rode away.

Ogbe clamped his huge hands. "Come now. We will get you out of those dusty clothes and get a good meal inside you."

The duo followed Ogbe into the hostel. The foyer was sparse, a plain wooden bench propped against the right wall, a pedestal with a washbowl to their left. Ogbe gestured towards the bowl and both men washed their faces and hands with the cloth towels handing on pegs nearby. A carpeted hallway extended before them. Ogbe removed his shoes and so did Shaigu and Pandare.

"I will take you to the baths first," he said. "One must be clean before a meal, don't you think?"

Shaigu didn't agree but nodded anyway, following Pandare's lead. He was starving. He would eat a piece of bread covered with mud from a pig sty if he could. He reluctantly followed Ogbe to a large room at the end of the hallway. A cool breeze escaped from the room, drawing Shaigu toward its source. A clear pool of water shimmered before them held in a bowl of hardened clay. Ogbe reached into a depression along the wall an extracted two gourds.

"Here, this is drinking water. The water in the pool contains special minerals designed to heal and refresh. They are good for the skin but bad for the stomach."

They indulged on the cool liquid then disrobed and enter the bath. The medicated liquid tingled against Shaigu's skin and he smiled. He immersed his head completely then shook it as he emerged. Shaigu grinned as he enjoyed the needed respite. Pandare's expression was the opposite.

"You enjoy yourself too much, brother," he warned. "Remember the teacher's words. The Enemy's seductions are many. It takes only one to corrupt the Spirit."

Shaigu waded close to his brother. "Why should they wish to seduce us? They don't know our purpose. We are poor disciples."

Pandare rolled his eyes. "The temptations exist without direction. It is the way of the Enemy. Society controls the mind by its structure. Amadou is the center, which is why he must be killed."

Shaigu lowered his eyes in shame. "You are right, brother. The depravations of the desert have weakened me. "

They spent the rest of the bath in silence then quickly donned their clothes. Ogbe waited for them as they exited the room.

"That's much better!" he said. "Now no one will think you are camels. Come, it's time to satisfy your stomachs."

Ogbe led them down the hallway. The aromas of the waiting meal reached Shaigu's nostrils before they entered the room and his mouth watered. Four long ebonywood tables stretched from one end of the room to the other, flanked on both side by benches. The room was empty save a woman spooning an aromatic stew into two bowls at the end of the table. She looked up and greeted them with a generous smile.

"Come,' she chirped. "It's best when it's hot."

Shaigu had to restrain himself from running to the table. He followed Pandare's lead, walking calmly to the table then bowing to the woman before sitting.

"We thank you for your hospitality," Pandare said. "It is rare to find such courtesy in this world."

"Courtesy is a sign of either abundance or scarcity," a male voice commented.

Shaigu turned to the source of the voice. A man entered the room draped in a large white cloak that contrasted starkly with his black skin. An embroidered cap graced his head; he looked at them with a strong and pleasing gaze. His strong chin was graced with a grey speckled beard. He gave their server a slight bow then sat before Shaigu and Pandare, placing his fly whisk on the table.

"You are the men from across the desert," he said.

"Yes," Pandare answered. "My brother and I traveled here hoping to become students of the great Adamou. It seems our journey was in vain."

The man's eyebrows rose. "How so? Surely he would grant you an audience after such an arduous journey."

"It seems that will not be so," Pandare said. "His student Kakou informed us that he is not taking new students under any circumstances."

"Ah," the man said with a smile. "Kakou. I should have known. Even the best students have their faults. Kakou is very talented but that does not allay his insecurities. He is always wary of anyone that might threaten his status. It seems I have more work to do with him."

Shaigu looked at this man with a puzzled gaze. What was he saying? Pandare's response was entirely different. He jumped to his feet and bowed deeply.

"Amadou!" he exclaimed.

Shaigu dropped his spoon and stood as well. He bowed, his eyes wide in surprise. The great Amadou had come to see them!

"Please, sit. There is no need for praise. I am a man just as you. Be thankful that Kakou's brothers witnessed his actions and chose to share what they saw."

Both men sat. Shaigu studied Amadou as he was taught. He was younger than he expected but not a young man by any means. This meant his skills were mature which would make him a formidable target. This would take time; months, maybe even years. He was not sure if he was up to such an assignment. He looked over at Pandare. His brother showed no signs of vigilance, only the enamored gaze of a humble admirer. He could see why the Great Teacher chose him for the task.

Amadou stood. Shaigu and Pandare began to do the same but Amadou waved them down.

"Enjoy your meals and rest. I will send someone for you in the morning. There are still questions to be answered before I make my decision. At least you'll get the chance. You have come far to seek my instruction. I will not turn you away without at least giving you the opportunity to prove yourselves.

"We thank you, teacher," Pandare said. "We thank you!"

Amadou left them to their meals. Neither man was hungry.

"That was unexpected," Shaigu said.

"Very," Pandare replied. "You did well, brother."

"I'm only glad he did not speak to me," Shaigu confessed. "I would have lacked your poise."

Pandare laughed. "I was shaking in my sandals. I was sure he saw through my words. I waited for him to strike us dead at any moment."

"I can see why the Teacher chose you," Shaigu's hunger returned and he ate his stew, enjoying the savory concoction.

"So what do you think of him?" Pandare asked.

"It's too soon to tell," Shaigu answered. "Besides, does it matter what I think?"

Pandare nodded then gulped a spoonful of stew. "True. But it is always necessary to understand a person. You must learn their strengths and weaknesses in order to exploit them and gain access to their confidence. "

"It is their weakness that draws our attention, because by applying our strength to their weakness we achieve victory," Shaigu finished.

Pandare smiled. "The words of the Teacher."

Ogbe appeared, bringing bread and beverage. "So you have met Amadou."

"Yes we have, and we are greatly honored," Pandare answered. Shaigu nodded as he slurped more stew.

"You should be," Ogbe replied. "Amadou rarely travels beyond his compound. He must be intrigued by you."

"We only hope he is intrigued enough to allow us to study under him," Shaigu said. "His reputation spans the desert and reaches into our mountain home."

Ogbe's eyes widened and he smiled. "The quiet one speaks! You must be impressed!"

"I have a habit of saying the wrong things," Shaigu said. "So I stay silent until I am sure of my words."

"That is a good practice," Ogbe answered. "If only more of us were more prudent."

Ogbe placed the bread and drink at their table. "Here is the rest of your meal. If you slow down you'll see that they complement the stew very well."

"We thank you again," Pandare said. "The people of this city are more generous than most."

"I could not say," Ogbe answered. "I have never been beyond the gates. Most of us haven't. "

Shaigu was surprised. "Not even into the countryside?"

Ogbe shook his head. "I am not a farmer nor do I own herds. And as you say, we are a generous folk. I can imagine that there are places just as pleasant, but I can't imagine any place better."

You have never seen the Teacher's garden, Shaigu thought. *And you never will.*

The duo finished their delicious meals then was lead to their sleeping quarters. They were given separate rooms; business was slow during harvest season so the space was available. Shaigu's cot was narrow but comfortable. As he laid his head on the cotton padded headrest he wished he had the luxury of the vision tent. This mission was nothing like he expected. He had imagined Sala a harsh place filled with crazed and depraved people; instead he and Pandare had been treated with respect and kindness by also everyone, the exceptions being the Salan guards and the suspicious Kakou. He had to be diligent, however. He more than anyone else knew that behind a veil of kindness could be a cruel truth. Was he not here to kill a man?

Sleep came easily to him and the morning arrived too soon. Someone shook him awake; he opened his eyes to Pandare's stern face.

"Wake up, my brother. Amadou has sent someone to bring us to his compound."

Shaigu groaned as he sat up then rubbed his eyes.

"So early?" he complained.

Pandare chuckled. "It is well into the day. I overslept myself. Ogbe must have put a sedative in the food we ate."

"I doubt it," Shaigu said as he stood and stretched. "If there is one thing I can do it is detect elixirs. We were tired, nothing more."

"Hurry," Pandare urged. "Our new master waits."

Shaigu followed Pandare through the hostel. Waiting at the entrance was Ogbe and his ever present smile.

"I hope your stay here was to your satisfaction?" he asked.

"Very much so," Pandare replied.

"Yes, it was," Shaigu said.

Shaigu did not think it was possible for the innkeepers smile to be any brighter but quickly discovered he was wrong.

"Excellent! Be sure to share your feelings with Amadou. " Both men bowed.

"We will," Pandare said.

They stepped through the door into the daylight and were greeted by a familiar face.

"Greetings to you," Kakou said.

Amadou's student forced a smile to his face. Pandare nodded respectfully while Shaigu looked away to hide his smug grin.

"Amadou wishes me to bring you to his compound. Come."

He turned away abruptly and walked rapidly away. Pandare and Shaigu scampered to catch up with him.

"Thank you for your help," Pandare said.

"Do not thank me," Kakou replied. "I still believe you both should be on your way back to wherever you came from."

"But Amadou disagrees," Shaigu said.

Both Pandare and Kakou turned to glare at him. Shaigu lowered his head and cursed himself silently.

"Amadou is my teacher," Kakou said. "But we do not always agree. He is a great man but he is not always right. Even he is not perfect."

They walked in silence afterwards, exiting the narrow street to the broad avenue that led to the city center. The homes along the street became grander as they progressed, large stone structures surrounded by high walls and well-kept vegetation. They passed through a crowded market where they almost lost their reluctant guide, but managed to find him on the other side of the crowded venue.

They finally reached Amadou's compound. Shaigu was not surprised at what he saw; it was modest and non-descript, a reflection of the teacher's façade. What did surprise him was the openness of the place. There was a constant flow of people in and out of the gates. The men and women were not unusual, but it was the presence of children that caught his eye. Boys and girls from infants to adolescents were everywhere, laughing, crying, working and playing among the adults.

"Does Amadou teach children as well?" Pandare asked.

"Of course not," Kakou replied. "These are his children, nieces and nephews."

"He allows him in the school?" Shaigu asked.

Kakou spun to confront the two, an annoyed look on his face.

"Amadou has no school. When you are selected as a student, you are chosen to be a part of his family. This is his family compound."

Kakou turned about and led them into the compound. A few curious eyes followed them as they entered. Their plain white garb made them stand out among the bright and varied colors of Salan dress. There were a number of building within the walls, each belonging to a separate family. Kakou led them to the largest, a rectangular structure that contrasted with the cylindrical homes. Amadou sat before the entrance surrounded by children, their wide eyes locked on his smiling face.

"I thought you said he didn't teach children," Shaigu observed.

"He does not teach them what you seek," Kakou snapped.

They stood behind the children.

"Stay here," Kakou said. "Amadou will talk to you when he is done with the children. I must tend to my duties."

He marched away, sharing a parting glare at them before joining a group of men at the compound gate. Together they left the compound.

Shaigu and Pandare turned to Amadou. He spoke to the children in the language of the city, his tone gentle and engaging.

They repeated some words and sang others, each child never taking their eyes off their teacher. Finally Amadou stood and the children did as well. He raised his arms and they scattered like gazelle, giggling and screaming as they ran to their homes.

Amadou greeted them with a wide smile.

"Welcome to my home," he said. "I see Kakou brought you all the way this time."

Both men bowed. "He was most attentive," Pandare said.

Amadou laughed. "There is no need to lie to me, Pandare. Kakou shouted loud enough to wake the ancestors when I asked him to bring you here. Do not expect to have his help. You will have to win him over."

"I don't think we can," Shaigu said.

"Anything is possible," Amadou replied. "All it takes is perseverance and persistence. But you are not here to know whether or not I will allow you into my family. I'm curious to know if I will, too."

Amadou gestured for them to follow him. They entered the rectangular building. The building was empty except for a collection of carved masks that hung from the walls. There were no chairs or stools, no pedestals or dais. They followed Amadou to the center of the room. They stood together, Amadou smiling.

"Teacher, what are we to do?" Pandare asked.

"We are waiting for someone," he answered.

"Who?" Shaigu asked.

"We are waiting for my wife, Timneet," Amadou answered. "No one enters the family without her approval.

"I am here," a woman's voice announced.

Shaigu looked to the entrance. Timneet sauntered into the building, a smile on her youthful face. The green head wrap hiding her hair contrasted with her smooth black skin and complemented the green patterned dress hugging her slim but shapely frame. Her numerous bracelets jangled with her steps as she approached them. It had been a long time since Shaigu had seen a woman so lovely.

"Sorry for the delay, husband," she said. "Your young

students can be quite mischievous."

Amadou laughed. "I told them a mischievous tale."

Timneet stood before Pandare and Shaigu. Shaigu stared into her caramel eyes, transfixed by her smile.

"Pandare, Shaigu, welcome to our compound." Shaigu jumped when she grabbed his hands and her smile widened.

"Don't fear, Shaigu," she said. "This will only take a moment."

Her grip firmed and she looked into his eyes. Shaigu could not look away, nor could he blink. After a brief moment she let go of his hands and turned her attention to Pandare. Pandare placed his hands in hers and received the same scrutiny. Once she was done she stood beside Amadou.

"Welcome to our family," she announced.

Pandare bowed to the couple. Shaigu bowed as well, joyous that he'd passed Timneet's mysterious inspection.

"Pandare, you will come with me," Amadou said. "Shaigu, please go with Timneet."

The two men looked at each other with puzzled expressions. Shaigu fought to hide his apprehension.

"This is our way," Amadou assured them. "Shaigu, please follow Timneet."

Shaigu glanced and Pandare and Pandare nodded. Timneet walked toward the entrance, Shaigu following. He caught up with her as they emerged into the sunlight.

"Mistress, where are we going?" Shaigu asked.

"I will give you a tour of our compound then we will assign you duties," Timneet replied. "We have a big compound and a bigger family. Everyone has a duty."

"Is this part of my teaching?" he asked.

Timneet's face became serious. "You are not ready for teaching yet, Shaigu."

Shaigu's eyes widen. Had he betrayed their intentions?

"There is fear in you, and doubt," Timneet continued. "I am sensitive to these things. Amadou feels it would be better for you to get used to our way before taking you on as a student."

She smiled again and Shaigu felt the tension inside him fading.

"Don't worry. This is normal. Your friend seems to be in a better place so Amadou will begin his instruction immediately. He will be given duties as well."

"So we will stay?"

Timneet smiled again. "Yes you will. Now come let me introduce you to our family."

Timneet led him through the compound, pointing out every man, woman and child and giving their names. Shaigu was overwhelmed; there was no way he would remember so many names and faces in one day. He could not concentrate on her words for he was still engrossed with Timneet.

"We are similar to your folks," she said. "Yet many of our ways are different. We have no king; we are ruled by a council of elders in which each caste and clan has a voice. Decisions are made by consensus. If there is a stalemate the eldest of the elders makes the final decision."

"I see," Shaigu said absently.

Timneet stopped and turned toward Shaigu. He almost ran into her.

"I am so sorry, mistress," he said.

"Make sure you are paying attention to the proper things," she said. A knowing smile came to her face and Shaigu eyes widened like a child caught in mischief.

"I...I am so embarrassed! Forgive me for my disrespect."

Timneet chuckled. "You are a man. Come, I'll show you the rest of the compound."

Their tour took the remainder of the day. By nightfall they returned to the building where they first met. Pandare and Amadou waited for them.

"That was quite a tour," Amadou said. "I didn't realize our compound was so interesting."

"Our new brother had many questions," Timneet replied. "And how was your day?"

"Productive," Amadou said. "Pandare is a promising

student. He will be placed with the seconds."

Timneet looked skeptical. "Are you sure?"

Amadou frowned. "Yes I am."

Timneet smiled again. "I will leave you with my husband," she said to Shaigu. "Tomorrow we will decide how you'll be helpful."

Timneet sauntered out of the room. Shaigu took his place beside Pandare before Amadou.

"You will share a room for now," he said. "Once you have become comfortable here you will be separated. Unlike the others you must learn our ways before you can begin to reach your potential. Rest well, sons. The day will begin early."

Amadou left the building, following Timneet to their home. Kakou entered the room soon afterwards and waved for them to follow him. They followed the student to a long reed walled building situated along Sala's western road. It was a dormitory, the home of the Teacher's students and assistants. They entered the building then Kakou led them to a room at the end of the hall.

"You will sleep here," Kakou said. "I will wake you in the morning."

The acolyte turned to walk away and then stopped.

"This is a great honor my Teacher bestows upon you. Do not disappoint him…or me."

Kakou stalked away then entered a room near the compound entrance.

"He does not trust us," Shaigu said.

"He is of no concern," Pandare. "One swift thrust and he is a memory. What have you learned?"

Shaigu squatted over the floor and took a short stick out of his shirt. The ground was hard packed but he was still able to scratch out thin lines without breaking his makeshift writing tool. Shaigu knew his spiritual skills paled in comparison to Pandare, but he had other skills that were useful, such as his uncanny memory of physical details. He quickly drew out a complete map of Sala.

Pandare studied the diagram while rubbing his chin. "It is

a good design, strong and easily defended. The road allow of easy traffic flow within the city but limits entrance. These Salans are no strangers to sieges."

"What have you learned, brother?" Shaigu asked.

"Nothing, though I am not surprised. Today was mostly a briefing of our duties and what this Teacher expects of us. I had hoped to glimpse a reason of why Teacher wishes this man dead, but he is shrewd with his talents."

"I must apologize to you and Teacher," Shaigu said. He bowed briefly after saying Teacher's title. "I should be with you as a student. Instead I have been made servant to his wife."

"There is no need to dwell on such misfortune, brother." Pandare patted Shaigu's shoulder. "We know our purpose here. At least he didn't reject you completely. He sees potential. Besides, we don't need to become completely close to either of them. We just need to get close enough to fulfill our task. Then we will see Paradise again."

Pandare's mention of Paradise made Shaigu think of the tent. When he looked at his brother there was a frown on his face.

"You must be strong, Shaigu," he admonished. "There may be a time we may need Teacher's reinforcement, but not now. Now sleep. Who knows what this man has in store for us."

Kakou woke them early as he promised, seeming to take pleasure in their discomfort. They ate a quick breakfast of ground corn then separated, Pandare following Kakou to the teacher's home while Shaigu waited for Timneet. She appeared with the rising sun, sauntering to him with a basket balanced perfectly on her head.

"Good morning, Shaigu," she sang. "Come. The day is late and we have much to do."

"Late?" Shaigu rubbed his chin. "But the sun is still rising!"

"You are not a farmer, are you?"

Shaigu shook his head.

Timneet gave him a sad smile. "Then today will be a very long day for you."

Timneet led him to the sorghum fields beyond the city walls. The people harvesting the grain seemed to have been at work for hours. Stacks of grains stalks lined the field edges, tied together with stalks and waiting to be loaded on nearby two wheeled donkey drawn wagons.

"You will load today," Timneet said.

Shaigu nodded and went to his task. The first few wagons were easy for the grain bundles were bulky yet light. As they day went on and the temperature rose the work became more laborious. By the time the first break came he was hungry, sore and exhausted.

Shaigu devoured the bowl of sorghum porridge given to him. The water was warm but refreshing after such hard labor. He looked into the sky at the sun directly above him and cursed. He had a half a day of work ahead.

"I see you are still alive."

Timneet stood over him, smiling down with the sunlight. Her mood seemed infectious and he felt less tired in her presence.

"You are right," he said. "This will be a long day."

"You will sleep well," she replied. Timneet reached into her dress and retrieved a bundle of cloth. She opened the cloth to reveal a large nut-like object. She handed it to him.

"It's a kola nut," Timneet explained. "It's bitter, but it will give you energy."

"Thank you," he said. Shaigu place the seed in his mouth then chewed. It was bitter, but not disgustingly so, and as Timneet said he felt a rush of energy. He smiled and Timneet clapped.

"You should be good for the rest of the day," she said.

She rejoined the others and continued harvesting. Shaigu finished his meal and continued gathering the sorghum bundles. Timneet sang and the others joined in. It was a song Shaigu was not familiar with sang in a language he did not know, but the sound soothed him and eased his burdens. Suddenly there were no more bundles to load. The sun was settling into the western dunes and the workers trudged to the city, their work done for the day. Timneet met Shaigu as he loaded the last sorghum bundle on the wagon.

"Not bad for your first time," she commented.

"Thank you," he said. Timneet's compliment made him proud. He always strived to do well, but his body or mind always seemed to fail him. At least he was good at collecting sorghum.

"You will tell Teacher, won't you?"

Timneet laughed. "Of course I will. But this was only one day."

A shrill voice interrupted them.

"Mama! Mama!"

A small girl ran to them, her hands cupped before them. Timneet face bunched with concern.

"What is it, Almaz?"

The girl ran up to Timneet and extended her hands.

"I didn't mean it!" she squealed.

Shaigu peered at the girl's hands. A dead bird lay on them.

"I was throwing clay balls at it to keep it away from the sorghum," she sobbed. "I didn't mean to kill it!"

Timneet knelt down and cupped Almaz's hands in hers.

"Close your eyes," she whispered.

Timneet leaned until her forehead touched Almaz's.

"When we take life, we must give life," Timneet whispered.

"We must give life," Almaz repeated.

Timneet blew on the bird. It twitched and then its wings fluttered. Timneet drew her head away just as the bird flew from Almaz's hands.

Shaigu was stunned. He'd seen Teacher do many things, but never had he seen him restore life. If Timneet possessed such powers, what was Amadou capable of?"

"Thank you, mama!" Almaz jumped at Timneet and Timneet caught her in an embrace.

"Careful with those clay balls," Timneet said.

"I will, mama."

Timneet put Almaz down and she skipped away. Timneet looked at Shaigu and pressed a finger to her lips.

"Not a word," she said.

Shaigu nodded.

The two of them walked back to the city and to the lodge. Timneet said goodbye and Shaigu went inside, still marveling at what he had witnessed. Pandare was there fast asleep. Apparently his day had been just as strenuous. Shaigu was relieved. He wouldn't have to lie to his brother about what he witnessed. He had no intentions of tell him. Timneet was innocent; they were here for Amadou. It would remain so.

And so the next days, weeks and months passed. Shaigu and Pandare barely spoke, each exhausted by the work given to them. Shaigu found himself so engrossed in his work that there were times he was unsure why he had come to Sala.

A respite finally came when the rainy season arrived. Shaigu awoke early as always, ready for another day of hard work. Pandare woke as well and began to dress. They prepared in silence, like two strangers occupying the same cramped space. Two hours passed before they began to realize that no one was coming for them. Pandare looked at Shaigu awkwardly before speaking.

"This is not what I expected," he finally said.

Shaigu nodded in agreement. "I thought I would hate them."

"I thought so as well," Pandare agreed. "Amadou is a wise man. He had taught me things I never knew."

"His wife is helpful as well," Shaigu said. "I do not understand why we must kill him."

Shaigu's words seemed to spark something in Pandare. His face went firm, his eyes focused.

"Secure the door," he ordered.

Shaigu pushed his cot against the door. Pandare opened his bag and extracted the tent. The room was cramped but there was just enough room. They made a small fire and placed the incense pot directly on the fire. Soon the tent filled with the thick fumes of illusion. Shaigu shut his eyes and opened his mind to the effect, eager to be in Paradise. Instead he found himself standing in a sorghum field surrounded by recently harvested grain. He heard a familiar laugh behind him and he turned to gaze into the face of Timneet. She stood before him; her arms opened wide, her smile sensual and inviting. He stumbled to her like a drunken man, wrapping his arm around her narrow waist as she lay arms on his shoulders and cradled his head. She smelled of sweet sorghum and jasmine and he inhaled her like air.

"Tell me your secrets," she whispered. "Share your life with me."

This was not the dream he was supposed to have. He tried to take control of the image as he had been taught, working his mind to create some familiar totem that would bring him back to Paradise. But every path was filled with Timneet.

Shaigu was thankful when the incense was spent. He kept his head low, afraid to look at his blood brother because of what his expression would reveal. When he finally looked up, he was surprised to see in Pandare's face what he was sure displayed by his.

"We must strike soon, brother," Pandare said with a quivering voice. "Sala has wounded our faith. We can only restore it by fulfilling our duty. Paradise will be closed to us until then."

Shaigu only nodded.

"Good night, brother," Pandare said. "Remember, we must strike soon."

Sleep did not bring Shaigu any respite. He dreamed of Timneet, her arms wrapped around him, her body wrapped about him like a comfortable blanket. In his dreams he told her everything and she listened. When he woke the next morning he was less sure of himself than when he laid down to rest. The incense failed him.

When he woke the next day Pandare loomed over him.

"Today is the day. I will go to meet with Amadou. You will go to Timneet and bring her to the house as well. When we have them both together we will kill them."

Shaigu fought hard to hide his shock.

"Both of them? We were sent to kill Amadou. Why must we kill Timneet?"

"Because she is his wife. Whatever secrets he possesses

she knows. It serves no purpose to kill Amadou if the knowledge he has remains."

Shaigu wanted to argue with Pandare, but to do so would reveal his feelings. He chose this journey to enter Paradise, but now his mind told him that Paradise was in Sala with Timneet. If Amadou was dead, he would have his chance. But Timneet must live. She would live.

"I will bring her," Shaigu said.

They dressed in silence. Shaigu moved slowly with eyes closed, trying his best to summon the visions and feeling that led him to this point. The Teacher had done so much for him; he rescued him from a destitute street life, delivering him to a world of knowledge and abundance. A world of much more awaited him if he could only accomplish a simple task. So much had changed since then.

He pulled a heavy blanket over his shoulders to protect from the rain. When he finally looked up Pandare stared in his eyes. He seemed so poised, so sure. Shaigu looked at his brother's hand and stifled the shiver that threatened to take over his body. Pandare held the blade in his hand, the hilt extended toward Shaigu. He took the knife and hid it within his clothes.

"Bring her to the main house," Pandare said. "Amadou and I will be waiting."

Shaigu left the dormitory, stepping into the pouring rain. He trudged through the muddy streets, the compound walls blurred by the downpour. He didn't need to see; he knew the way by heart. He'd walked it so many times accompanied by the woman that he was about to kill. He found the compound with the gate opened as it always was, always welcoming anyone who wished to enter. He crossed the wide courtyard to the carved door then knocked. The door opened, revealing Timneet's concerned face.

"Shaigu, what are you doing in such weather? Come inside."

"No, Timneet. Master Amadou sent me for you. He said it is urgent."

It upset him how easy the lie came from his lips and how

easy he controlled his emotions.

"Now?" Timneet looked skeptical. "What could be so important?"

"I don't know," Shaigu replied with a shrug.

Timneet sighed and left from the door. She returned with a cloak and umbrella. Shaigu took the umbrella then escorted her to the main house. He stood before the door and looked into her questioning eyes.

"Shaigu, I'm getting wet."

He opened the door. Timneet walked in then stopped.

"Amadou, why is so important that you sent for me in the rain?"

Amadou looked back with questioning eyes. "Sent for you? Pandare said you sent for me."

Shaigu moved behind Timneet, blocking the door. Pandare looked at him and nodded.

"For Paradise!" he shouted.

Shaigu pulled the knife from his shirt. He stepped toward Timneet as Pandare plunged his knife into Amadou's chest. Amadou did not look at Pandare. Instead he turned and looked into Shaigu's eyes.

"Timneet,' he gasped.

Timneet turned toward Shaigu. She looked at him with amber eyes that transformed from confusion, to shock, disappointment and finally rage. Shaigu froze, unable to move his hand. At first he thought it was because he didn't want to, but then he realized it was because he couldn't. He tried to pull his hand back but it refused to move. Then it was swallowed by searing pain. He cried out as his bones shattered, the knife tumbling from his crushed hand. He fell to his knees, gripping his wrist. He looked up to Timneet but her attention was no longer on him. She looked at Pandare now, who hovered over Amadou. She extended her right hand and Pandare's downward knife stroke stopped. His face strained as he tried to push through the invisible force. Timneet closed her hand and Pandare dropped his knife. His hands went to his throat. She lifted her arm and Pandare rose from the floor, his hands digging to stop the pressure crushing his throat. Then Timneet swung her arm as if swatting a fly. Pandare sailed across the room and collided with the wall. There was a hollow cracking sound and blood splattered the wall behind his head. His arms fell to his side and his head tilted awkwardly. Timneet dropped her arm and Pandare's lifeless body fell to the floor.

The door burst open and Amadou's acolytes and family poured in. They saw Amadou's body and the room filled with cries of pain and rage. Some ran to their fallen master but others hovered over Shaigu, their intent clear. Timneet raised her hand before they could kill him. She knelt beside him.

"Who are you? Why did you do this?" Her voice trembled.

Shaigu cleared his throat. "We were sent by out Teacher, to rid this city of that which would drag it down to evil."

Timneet closed her eyes and shook her head. "That old fool. He never forgave us, I see."

She stood over him. "He has failed. Amadou will live. I will see to that. You would have done better to strike me first. It is I the Teacher wishes dead."

Shaigu looked up at her in shame. She stared back then her eyes widened.

"You couldn't do it, could you? Even if I had not stopped you."

Shaigu nodded his head.

"Then I was right. There is some goodness in you. Goodness...and love."

She extended her hand. "For that reason only you will not die, at least not today."

Timneet closed her hand and Shaigu blacked out. When he opened his eyes again bright sunlight stabbed them, forcing them closed. His back burned; he sat up quickly and opened his eyes again. He was surrounded by sand and dunes, the sun high overhead. He looked at his hand; it was still broken. He searched for some sign on how he arrived in such a desolate place but there was no sign. Then he saw the vision tent. He struggled to it, setting it up as fast as he could with his crippled appendage. His incense was in its bag but there was no food or water.

Shaigu set up the incense pot. There was one spark stick; he used it to light the incense. The smoke rose about him and he inhaled. The pain in his hand subsided then dissipated. Timneet said he would not die today, which meant his love for her meant something. He inhaled again and drifted into a vision. He dreamed of Paradise. He dreamed of Timneet.

The Hand of Sa-Seti

By Balogun Ojetade

"That's *it*, my brother and sister! Stay in step, just like that!"

The massive war elephants lumbered across the plot of land, cheered on by their "brother", Akhu and his apprentice, Amat.

Akhu was a genius. One of many in the wondrous country of Menu-Kash, yet Akhu had a knack for invention never before seen in the history of this land of grand pyramids, libraries filled with tomes of mystic texts and schools of healing, art, culture and science. The elephants – Fusii and Gahs – had been Akhu's companions since he was a toddler. They, like Akhu, possessed intelligence greater than any other of their species. Akhu's uncle – the revered and feared leader of the armies of Menu-Kash, General Mu Ankh-Kara – had charged the elephants with protecting Akhu when his parents failed to return from an exploration of Sakadaah – the cold desert in the northwest.

"Amat, now!" Akhu commanded as he yanked on a lever that protruded from the arm of the ebony couch in his litter. Amat mirrored Akhu's movements and suddenly, the litters began to smoothly slide sideways toward the ten-foot gap between elephants. Akhu jumped to his feet. Amat followed suit.

The litters came together with a click, forming a covered bridge.

"It works, my Neb!" Amat shouted, jumping up and down with glee.

Akhu hugged his apprentice and kissed the top of her cleanly shaven head. Amat's cocoa skin tinged red. "We did it Amat!"

Gahs raised his head and a sound like a blaring trumpet escaped his throat.

"Apologies, Gahs," Akhu shouted, winking at Amat. "You performed brilliantly! You too, my sister!"

Fusii nodded her massive head and raised her trunk in approval.

"This will make a perfect base for *Ra's Rain*, my Neb."

"Yes, it will," Akhu replied. "Let's set up the tripod and…"

A deep, roaring noise – like the sound of a gale wind – stifled Akhu's tongue.

Akhu drew his scimitar from its sheath and slashed inward, toward his chest. The steel blade crashed into a massive, stone maul. An outward slash sent the war hammer careening back toward its thrower – a hulking figure standing in the grass below.

Akhu somersaulted from the litter-bridge toward the large man beneath him. The man reached up and caught the shaft of his maul as Akhu landed in a kneeling position before him. Akhu placed his sword at the man's feet and bowed his head.

"Uncle," Akhu said.

"Fast reflexes, boy," the man said, pulling Akhu to his feet.

"I was trained by the best, my Neb," Akhu replied, smiling warmly.

"That you were, boy! That you were!"

Both men laughed as they embraced each other. Akhu's uncle looked up toward the bridge.

"Apologies if I frightened you, Amat."

"Apology accepted, General Mu," Amat replied. "How are you today, my Neb?"

"My heart is heavy, Amat," General Mu sighed. "For today, I have to leave *you* lot to kill a dead man."

Akhu's brow furrowed as he stared into his uncle's piercing, brown eyes. "You speak in riddles, uncle Mu. Kill a *dead* man?"

"The Shekhem's daughter has been kidnapped by the wizard, Sa-Seti."

"*The* Sa-Seti? Shekhem of seven centuries ago?" Akhu inquired.

"Yes," General Mu replied. "It appears that rumors of Shekhem Sa-Seti's death have been…exaggerated."

"Undead?" Akhu asked, shaking his head in disbelief.

General Mu answered with a nod.

"I will accompany you, then."

"No," General Mu said with a wave of his maul. "The Shekhem would have my head if the most brilliant mind in Menu-Kash died on my watch. Besides, how tough can one mummified sorcerer – with untold magic power – be?"

"Tread carefully, uncle Mu."

"Always, son," General MU said, embracing Akhu. "Always."

General Mu turned away from his nephew, tossed his maul over his thick shoulder and sauntered off.

Akhu looked up to the litter-bridge at Amat. "Let's run *Ra's Rain* through its paces. We may have use for it soon enough."

Akhu lay in his bed, but sleep eluded him. Three days had passed and General Mu and his elite Jackal Squadron – warriors specialized in the hunting and killing of practitioners of dark magic – had not returned home.

Suddenly, Amat rushed into Akhu's sleeping chamber. Her face was a mask of worry. "My Neb, please, forgive the intrusion, but…"

Akhu sprang out of bed. "What is it Amat? What's wrong?"

"Your uncle has returned, my Neb, but he is…not well."

"Not well?" Akhu echoed. "What, exactly, is wrong with him?"

"He is in the courtyard, my Neb. Please, follow me."

Amat turned on her heels and darted out of the room. Akhu followed her out to the courtyard. General Mu sat on his haunches. His tan, linen vest and trousers were drenched with sweat and he shivered violently as the cool, night air slithered across his chest and down his back. The General's maul and his red, studded leather armor lay in a heap beside him. General Mu's helmet had rolled from his lap and lay, bottom up, a few feet in front of him.

Akhu ran to his uncle and knelt beside him. "Uncle Mu! What happened? What's wrong?"

"They…they came at us from all directions," General Mu replied. "*Thousands* of them!"

"Thousands of *what*?" Akhu asked.

"Beetles," General Mu groaned. "Beetles the size of men! Beetles that *were* men! Goddamned *beetles*!"

General Mu collapsed onto all fours. Sputum erupted from his mouth and cascaded into his helmet.

Akhu and Amat pulled the ebon-skinned goliath to his feet. "Let's get you to bed, uncle," Akhu grunted as he struggled to support General Mu's massive weight with his shoulders.

"You must see the Shekhem, boy," General Mu croaked. "Take my scepter; show it to the guards. They will let you pass. Warn the Shekhem, boy!"

"Warn him? Of what?"

"Sa-Seti allowed me to live so that I could deliver this message to the Shekhem – he has three days to return Sa-Seti's hand, or Ta-Sut is dead and all of Menu-Kash will soon follow."

****

Shekhem Tehuti Ur-Amun rubbed his goatee with his right hand, which – as always – was encased in a crimson, silk glove. He studied Akhu, who knelt before him.

"And what is General Mu Ankh-Kara's condition now?"

"He is feverish; nauseous; and grows weaker with each passing hour, your Majesty."

"A curse?"

"It appears so, your Majesty."

"Perhaps the General's talk of me returning Sa-Seti's hand is just the ranting of a man wracked by fever, then."

Akhu shot a glance at the Shekhem's gloved appendage. "I think not, your Majesty."

The Shekhem smiled wryly. "You have always been a clever boy Akhu Ankh-Kara, a clever boy indeed. What, exactly, do you know of my hand?"

"Just what every citizen of Menu-Kash knows, your Majesty – you were wading in the River Ise, presenting an offering to Pademak, when a crocodile sprang from beneath the surface of the water and attacked. You killed the crocodile, but suffered severe and disfiguring injuries to your right hand."

The Shekhem rose from his golden throne. Akhu bowed his head in reverence.

"Stand up, son," the Shekhem commanded.

Akhu rose to his feet. The Shekhem stared into Akhu's eyes. "What I tell you now never leaves this room. Understand?"

Yes, your Majesty," Akhu replied.

"The story of my hand is a...fabrication," the Shekhem began. "The truth is – I heard my father speak, in whispers, of a powerful sorcerer who once ruled Menu-Kash. It was said that this sorcerer had been kissed upon the right hand by the Goddess Ise, herself and thereafter, the sorcerer-king could see the past and future."

"I have heard the legends, your Majesty," Akhu said.

"Yes, but only Shekhem know that sorcerer's identity. There have been twelve sorcerer-kings, but all of our powers pale in comparison to the third."

"Sa-Seti," Akhu said.

"Indeed. It was *his* hand that Ise kissed. It was *his* hand that held the key to the powers of precognition and post cognition. And it was *his* tomb that I raided for that hand over thirty years ago."

"But what does that have to do with *your* hand, your Majesty?"

The Shekhem paced back and forth, his bare feet making slapping sounds on the cool marble with each step. "The ritual to claim Sa-Seti's hand as my own required a sacrifice. I sawed off Sa-Seti's hand and placed it in a calabash..."

The Shekhem returned to his throne and flopped down in the huge chair. Beads of sweat ran down his forehead as he continued to speak.

"Then, I...I severed my own hand and placed it atop Sa-

Seti's. Suddenly, the world went black. When I awakened, I was at home in my bedchamber. I felt no different, but when I looked beneath the covers to peek at my stump, I found this…"

The Shekhem snatched the glove from his hand. Akhu stared at it in disbelief. The Shekhem's hand was withered and the digits were twig-like and twisted, ending in long, cracked, yellowish-pink nails. At the center of the leathery palm was a large, fully developed, alive and alert human eye. The eye's piercing greenness both fascinated and disgusted Akhu.

"With the hand of Sa-Seti, I can indeed see the past and the future, but only of others; not of myself or my bloodline," Shekhem Tehuti whispered.

"To have your daughter returned to you alive, you must sever that accursed hand and return it to its rightful owner, your Majesty," Akhu said. "I am a skilled surgeon. I can…"

"I'm sorry," The Shekhem said, interrupting him. "I…I don't know if I can do that."

"You don't know, your Majesty?" Akhu said, lowering his gaze to hide his disgust for this man, who had just proven to be a thief, a liar *and* a coward.

"Look, Akhu," the Shekhem sighed. "I love Ta-Sut with all my heart – she is my firstborn and heir to the throne – but the many outweigh the one. With insight from the hand of Sa-Seti, I have brought Menu-Kash unimaginable wealth and glory and I have kept this great land of ours safe. And – one day soon – I will heal the festering wound carved into this world by Pademak and restore peace to all of Ki-Khanga."

Akhu knelt in salute. "If you speak it, it is so, your Majesty."

The Shekhem slipped the crimson glove back over Seti's mummified hand. "Leave me now, Akhu. I must devise another plan to rescue my beloved daughter from the clutches of that monster."

Akhu sprang to his feet and – as custom dictated – walked backward out of the Shekhem's throne room.

****

A cool breeze sent a chill down Akhu's spine, awakening him. He sat up on the couch in his litter, stretched his sinewy arms and then peeked over the back of the couch at the top of Fusii's head. The steel plates of her barding glowed a soft red as the armor reflected the tint of the morning sky. Her trunk was raised high, set to deliver another blast of air.

"I'm up, sister; I'm up!" Akhu chuckled. "Why have you awakened me?"

A soft, whistling sound made Akhu snap his head toward Gahs. Amat stood in her litter, pointing toward something in the distance. Akhu followed Amat's finger. A towering obelisk loomed in the distance – the tomb of Sa-Seti.

"Strange…the tomb is surrounded by some sort of black liquid that ebbs and flows like an ocean tide."

"That is no liquid, my Neb," Amat replied. "Take a closer look."

Akhu pulled a small, bronze telescope from a pouch on his belt. He raised it to his eye and what he saw made him gasp.

"Beetles! Beetles the size of a man's hand!"

"Hundreds of thousands of them, my Neb," Amat sighed. "Perhaps, millions."

"Prepare yourselves!" Akhu shouted as he pulled the lever on the arm of his couch.

Amat pulled her lever and the litter bridge snapped into place.

Akhu snatched a large tarpaulin from under his couch and dragged it to the center of the bridge as Amat set up an iron tripod.

The war elephants galloped forward as Akhu and Amat continued to work, busily sliding tubes, gears and large canisters – all from the tarp – into place. Gahs let loose a powerful roar, which shook the ground beneath him. Akhu looked up from his work. The beetles had taken flight and a dark, clicking cloud closed upon the litter bridge.

"I'll finish assembling *Ra's Rain*," Akhu shouted. "Fuel the *Horns of Sekhmet* and the *Steamsword*!"

Amat was a blur, grabbing a large calabash from her litter and emptying its contents into vents in the helmets of the elephants' barding.

Akhu hoisted *Ra's Rain* onto his shoulder then tossed the long, iron barrel of the weapon onto the tripod, fitting holes bored into the barrel's bottom onto the tripod's hooks. The massive weapon locked into place.

A shadow darkened the litter bridge.

"The creatures are upon us, my Neb!" Amat yelled.

"I suggest you work a little faster, then!" Akhu replied as he screwed a tube into the spigot of a steel barrel that sat over a roaring flame.

The sulfurous stench of feces assaulted Akhu's nostrils. He turned his gaze skyward. The clicking, black cloud of beetles was descending upon the litter. Akhu snatched back the canopy and stood behind the canopy of *Ra's Rain*.

"Fusii…Gahs…*now!*"

The twin war elephants raised their armored trunks skyward. A column of fire erupted from the nozzles connected to the barding covering each elephant's eight foot long proboscis.

The *Horns of Sekhmet* proved effective as the flames engulfed the beetles, roasting hundreds of them and injuring hundreds more. The dead beetles – and their living kindred fell to the earth, where Gahs and Fusii set about crushing the creatures under foot. Amat tossed the *Steamsword* to Akhu with one hand as she pulled a large, wheeled crate with the other. Amat pulled the crate, which was filled with fist-sized, steel balls, next to *Ra's Rain*.

On the ground, the beetles crawled together with military-like precision, forming a hundred or so patches of blackness upon the grass. Each group of beetles then began to fuse together, writhing and clicking as their bodies became one. After a few moments, a hundred large, chitinous black balls lay upon the field of battle.

The clicking ceased. The balls were still.

Akhu brought his telescope to his eye and studied the balls intensely. "Gahs, please, do us the honors."

Gahs nodded and then raised his right foreleg. He slammed

his foot down, beating a small crater into the grass. The force of the powerful stomp sent a shockwave across the battlefield, sending the beetle-balls bouncing upward. The balls fell back to the earth and then…no sound…no movement.

"Uh-*huh*," Amat grunted as she rubbed her smooth scalp with the palm of her hand. "So…do we move on? Do we…wait for something to happen? Umm…"

"Perhaps the creatures are displaying a gesture of surrender. I guess we press on," Akhu said with a shrug. "Brother…sister… please, takes us forward and step on those things as you go."

Suddenly the balls started to vibrate violently and a loud clicking rose from each ball.

"Or…not," Akhu sighed.

"I knew this was too easy!" Amat spat.

"One can only hope, Amat," Akhu replied. "Load up *Ra's Rain*; I'm going down for a closer look."

Akhu drew the *Steamsword* and leapt to the ground. He landed with a dull thud. "Send down a line!"

Amat lowered a thin flexible tube to Akhu, who slid its open end over a spigot on the sword's leather-wrapped, steel pommel.

"Give it some heat," Akhu shouted.

Amat turned a lever on the heated barrel that sat on the litter-bridge. A few moments later, the *Steamsword*'s blade began to glow with a reddish tint, heated by the hair-thin copper veins running the length of the flat sides of the weapon.

"That's enough," Akhu said, pulling the tube from the sword's pommel.

Amat turned off the heat and drew the line back up.

"Get ready!" Akhu shouted. "I am about to try something."

Akhu leapt toward a beetle-ball, raising the *Steamsword* above his head. As he descended, Akhu brought the tip of the sword downward, thrusting it hilt-deep into the ball of fused insects. The ball burst into flames and the burning beetles separated with a loud series of clicks.

"I thought so," Akhu shouted to his comrades. "The beetles are metamorphosing into something. We need to kill them now. Something tells me, we do *not* want to be here when the metamorphosis is complete!"

Suddenly, the beetle-balls unfolded in unison. Within seconds, standing before Akhu was a platoon of hulking humanoid creatures with large, wicked-looking mandibles, razor-sharp claws and spiked, black, armored exoskeletons.

"Too late, my Neb," Amat shouted.

Akhu rolled his eyes. "You *think*?"

The beetle-warriors charged forward. Akhu and the elephants surged forward to meet them. Akhu slashed fiercely with the *Steamsword*, setting beetle-warriors ablaze with each strike, as Fusii and Gahs butted, gored and trampled the monsters with abandon.

Score after score of beetle-warriors fell under the onslaught of Akhu and his elephant companions.

The creatures suddenly broke engagement and retreated. Akhu reheated the *Steamsword* and Amat refueled the *Horns of Sekhmet* as they watched the beetle-warriors – about an acre away – fuse into each other once more, their carapaces softening and melting into one another until all the surviving beetles had formed one massive ball, which sat taller and wider than Fusii, Gahs *and* the litter-bridge.

"Oh, no!" Akhu exclaimed. "Brother…sisters…charge that thing! Destroy it!"

Akhu sprinted across the grass toward the monolithic ball. Fusii and Gahs galloped forward behind him, sending chunks of rent earth flying behind them.

Akhu closed within two yards of the massive ball and then exploded into the air, the *Steamsword* raised above his head. The ball unfolded into a spiked, black titan that towered over the party of stunned would-be liberators. The creature stood as tall as an elder eucalyptus tree and twice as wide as the great tree's trunk. Akhu thrust his sword into the creature's foot. The monstrosity snatched Akhu with a claw and lifted him skyward.

Akhu screamed in agony as the crushing pressure of the creature's claw threatened to shatter his ribcage. He thrust the *Steamsword* into the giant beetle's claw. The creature screamed a series of quick clicks and then released its grip, allowing Akhu to plummet toward the ground far below. Akhu stabbed the *Steamsword* through the monster's armored torso and sank the weapon deep into the giant's chest, halting his descent. The creature clicked loudly, reeling backward from the pain in its chest.

"I pray you're ready, Amat!" Akhu shouted as he dangled from the hilt of the *Steamsword*.

"Ready, my Neb!" Amat replied.

Akhu twisted the hilt of the sword. Suddenly, a hissing sound rose from inside the monster's chest. The creature roared in anguish and a cloud of steam billowed from its mouth.

"Now, Amat! Now!" Akhu shouted as he released the *Steamsword*'s hilt. Akhu's fall toward the earth resumed.

Amat pulled the release lever on *Ra's Rain* and a volley of fist-sized iron balls erupted from the weapon's barrel. The balls flew into the monster's mouth and a moment later, holes burst open in the colossus' neck, chest and belly as the iron balls exploded, releasing hundreds of smaller, exploding balls. Akhu closed his eyes and whispered a quick prayer as the earth drew closer. Suddenly, a powerful force snatched him out of the air and held him aloft. He opened his eyes. Fusii was holding him in her massive trunk. Akhu leaned forward and kissed Fusii on the forehead.

"Thank you, big sister!"

Fusii gently lowered Akhu to the ground and patted the top of his head with her trunk.

Gahs raised his thick proboscis toward his sister. Fusii slapped the tip of Gahs' trunk with her own in the elephantine equivalent of a "high-five". Akhu perused his surroundings. The ground was littered with thousands of smoldering beetles.

"Good job, everyone!" He shouted as he jogged off. "Meet me at the tomb. If I have not come out within a half hour, use *Ra's Rain* to raze Sa-Seti's tomb to the ground!"

****

The interior of Sa-Seti's tomb was, surprisingly, well-lit by some mystic form of illumination and the monument smelled pleasantly of frankincense and myrrh.

"Strange," Akhu whispered.

"What did you expect," a rich, baritone voice asked. *"Something akin to a vampire's rectum?"*

Akhu whirled toward the voice. Sitting upon a golden stool was a beautiful, cinnamon-skinned woman with curly brown locks that fell past her shoulders.

"Ta-Sut!"

"Well...*sort* of," the woman giggled.

"Sa-Seti."

"You *are* a smart boy!"

Akhu pointed the *Steamsword* at Ta-Sut's chest. "Release her, demon, or I will..."

"You'll what?" Sa-Seti asked, interrupting him. "Murder the daughter of your Shekhem?" Ta-Sut's mouth moved, however, it was Sa-Seti's voice that continued to escape it.

"The Shekhem will not negotiate with demons! He will not relinquish the hand." Akhu said.

"I knew he would not," Sa-Seti replied. "That's fine. I have no use for it anymore."

"Then, why kidnap his daughter?"

"To lure *you* here."

Akhu's eyebrows furrowed. "Me? Why?"

"Because you are the only man in Menu-Kash with the wits to defy him."

"I would never betray my Shekhem!" Akhu spat.

"Your Shekhem will, one day, crush this world beneath his boot-heel if he is not stopped!" Sa-Seti hissed.

"What?" Akhu asked, confused. "Why do you say such things?"

"Although my physical form is long gone, I still maintain much of my power," Sa-Seti began. "Recently, I had a vision of

Shekhem Tehuti Ur-Amun. He had three faces. Each face ordered a different army to rape, murder and pillage all the lands of Ki-Khanga. I knew, then, that he must be stopped."

"And how do you know I will come against him? How do you know I won't tell the Shekhem what you have told me?"

"Shekhem Tehuti needs my hand to see the future," Sa-Seti replied. "I, myself, do *not*. Besides, your test against my scarab-warriors confirmed that you are more than capable."

"And what of my uncle?" Akhu inquired. "He is dying because of your 'test'."

"He is dying because I cursed him with a *rot* spell when he fought his way into my tomb and nearly foiled my plans," Sa-Seti replied. The antidote is the ichor of a white dove. He must fully drain a dove of its blood every three days for the rest of his life or his condition will worsen and he will die. If he does this, however, his health will stabilize rapidly."

"And what of Ta-Sut?"

"She is free to return home with you," Sa-Seti replied. She will not remember this conversation. Just tell her and everyone else that you destroyed me."

Akhu nodded in reluctant agreement.

"I will leave you now," Sa-Seti said. "Oh…one last thing…"

"Yes?"

"That apprentice of yours will make a fine wife and a great Shekhem one day."

With that, Ta-Sut fell limp. Akhu caught her in his arms.

"Wait," Akhu shouted. "Amat…wife? *Shekhem*?"

****

"The citizens of Menu-Kash salute you, Akhu Ankh-Kara!" Shekhem Tehuti said as he thrust a golden scepter toward Akhu, who knelt before him. General Mu – whose strength had seemingly returned – knelt beside him.

Akhu took the scepter in his hands, stood and raised the scepter high into the air. The sea of citizens cheered wildly for their hero, who defeated the most powerful sorcerer that ever lived and rescued the Shekhem's daughter from the monster's clutches. General Mu embraced his nephew, lifting him off his feet.

"I now promote you to the rank of Lieutenant, under the command of your uncle, the mighty General Mu!" The Shekhem shouted.

The crowd roared excitedly once more.

"Celebrate well tonight, gentlemen," the Shekhem continued. "For tomorrow, you will have the privilege of retrieving a powerful relic for your Shekhem from the exotic lands to the west!"

The hairs stood on the back of Akhu's neck and a chill clawed its way up his spine. "A relic, your Majesty?"

Shekhem Tehuti placed his crimson gloved right hand on Akhu's shoulder. "You will find – and bring to me – the mask of Itu-Nusani Mujo – *The Three-Faced One*."

The Signal

By Milton Davis

When Fort master Edfu's guards burst into his bedchamber carrying the dark skinned woman between them that cold winter morning he was completely surprised. He sprang upright in his bed, pulling the thick woolen sheets up to his neck to cover his grey hair covered sagging chest. The chamber slave sharing his bed squealed more from shock than discovery. Edfu's preference for his help was well known in the fort, even to his wife, which was why they maintain separate bedrooms. Still, the intrusion angered him.

"What is the meaning of this?" he yelled.

The intruders, two of his senior rampart guards, nodded respectfully. They held the arms of the woman as she sagged between them. Blood dripped from her mouth, her clothes torn and soiled. Whoever she was she apparently put a grand struggle. The guards showed signs of damage themselves. The tall man's right eye was badly bruised and barely opened while the shorter, thicker man grimaced from some unseen wound. They leaned on their pikes, their chests heaving.

"Sir, we're sorry to intrude," the tall one said. "But you ordered us to come to you immediately if we found one of them lurking about."

Edfu's eyes widen and he shivered. The blanket fell from his hands and he jumped from his bed naked. The rumors began three years ago after the fall of Menu Kash and had grown more numerous every year. Shaall fortress was one of forty citadels established by Ras Wolde'ab to enforce the boundaries between the Haisetti highlands realm and the volatile Kashite kingdom. The fortified cities recently took on more importance when rumors of a strange cult began to sift west. This cult, the Joka Watu, seemed focused on conquering Ki-Khanga and forcing its inhabitants to follow its practices. The Ras scoffed at the rumors until the refugees began arriving. Initially they were allowed entry, for there were lands in the kingdom that needed the labor these unfortunate folks provided. Eventually the flow became too much and the ras attempted to stem the flow without success. With more refugees came more rumors of the invaders. They called themselves joka watu and they rode beasts that flew like the fabled eagles of Targa but were much larger. Wolde'ab assured his people they had nothing to fear; their kingdom was stronger than any threat the Kashites' conquerors could raise; their plateaus stood strong liked that of the Creators. And as far as flying beasts were concerned, Ras Wolde'ab laughed. He would not be frightened by children's tales.

"Show me," Edfu ordered. The tall man grabbed the woman's head and tilted it to the side. She moaned as the other man dug through her hair just above her right ear.

"Here it is," he said. He pushed the hair back, revealing a small horn curled tight against the woman's scalp.

"Take her to the tower!" Edfu said too quickly. "Once you secure her send a message to Folasa to meet me immediately. Go!"

The guards bowed and dragged the woman from the chamber. Edfu hurried to his closet, the chambermaid following to perform her official duty. She selected his clothing and began dressing him. Edfu hoped she hadn't witness what he'd been shown.

"She's a joka watu, isn't she," the woman asked.

Edfu gritted his teeth. "You saw nothing, Carva, you hear me? If I hear any word of this outside these walls I'll throw you in the tower beside her, understand?"

The chambermaid dropped his shirt then quickly retrieved it.

"Yes, ras," she stammered.

Edfu fidgeted as Carva finished dressing him. He stepped into his pants then tapped his foot as she buttoned his shirt, tucked it into his pants and fastened his belt.

"Now get out of my way!" Carva scrambled and cowered against the wall. Edfu stormed out of the opulent room and into the wide hall decorated with the portraits of his family lineage. Edfu's father answered the Ras's call among the nobles for the building of the fortresses. It was an opportunity for their minor house to rise in the ranks and he took to the task, sending most of the family inheritance to construct Shaall. The result was a citadel that rivaled the Ras's palace at Haiset. When the Immaculate Potentate inspected his borderlands he chose Shaall as his temporary residence. The visit brought honor and danger to the family. The Shaalls were now the envy of the minor and major houses; Fort Shaall was the mightiest fortress on the border which would make it the target for any attempt of invasion.

Edfu reached the top of the stairs when his wife emerged from the darkness. Dame Celia Udufu was a decade younger than Edfu and a much kinder person. Edfu knew she did not favor marriage to him nor him to her, for his carnal desires were beyond the prudish woman's skills. Still they both performed their duties, siring three girls and four boys, a sizable litter for lineage and enough to cause sufficient political intrigue upon his death. Their marriage formed a bond between Fort Shaall and the nearby Fort Atillia, insuring support between the citadels should an invasion occur. After the last child Edfu decided he'd given enough of himself to his people. Though they remained married, Edfu took up residence in the west wing of the castle, joining his wife only for official functions.

"Is it true?" She was dressed impeccably as always, a trait that annoyed Edfu to no end. She always gave the appearance that she should be enjoyed from a distance, like a valuable painting or statue. He was sometimes amazed that they were able to have children.

"This in none of your concern," he quipped. "Go back to sleep."

"You seem to forget I'm the Mistress here!" she shouted.

Edfu strode to her, his anger forcing his hands into fists. Celia looked at them and grinned.

"What are you going to do, Edfu? I'm not one of your servant girls. Strike me and a thousand chariots will be at the gates demanding your blood. "

Edfu's chest heaved as he fought to control himself. What she said was true but he was struggling to decide if it mattered.

"Come then," he growled. "If you mean that we have captured a joka watu then, yes it is true. You can watch while Folasa and I torture her for information. I'm sure you'll enjoy that."

The mention of Folasa brought a sneer to Celia's perfect face. "Must you use the witch?"

Edfu stormed past her, ignoring her glare.

"Like I said, Celia, go back to bed. You have no stomach for this."

He felt her eyes on his back as he descended the stairs into the grand foyer. When he gazed upward she was still there, contempt evident on her face.

His stable boy awaited him with his horse, flanked by two of his guards but he waved the boy away. His guards dismounted and walked with him across the courtyard to the dungeon tower. A guard opened the massive oak door and the trio descended into the tower. They reached the lower floor and were enveloped by the dank smell. A torch rested beside a nearby cell; Edfu grinned when he heard powerful phrases chanted by a familiar voice.

"Leave me, "he ordered.

His guardsmen bowed and withdrew. Edfu sauntered to the cell to behold a familiar sight.

Folasa knelt before the bruised and chained joka watu, her hand clutching the woman's head. Her eyes were closed as she chanted, her head thrown back, her dreadlocks cascading over her narrow shoulders and down her back. The dragon woman convulsed with each word, an eerie smile locked on her face. Folasa's voice became louder and louder, her fingers pressing hard against the woman's head. Her rhythmic chant degenerated into an angry rant.

"I can't! I can't get through! I..."

Edfu stepped into the cell and grabbed Folasa's wrists. He pulled her hands away from the joka watu's head. The infiltrator slumped against the wall; Folasa fell into his arms.

"Are you alright?" he asked.

Folasa looked up into his eyes and smirked.

"You'll do anything to get me into your arms."

She pulled away and stood. She looked down on the quivering woman with a frown.

"She's a tough one."

Edfu stood behind her, admiring her form. They'd been lovers long ago but obligations had driven them apart. She was the only woman he considered his equal and even then he did so grudgingly. Without her skills she'd be just like the rest of them.

"Is she a witch?" he asked.

"No, but she has been conditioned by one. Her mind is a maze of spells implanted to protect her from someone like me."

"So you cannot do it."

"I didn't say that," Folasa replied. "She needs more conditioning. Nothing too extreme, just something that will weaken her mentally."

"I'll have her flogged then we'll starve her," Edfu said. "You can come back tomorrow. Time is of the essence. I need to know where these bastards are as soon as possible."

Edfu turned to leave. "When you break her bring me your report."

"I'll send someone."

Edfu turned to look at her and was met with a devilish grin. "No, I want you to deliver the report."

"Keep you mind on the situation, Fortmaster," Folasa replied. "I'll consider it."

Edfu left the cell chamber. The dungeon master was in a bawdy conversation with his guards, laughing and swearing loudly. Edfu cleared his throat and the three fell silent.

"Melos, send the flogger to the joka watu's cell," he said. "I will return tomorrow."

The dungeon master bowed deeply. "As you wish, Fortmaster."

Edfu began climbing the stairs, his guards close behind.

"Sir," Melos called out. "Are the joka watus coming?"

Edfu stopped and smiled at the dungeon master. "Not if I can help it."

Folasa entered her room in the dungeon tower and sighed. It was enough attempting to break a prisoner's mind than to also have to deal with Edfu's advances. They were not totally unwanted; she and the Shaall patriarch had had their time together before his marriage. It was an innocent dalliance to her; it meant much more to Edfu. Her time spent with him was a combination of enjoyment and investigation. There was nothing he wouldn't do which left his mind exposed to her mental probing. At the beginning he had much to share for he was close to the nobles. Since he'd become patriarch his contacts diminished, as did her interest. But this joka watu was something different. There was no boredom with this one. Her mind was a maze, a construct deliberately designed to be difficult to decipher. These joka watus left nothing to chance. If she wasn't careful she could kill the prisoner before she divulged any information.

There was a knock at her door. She opened it to tower guards carrying a large bathing tub. Folasa stepped aside then they entered, placing the tub below the room window.

"Compliments of the Fortmaster," the guard said. A string of servants carried in steaming buckets of water, filling the tub with quickly and exiting just as quick. Folasa shuttered her door then went to her cupboard. She opened the elaborately carved doors and perused her selection of oils, finally selecting a rare concoction of flower essence and emollients given to her by a wandering wizard long ago. She sauntered to the tub and slowly poured the liquid into the water, a grin coming to her face as the intoxicating aroma embraced her. She undressed and eased into the hot liquid.

Soothing warmth permeated her body and released the tension infused in her body by the interrogation. Edfu was a harsh man, but he was very attentive to those he cared for. He knew how much she loved to bath after a reading, as if to wash away the evidence of what she had to do to obtain knowledge.

The image of the joka watu's mind persisted despite her relaxed state. Never before had she experienced such a complex web of blocking spells. Who were these strange folk? They worshipped images of the very creatures they sought to destroy and were determined to force everyone to bend to their belief. They sought no riches, fame, or land, only total submission to their ways. And now they were at the edge of the frontier, probing the boundaries and devising plans. Folasa shuddered; could it happen? Could these joka watus defeat Woleo 'ab and bring the Haisetti under their spell? She imaged herself like the prisoner, her mind twisted by spells, her thoughts not her own. She opened her eyes and sighed. There would be no rest tonight. She stepped out of the bath and found a towel to dry herself. There could be no rest until she broke the joka watu's mind. The fate of the kingdom depended on it.

Edfu kept the next day as routine as possible. He met with the village elders to for updates and grievances then toured the keep in his daily inspection. Occasionally his attention would be drawn to the dungeon tower but he would divert it. Folasa was an expert and his days of interrogation were long past. The afternoon was spent with Carva, and the evening with his wife and children. By the time evening approached he was exhausted, his fatigue more from his thoughts than his actions.

Edfu slept fitfully that night. He slept alone which was not normal for him, especially in times of duress. He climbed out of bed and put on his robe. He went to the ramparts, the stair climb winding him more than he expected. He leaned against the rampart wall to catch his breath. The valley glowed like the sky, the village lights flicking between the trees. Any other night he would look out on the view with contentment, but shadows lurked between the trees, shadows with the eyes and ears of an approaching enemy. He could no longer deny it; the joka watus were coming. In the morning he would double the patrols and call out the militia. Folasa would break their captive and he would have the information he needed to preempt their attack. All would be well, he assured himself. The joka watus had never confronted a prepared foe. Fort Shaall would be prepared.

He was settling back into is bed when he heard the scream. It cut through the humid night like a jagged knife, ripping him from his drowsiness. He knew its origin; in moments he was dressed and running through the keep. Again his men met him in the foyer, this time in full armor and weapons.

They ran to the dungeon. The door was ajar, hanging on one hinge.

"Call out the guard," he ordered. He rushed into the dungeon and stumbled over the dungeon masters body, his head twisted at an unnatural angle. He ran to the cell and froze. Folasa laid sprawled again the wall, blood running from her nose, ears and her lifeless eyes. The joka watu was gone.

Edfu ran up the stairs and out into the courtyard. His men crowded the area, all of them looking upward to the observation tower.

"What are you doing?" he shouted. "Get to the ramparts now!"

They looked at him, a glazed expression on their faces. Edfu ignored the chill spreading from his back and into his limbs. He grabbed a sword from the nearest man and ran as fast as he could to the rampart steps. Once he reached the ramparts he sprinted to the observation tower. Movement from below caught his eye and he dared to look. Thousands of lights moved through the night, each one heading for the fort walls. Edfu stopped before entering the tower, his throat tight with rage.

"Get up here, damn you! Protect this fort!"

His shout seemed to break the trance. The courtyard erupted in sound, shouting men, ringing steel and desperate cries.

Edfu attacked the staircase, ignoring the pain rising in his lungs. He reached the top exhausted but ready to fight.

The joka watu stood before him, the same demented grin on her face he'd seen when Folasa tried to crack her mind. Blood ran from her wrists, pouring over her hands and dripping on her feet and the stone. He held a torch in her right hand and a small dagger in her left. Edfu looked at it more closely. It was Folasa's.

"Die, Cleave spawn!" He ran at her, sword held high. The joka watu raised her torch then emitted a piercing screech that hit Edfu like a bolt and sent him reeling. She raised both arms high then lit herself afire. The fire consumed her with unnatural alacrity, blazing like a bonfire. Edfu looked on, stunned by the woman's crazed action. As he climbed to his feet he heard another screech tear from the sky overhead. An undulating light appeared in the distance moving rapidly toward him. Edfu was transfixed by the sight, the sword loose in his grip. The shape came closer and his mouth gaped. It was a dragon. The beast passed over him and the keep then circled around to pass over again. As it made its second pass Edfu saw that it was not a real dragon, but some type of craft fashioned to resemble it. There were people inside and on top of it, working various levers and pulleys. Flaming arrow rose from the darkness, impaling his men on the ramparts and falling into the keep to set whatever they touched aflame. The bonfire that was once the joka watu continued to burn, a beacon for the beast. Edfu took off his cloak. Maybe he could douse the flame with the thick fabric. He stepped toward it and halted. Something emerged from the fire, a flaming human form. It came toward him, its arms opened wide. Edfu stepped back, waving his sword frantically.

"Stay away, stay away!"

But the flaming figure continued to come, pushing him against the rampart wall.

"Damn you! Damn you all!"

A searing pain erupted in his back. Edfu twisted back and forth, trying to see what was causing him so much agony. The flaming figure halted its advance and a cackling sound came from its head. Fire wrapped around Edfu's waist and he cried out in terror and pain. He burned. The fort burned. He tore at his blazing robe but it was fused to his skin. There was only one hope for him. Far below in the darkness, below where he stood, was a small pond. He struggled upon the rampart. Over him the joka circled as if waiting. He lost his reason to pain. He jumped.

Fearless

By Balogun Ojetade

Keita Bojang, great Mansakeh of the Kingdom of Mali, sat before Jubeh, the Royal Diviner. The old, blind man had been summoned to the palace to consult the oracle on the recent birth of his son, Anjai…and on the passing of Anjai's mother, Maala.

Anjai stared into Jubeh's sightless eyes as the old man placed the boy's tiny, right foot into a bowl of warm sand. Anjai cooed and giggled as the sand tickled his plump, little toes.

Jubeh grabbed a fistful of the sand and tossed it onto the floor. He rocked back and forth as the Alifaa Faloloo – the ancestors – spoke to him. Great King Keita cradled Anjai in his arms and awaited instructions from the spirits.

Jubeh's rocking stopped. His head fell against his shoulder and his chest heaved as he took a deep breath.

"Anjai is to exceed, in skill and wits, all the children of this great nation, past and present."

Mansakeh Keita smiled and then kissed Anjai on the forehead.

"However," Jubeh sighed. "He will bring you much heartache, as he will leave this world long before you."

The Mansakeh's jaw fell slack. "What?! How?"

"He will be killed by an animal," Jubeh replied. "Either an ape, a crocodile, or a dog. The ancestors will not say, specifically, which."

"What can we do to prevent this?" Mansakeh Keita asked, wiping tears from his cheeks.

"Nothing, Great One," Jubeh replied. "The ancestors have decreed it so."

"I am Keita Bojang," the Mansakeh spat. "Mansakeh of Mali, the greatest nation in all Ki-Khanga. There is *nothing* that I cannot do!"

"Great One, the ancestors have spoken; we…"

"*I* have spoken!" Mansakeh Keita shouted as he sprang to his feet.

Anjai kicked his feet and giggled.

"What the ancestors have revealed is a warning; nothing more," the Mansakeh said. "I will ensure my son's safety and he *will* rule Mali upon my passing."

"Yes, Great One," Jubeh sighed.

The great king sauntered out of his chamber and stumbled into the courtyard, where he rocked Anjai into a deep and peaceful sleep.

****

Anjai whirled, kicking up clouds of red dirt as he rent the air with his broadsword. He drew a figure-eight pattern in the air with the razor-sharp steel and then thrust the sword into the stiff, leather scabbard that hung from his belt.

"Your technique is superb," a familiar voice bellowed.

"Thank you, father," Anjai said, turning toward the Mansakeh. "Perhaps, one day soon, I will be blessed to use what I have learned over all these years on the battlefield, in service to the great Mansakeh Keita."

The Mansakeh hung his head. "Son, you *will* leave this compound one day. Please, be patient."

"But, I am terribly lonely, father," Anjai sighed. "I live half a day's ride from Timbuktu…from *you*; and there is not another living human soul anywhere near here."

"You have your housekeeper and your personal guard," Mansakeh Keita said. "And I visit as often as I can."

"Uli and Asuru are not big on conversation, father," Anjai

said. "And this is <u>your</u> first visit in two moon cycles."

"Shall I throw a celebration in your honor, then?" the Mansakeh asked. "I can bring the best drummers and dancers and the most beautiful women in all Timbuktu, including that young woman who had you so smitten at your last celebration – the daughter of the Alikaalah of Diari – what is her name…"

"Akinah," Anjai replied.

"Akinah! That's it! I can invite her."

"No, father," Anjai said, shaking his head. "My desires are less…complex."

"What, then?" the Mansakeh asked.

"I want a puppy," Anjai answered.

Mansakeh Keita's brow furrowed and the corners of his mouth curled downward. "No, son; no puppies…*ever!*"

"Why not?" Anjai asked. "A friendly puppy…"

"Will become a *dog*," the Mansakeh spat. "And a dog may be the death of you!"

Anjai's heart raced. Sweat ran down his forehead and dripped from the tip of his nose, leaving tiny pools in the sand between his feet. "The death of me? How so?"

The Mansakeh paced back and forth, rubbing his temple with the tips of his fingers. He squeezed his eyes shut, as if to prevent from seeing the painful truth.

"When you were born, the Royal Diviner told me that you would meet your fate through an encounter with an ape, a crocodile, or a *dog*."

"Then, it is possible that a dog will not be the culprit?" Anjai asked.

"It is possible," Mansakeh Keita answered.

"Then, I am willing to take that chance," Anjai said. "If I raise it with love and kindness, would it dare harm me?"

"You have a point," the Mansakeh said, rubbing his smooth, ebon chin. "Alright, then, I will send forth my wisest advisors to find the friendliest, most intelligent newborn puppy in all Mali!"

****

Anjai's heart soared the moment he laid eyes upon the playful, stark-white Azawakh pup that the Wise Ones had chosen for him. "He is beautiful, father! I know we will become the closest of friends.

"What will you call him, son?" the Mansakeh asked.

"His name is…'Fatinga'," Anjai replied.

"Fearless," Mansakeh Keita said, with a nod. "That is a good name."

Mansakeh Keita placed a hand upon his son's sinewy shoulder.

"Son, while the Wise Ones searched high and low for your pup, they heard that the Alikaalah of Diari seeks a young man to wed his daughter. The Alikaalah is a dear friend and has led Diari well on my behalf. It would please me if you married Akinah."

"When will you arrange the marriage, father?" Anjai inquired.

"It is not that simple," the Mansakeh replied. "The Alikaalah of Diari loves tests of strength, bravery and wits; thus, he has put forth a challenge."

"Which is?" Anjai asked, raising an eyebrow.

"The first to scale the wall of the Alikaalah's palace and climb through his daughter's window – which is on the uppermost floor – wins her hand in marriage," the Mansakeh replied.

"How high is this wall, father?"

"Seventy cubits," the Mansakeh replied. "One hundred and five feet."

"Has anyone tried such a treacherous climb?" Anjai asked.

"Many," the Mansakeh answered. "They all fell to their deaths. Does that frighten you, son?"

"No, father," Anjai replied. "Not one bit."

"*That's* my boy," the Mansakeh said, beaming. "The Bojang bloodline is notorious for exceptional bravery!"

"It is not bravery that makes me so assured father," Anjai said. "It is knowing that I will die by ape, dog or crocodile…

not by a fall."

"Ha!" The Mansakeh bellowed. "Sometimes, a fox's head serves a warrior better than a lion's heart."

****

The carriage ride to Diari was the happiest moment of Anjai's life. He was finally free of the confines of his compound. He thrust his head out of the window of his carriage, relishing the kiss of the desert breeze upon his face. His camels raced across the network of sand roads, spurred on by the expert handling of Anjai's bodyguard, Asuru.

After a day-and-a-half ride, Anjai arrived in the bustling town of Diari – the *City of Gold* – the location of the largest gold mine in all the lands of Ki-Khanga. The palace of the Alikaalah was constructed entirely of gold. Its interior and exterior walls, floors, doors and ramparts – all gold.

Anjai's carriage was met by Idris Ul-Arbah, Chief of the Palace Guard, as it approached the palace. "How may we help you, kind sir?"

"I am Anjai, son of Mansakeh Keita Bojang," Anjai replied. "And I have come to win the hand of the Alikaalah's daughter."

Idris dropped to one knee. "Welcome, Your Highness. Will you need accommodations for the night?"

"No," Anjai replied, stepping down from his carriage. "I will scale the wall after a brief stretch."

"As you wish," Idris said, rising to his feet. The Chief of the Palace Guard turned and sauntered back through the palace gates.

Anjai bent forward and touched the ground with his palms, stretching the muscles in his back and legs. He held the position for a few minutes and then stood bolt upright. "I am ready, now."

Asuru nodded.

Anjai sprinted toward the eastern wall of the palace – his father's informants had told him that Akinah's chamber was on that side – which was dotted, from-top-to-bottom, with golden spikes, each as thick around as a man's wrist and protruding two feet out of the wall. He exploded upward, thrusting his arms above his head. He grabbed one of the spikes with both hands and pulled himself up until his feet rested firmly on a spike beneath him. He exploded upward again and again, grabbing the spikes over his head and pulling himself ever closer to Akinah's window.

Finally, he reached it. He swung his legs toward the open window and tumbled inside. Anjai landed with a dull thud as his buttocks struck the golden floor.

He fought off the pain and pulled himself to his feet. Sitting on a bed of plush, pastel-colored pillows was Akinah, who was even more beautiful than Anjai remembered.

"I am Anjai," he began. "Son of Mansakeh Keita Bojang…"

"I know who you are," Akinah giggled. "Cease with the formalities; we are to be married in less than a fortnight. Soon, I will be scolding you for passing gas in our sleeping chamber. How informal can you be?"

"Gods, you are so beautiful," Anjai said, taking a seat beside her.

"More importantly, I am highly intelligent, skilled in business and spent eight years in Fez, training under the greatest wizards to ever traverse the sands of Ki-Khanga," Akinah said.

"Does my complimenting you on your beauty offend you?" Anjai inquired.

"No," Akinah replied. You merely speak truth. However, if you are going to shower me with compliments, please be fully accurate in your descriptions."

Anjai laughed. For the first time since he left his compound, he looked forward to returning home, for he would return with a magnificent friend and partner to share it with.

****

Akinah awakened with a start. A frightening din came from the kitchen below. She recognized the noise as the snarls of an angry canine. Something had Fatinga quite vexed.

Akinah now loved the dog – and he, her – but when Anjai first told her of the ancestors' decree on how her husband would die, she begged Anjai to kill the Azawakh. She was now happy that he refused, for the dog had proven time and again to be a loyal and protective companion to the couple.

Akinah gently shook her husband's broad shoulders, awakening him.

"What is it, my love?" Anjai asked, rubbing his eyes.

"It is Fatinga," Akinah whispered. "He is growling at something in the kitchen."

Anjai sprang from the bed and grabbed a pair of cotton trousers. "I hear him!"
Akinah stood and threw on her silk robe.

"If I ask you to stay here, will you oblige?" Anjai asked, as he snatched his broadsword its ivory stand.

Akinah pursed her lips and raised an eyebrow in reply.

"I thought not," Anjai said with a shrug. "Let's go!"

Anjai darted down the stairs. Akinah followed closely behind him. They sprinted toward the kitchen. Fatinga stood defiantly, baring his teeth and snarling at a half dozen squat, husky figures, which lurked in the shadows.

"Show yourselves!" Anjai demanded as he inched closer to the kitchen.

The figures lumbered out of the shadows. They were chimpanzees, but their eyes revealed an intelligence and a brutality possessed only by man. All except one were black as pitch, with wrinkled, pink faces, twisted into harsh scowls. At the head of the apes stood one who was slightly taller than its brethren and of a sandy complexion. The sand-hued chimp raised its right arm high. Dangling from its fingers was the severed head of Anjai's bodyguard, Asuru.

"Belong you, him does?" the sand-colored creature snickered in the native, human Ki-Khanga tongue.

"He was my bodyguard, monster!" Anjai spat.

"Him not guard you body too good," the chimpanzee said.

A shrill laughter erupted from the other chimps.

"Leave now, ape and we will let you live," Anjai said.

"We leave, you mate come with," the leader ape said. "She Gold King baby; we trade she with Gold King for lot gold; lot food."

"No," Anjai said.

"Wokay," the sand-hued ape said with a shrug. "We kill and take mate, then."

The chimpanzees charged forward. Fatinga leapt toward one, sinking his fangs into the ape's neck as he ripped at the creature's belly with his rear paws. The ape let loose a hissing gurgle as blood erupted from its neck and its entrails spilled onto the floor.

Anjai rolled forward, delivering a powerful thrust as his momentum brought him to a kneeling position. His sword sank into the chest of a charging chimpanzee. The creature shuddered and then slid off the blade, collapsing, with a loud thud, onto its back.

Akinah waved her hands in wide circles in front of her, as if she was scrubbing the floor with her palms. A huge hole opened beneath the feet of a pair of chimpanzees that sprinted toward her. The apes plummeted into the deep hole. A moment later, the cavity closed over them, muffling their cries of terror.

The sand-colored ape and the surviving pitch-black ape spun on their heels and dived out of an open kitchen window. Their cries pierced the night calm as they scurried off into the shadows of the desert oasis.

"Is everyone alright?" Anjai asked, his eyes darting from Akinah to Fatinga.

"I'm fine, love," Akinah replied.

Fatinga replied with a throaty bark.

"At least we know that it won't be any ape that is the death of you," Akinah said.

"They can always return," Anjai said.

"And we will fill ape-heaven with them all," Akinah half-quipped.

"Get some rest, you two," Anjai said. "Tomorrow morning, we burn these foul creatures and bury Asuru."

****

The day was exceptionally beautiful. Anjai was invigorated by the gentle breeze, which caressed and cooled him as he breast-stroked in the warm waters of the Sati-Baa River.

Akinah gathered moist sand from the shore in a calabash. She poured the sand onto the ground and sculpted it into little figurines. Fatinga paced back-and-forth along the shoreline as he kept a watchful eye on Anjai. The dog unleashed a high-pitched howl.

Akinah looked up from her sculptures and spotted the head of a large crocodile break the surface of the water just a few yards from her unsuspecting husband. Fatinga howled again.

"Anjai," Akinah shouted, pointing at the massive crocodile. "Behind you!"

Anjai peered over his shoulder. He screamed in terror and began to swim furiously. The crocodile was hot on his fluttering heels.

Akinah glanced at her sand sculptures. They had fused together, forming themselves into the perfect likeness of a crocodile. The sorceress stomped the tip of the sand crocodile's tail. A moment later, the real crocodile hissed and thrashed in agony. The water around the crocodile became a deep crimson. With a swipe of the back of her hand, Akinah knocked off a piece of the sand sculpture's jaw. The real crocodile thrashed violently in the water as its lower jaw disjointed and then fell from the crocodile's head. The wedge-shaped mass of flesh, bone and teeth floated up-shore as the crocodile sank beneath the surface of the water.

Anjai swam to shore. He scampered out of the water and then sprinted into his wife's open arms. "You saved me!" He planted brisk kisses upon his wife's forehead and cheeks. He then knelt next to Fatinga and rubbed his neck. "You did well, little brother. Thank you!" Fatinga wagged his tail.

"As long as you have Fatinga and me around, no harm will befall you," Akinah said. "You will live to see your grandchildren grow old. We should tell your father about…"

A sound, like distant thunder, rent the air.

"Someone approaches," Anjai said, pointing toward a fast approaching mass in the distance.

A woman on camelback galloped toward them. Her leathery skin was as dark as the smooth, mahogany saddle upon which she sat.

"Your Highness," the woman called, bringing the camel to a stop a yard from them.

Akinah recognized the woman as Nura, her father's Emissary. "Yes?"

"Your mother has fallen very ill," Nura replied. "She asks for you; your father has commanded that I escort your carriage to Diari at once. I have already alerted your driver. He and your housekeeper are packing your travel bag as we speak."

"I will ride with you," Anjai said.

"No, my love," Akinah said. "There is an old woman along the way who possesses a deep knowledge of healing herbs. I will hire her services, see that my mother is well-cared for and return home in less than half a fortnight.

"Fine," Anjai said. "When you return, I would like to begin laying the foundation for those grandchildren whom I will usher into old age."

Akinah blushed as she jogged toward their compound. "Why wait? Escort me back to the compound and let's lay that foundation before I depart."

"As you command," Anjai said, chasing her.

Fatinga trotted behind his masters, gleefully wagging his tail.

****

Anjai awoke to the smell of fresh horned melon and yogurt with a hint of vanilla. Uli had prepared his favorite breakfast. He darted out of bed, threw on a pair of loose-fitting, linen trousers and a waist-length tunic and then darted down the stairs, not stopping until he reached the dining room.

"I saama," Uli said in greeting. *"Good morning."*

Anjai returned the greeting – "I saama."

The elderly woman bent slightly at the waist in salutation and then left Anjai to enjoy his meal.

Anjai devoured the food, gulped down two cups of water and then jogged out the door. Fatinga burst out the door behind him.

"How far shall we run, Fatinga?" Anjai asked, patting the dog's head. "Two miles?"

Fatinga barked in approval.

"Two miles it is, then," Anjai said.

Man and dog trotted along the sand and gravel road leading out of the compound.
After a short while, Fatinga stopped running. He stared up at the palm trees that lined the trail. A low growl rose from his gut.

Anjai knelt beside Fatinga. "What is it, little brother?"

From out of the trees descended a score of pitch-hued chimpanzees. The apes landed in a series of dull thuds, kicking up clouds of sand and red dirt as each hit the ground.

When the dust cleared, an army of apes stood before Anjai. Standing a yard ahead of the chimpanzees was their sand-colored leader.

"'Member we Mkeko?" The leader of the apes asked. "We Mkeko 'member you. You kill we Mkeko; now, Mkeko return favor!"
The apes lurched forward in unison.

"Fatinga, run!" Anjai commanded, as he dashed off the trail.

Anjai exploded into a full sprint, with Fatinga running close behind him. The Mkeko gave chase, some trotting across the sand and dirt, others swinging and leaping through the trees. Anjai ran on and on; out of his compound; across the oasis upon which his home was built…and into a pool of quicksand. Anjai tried to swim out of it, but the grainy liquid was too thick. Within moments, only his torso was visible above the surface. Fatinga barked at Anjai, as if to scold him for putting himself into such a dangerous predicament. Soft footsteps approached. Fatinga whirled toward the sound. The sand-colored chimpanzee was coming. Fatinga snarled viciously. The ape stopped a few yards from the dog and pointed at Anjai, who had now sunk to his chest.

"You run right where we Mkeko want, silly man. Now, we Mkeko wait for Gold-King baby come home; we Mkeko take daughter; trade for lot gold; lot food. Bye-bye, silly man."

The sand-hued chimpanzee turned and walked back toward the army of Mkeko, which awaited him in the distance.

"Fatinga," Anjai called. "Run back to the compound. When Uli sees you arrive without me, she will come looking."

Fatinga did not budge. He stood his ground, growling to keep the surrounding Mkeko at bay.

Anjai sank farther. Sand rushed into the top of his tunic. "Fatinga, hurry!"

The dog refused to leave its master alone and unprotected. It fearlessly stood its ground.

Sand slapped Anjai in the chin.

"Fatinga…please."

Fatinga did not budge.

As Anjai sank completely beneath the surface of the quicksand, he realized that the ancestors, indeed, spoke truth. He had met his fate through a dog. A protective, loyal and fearless one.

The Greatest

By Milton Davis and Balogun Ojetade

They came from all over Ki Khanga, from the arid plains of Fez, the forested peaks of Haiset, the windward Kiswala islands and the dense forests of Kongo. Some even trekked from as far as Kamit, daring to cross the stormy straits separating the mysterious island from the mainland. No matter their origin, their destination was the same; the grand city of Sati-Baa. It was Baa Fest, the month long celebration, the time between seasons when the citizens of Sati Baa celebrated their good fortunes and the blessing of the Twin Rivers.

For three weeks revelers poured into the city, indulging in the excesses of food and entertainment. But on the fourth week the visitors transformed. It was the buildup to the final event of the celebration, the Ibuthodili, The Gathering of Warriors, the greatest wrestling competition in all Ki Khanga. People flowed toward the massive amphitheater like a swollen river during rainy season. Though the tournament would not begin for another two days the potential spectators began the trek early to get choice seats. It was a lively spectacle; people dressed in the colors of their regions played instruments and sang the songs of their homelands and praise songs for the wrestlers they supported. As prone to happen under such circumstances arguments and fights broke out but were quickly suppressed by friends or the numerous constables lurking among the throng.

Despite the controlled chaos a loud rhythmic drumming rolled over the cacophonous crowd, drawing its attention. A large procession worked its way through; their clothing and manners making them stand out even among the most richly dressed. A short wide man wearing a shimmering red cloak edged in gold and precious stones led the procession, leading a dozen men and women who danced with an energy which seemed unnatural. Bordering them were drummers dressed in white vests, pants and headbands, flailing away at their djembes. Following them were twelve stout men bearing a litter of ironwood. Atop the litter sat a man whose presence and stature marked him as a contestant, a wrestler come to challenge his peers.

"Make way! May way!" the cloaked man shouted, his loud voice drowning out the curious murmurs of those nearby. Most were impressed by this unexpected sight, but not all. A trio of drunken men staggered before the entourage. The tallest of the three stood before the hawker then took a swig from his gourd.

"What is this?" he slurred. "Another victim for Kankan Musa?"

The djele grinned. "You see the coming of victory. Behold the greatest wrestler of all time, Kola Kujo!"

The mention of the wrestler's name sent the dancers and drummers into a frenzy. They chanted in sync to the drums. "Kola...Kujo...Kola...Kujo...Kola...Kujo!"

Their mood was so infectious that those nearby took up the chant and danced as well. The drunken man and was not amused.

"Kola Kujo?" he said. "I've never heard of him. He looks like a wet chicken compared to Kankan Musa!"

The djele laughed. "Your words are like tiny farts in a storm. In two days all of Ki Khanga will know the name Kola Kujo!"

The djele shoved the drunken man aside as the Kola Kujo entourage plowed its way to the amphitheater. Spectators followed in its wake, chanting and singing along. Kola Kujo remained silent and unemotional under his beaded veil. The procession advanced up the road to the amphitheater then veered toward a three story stone building beside the venue. It was the Wrestler's temple, the facility where the competing wrestlers resided, trained before and during the tournament. A few of the wrestlers emerged from the temple, drawn out by the crowd and the commotion. The constables hidden among the throng made themselves known. They formed a human barrier between the throng and the Wrestler's temple armed with their lethal throwing clubs. They parted to let Kola Kujo and his entourage through. The djele led them up the hill to the temple entrance. They were greeted by a stout man whose thick arms and broad chest hinted at a past as a wrestler.

"What is this?" the man said.

The djele approached the man then prostrated before him, touching his forehead to the ground as if greeting an oba. The gestured had the desired effect; the large man unfolded his arms, placing his hands on his waist.

"You do us great honor by greeting us, Trainer," the djele said. "I am Jomoke Ehioze, master djele of Egbado. And this is..."

"Kola Kujo," the trainer said. "I am Yigo, master trainer of the temple. You're late. You should have been here two weeks ago."

The bearers lowered Kola Kujo's litter. Two of the dancers hurried to the litter then rolled out a cotton carpet decorated with abstract drawings of turtles and crocodiles to Jomoke's side. As Kola Kujo stood the others fell to their knees. The warrior took his time walking off the litter to Jomoke's side.

"I apologize for our tardiness," Kola Kujo said, his voice as masculine as his physique. "My preparation for battle rivals that of Tyraks and is just as effective. Although I come with respect for my fellow wrestlers, I fear for them."

Yigo looked puzzled. "Why is that?"

"Because like the Tyraks, I fear that I have been rendered invincible."

The trainer's laugh was drowned by a deeper, more powerful voice. Kankan Musa strode through the temple entrance, followed by the other wrestlers. Yigo stepped aside and Musa took his place before Kola Kujo. Musa was a head taller that Kola Kujo and twice as wide. If the Kujo was intimidated by the champion wrestler he did not show it. He looked up into Musa's face then smirked.

"You are smaller than I imagined," Kola Kujo said.

"And you are exactly as I expected," Musa said.

"Your reputation has traveled throughout Ki Khanga," Kujo said. "It will be an honor to face you for the championship."

Musa and the other wrestlers laughed.

"I think there are a few dozen wrestlers that would disagree with you," Musa said.

"It doesn't matter if they agree or disagree," Kujo said. "This match is destined to happen. I'm sure you'll be a worthy opponent and handle your defeat well."

"My...defeat?"

Musa's hands balled into massive fists. Before he could strike Yigo and Jomoke stepped between the two men.

"This is not the ring," the trainer said. "I don't like your attitude, Kola Kujo. I suggest you find different lodging."

"I had no intentions of residing in the temple," Kola Kujo said. "The purpose of our journey was to invite my comrades to our camp for the greatest feast they have ever witnessed. It is my gesture to them, an apology in advance for the vicious beatings they will suffer at my hands during the tournament."

Yigo rolled his eyes. "It is their decision. For now I must ask you to leave."

Kola Kujo looked past the trainer to the disgruntled wrestlers.

"The feast will begin at dusk," he said. "Our camp is at the lake's edge near the ironwood grove. It would honor me if you would attend."

Kola Kujo bowed then returned to his litter. The bearers lifted him to their shoulders turned toward the road then waited patiently as the dancers and drummer took their places. Djele Jomoke prostrated once again before the trainer and Kankan Musa.

"I hope you will come," he said. "It will be a grand feast!"

The drummers played and Jomoke scurried to take his place in front of the entourage. They pranced away; Kola Kujo perched as steady as an eagle on its perch.

"That man is crazy," Kakan Musa said.

"He is," the trainer replied.

"I think I'll break both his arms," Kankan Musa said.

"You won't get the chance," Yigo said. "He won't make it beyond the first round. If he does, I'll break my own arms."

The men laughed then returned to the temple, the other wrestlers close behind.

Kola Kujo's procession marched out of Sati-Baa to their encampment near the lakeshore. Despite their long journey the drummers and dancers continued their celebration while the porters and others unpacked the cooking pots, laid out the tables and built built fires to prepare the feast. Kujo and Jomoke stood side by side, both with arms folded as they observed the activity. One of the cooks ran up to them, prostrating before asking a question.

"Great Kujo! I fear we may not have enough goat for the signature meal."

"Jomoke!" Kola Kujo called out.

Jomoke pulled his robe aside, revealing a heavy coin pouch. He extracted three coins, thought for a moment, and then took out another coin.

"Here, Noma," Jomoke said. "Bring back the fattest goats you can find. This will be a feast befitting Kola Kujo's upcoming victory."

Jomoke looked to Kola Kujo for approval. Kola Kujo nodded his head and Noma hurried away to the market.

As the sun settled behind the Cleave Mountains the banquet guests arrived. Jomoke met each wrestler as he and his entourage arrived, honoring them with platitudes and grand gestures deserving of their rank. The dancers transformed to servers, leading them to their tables, careful not to seat rivals too close to each other. When everyone was seated the dancers gathered at the center of the tables. The drummers played a different tune accompanied by Jomoke's melodic kora playing and the shrill piping of wooden flutes. Kola Kujo entered the center of the circle, this time clothed in a pair of white pants with cowrie shells about the hems. A flowing kente robe hung from his broad shoulders; he wore a black cap decorated with star shaped gold buttons. He counted the attendees; ten wrestlers had accepted his invitation, more than he anticipated. He raised his arms and the music ceased.

"Welcome, my friends!" said. "There is a saying in Oyo that states if you have friends you will never be alone. Tonight I invite you all to be my friend. In two days we will be adversaries. But after tonight, we will all be friends. Eat and drink you fill!"

The drummers and kora players filled the night with music as the revelers feasted. Kola Kujo sat at the main table with his adversaries, sharing stories of previous matches and victories. Oddly enough Kola Kujo added nothing to the conversation. He smiled, clapped laughed yet did not add to the storytelling.

Finally Tarik Al Jaheen, the towering black bearded wrestler from Fez slammed his cup on the table, bringing the festival to silence.

"Great Kola Kujo," he began, 'I take the liberty of speaking for my friends. Thank you for this wonderful repast and the amazing entertainment. The skill of your drummers is unmatched, and your dancers bring new meaning to the words talent and beauty. Had I known the women of Oyo were so lovely I would have loaded four more camel with a dowry!"

The revelers laughed as the female dancers pretended to be coy.

"Yet we have heard no stories from you, new friend," he continued. "How is it that you come to be so celebrated in your homeland? What great wrestlers have you defeated to earn the honor to compete with us?"

Jomoke was about to speak in Kola Kujo's stead when the wrestler waved him down.

"I have no stories to tell," Kola Kujo confessed. "All my life I wanted to be a wrestler. My father, Oba Dende, spared no expense with my training. I have studied under all the great wrestlers of Oyo. Some that were my teachers are now my students, so amazing are my skills."

"That is nice to hear and probably better to say," Al Jaheen said. "But we still have not heard your stories."

For the first time since his arrival Kola Kujo was hesitant.

"I have fought no matches," Kola Kujo finally said. "This will be my first tournament."

Al Jaheem's mouth fell open. "You have never fought a match yet you are allowed to compete in the greatest tournament of all Ki Khanga? Suddenly your food has lost its flavor."

Jomoke quickly stepped between the two wrestlers.

"Honorable Jaheem," he said. "I believe you misunderstand."

"No, I don't think I do, djele," he replied. "Every man in this tournament has fought hard to have the privilege to compete in the Ibuthodili. Some never get the opportunity. And now your master dances up on the back of his rich baba with no experience and expects to fight against us? I will not tolerate it!

"We understand your concern," Jomoke said. "But the rules of the Ibuthodili state that each region can send its greatest wrestler, regardless of skill or experience. Kola Kujo is Oyo's greatest wrestler, so he is granted the opportunity to compete."

Al Jaheem stood suddenly,

"You have no reason to be here, Kola Kujo," Al Jaheem said. "If I meet you on the dirt, I will give you no respect."

"Nor will I you," Kola Kujo replied.

Al Jaheem pushed himself from the table then stormed away. The other wrestlers followed, more than a few taking a few bowls of food with them. Kulo Kujo frowned as he watched them walk away.

"How disappointing," he said. "I was hoping to defeat them all with respect. Now it seems I must have contempt for them."

Kola looked about at his worried entourage.

"Do not be discouraged!" he shouted. "Let us continue to celebrate the coming victory!"

The people cheered and the celebration continued well into the night.

On a normal day it should have been the sun's warm touch waking Kola Kujo. Instead it was an insistent shaking and angry voice stirring him from a decadent slumber.

"Wake up, Kujo! Wake up now!"

Kola Kujo jumped up, grabbing Yigo in a choke hold. The trainer attempted to reverse Kujo's hold to no avail.

"See?" he managed to say. "This man is dangerous!"

Kola Kulo eyes cleared. A man stood before him, a black skinned man wearing a constable uniform and holding a throwing club festooned with lake shark teeth.

"Who are you?" Kola asked. "And why are you here?"

"I'm Kofi Essien, senior constable of Sati-Baa. Yigo accuses you of poisoning the wrestlers who attended your feast last night. I'm here to investigate his accusations and if they are true, arrest you."

Kola looked dumbfounded. "Poisoned them? I did no such thing! When they left our feast they were angry and healthy. And now you say they are dead?"

"Not dead, but they might as well be," Yigo said. "They won't be able to compete, which was your plan all along!"

"Plan?" Kola shook his head. "My only plan was to compete in the tournament, defeat everyone and return home as champion."

"Kujo, do I have permission to search your camp?" Kofi asked.

"Of course," Kola replied. "You will find nothing."

The Sati-Baa constables spread out through the encampment, searching the grounds and baggage under Yigo's scrutiny. Kola and his people sat calm during the search until a loud exclamation drew there attention.

"Aha!"

Yigo hurried up to Kola bearing a yellow root in his hand.

"This is what you poisoned them with!" he said.

Kola tilted his head as he took the root from Yigo's hand.

"This? You must be mistaken. This is oburi root."

"Exactly!" Yigo said. He turned to Kofi. "Oburi root is a strong laxative. In proper quantities it can be very poisonous."

"Nonsense!" Kola said. He broke the root in half the tossed the larger piece into his mouth. Yigo looked on in horror as Kola Kujo chewed the root.

"Oburi is a delicacy in Oyo," he said. "We eat it every day, from the time we are children."

Kofi grinned. "Apparently you've developed a tolerance to it."

The old constable turned to Yigo. "I can't arrest a man for ignorance, although it would make my life much easier. Nor can he be disqualified from the tournament."

"How can we have a full tournament with only half the wrestlers?" Yigo asked.

"That's your problem," Kori replied. "All I know is that you will have a tournament. I'm not about to deal with thousands of angry Ki Khangans if the tournament is cancelled. Besides, the Ibuthodili has never been cancelled since it began 600 years ago. Do you want to go down in history as the first Trainer to do so?

Yigo trembled then pointed his finger at Kola Kujo.

"Report to the stadium first light tomorrow morning. Your match will be the first...and your last!"

Kola Kujo swallowed the root. "I will be there, great trainer. The journey to my victory will begin tomorrow!

****

Kola Kujo sat, spread-eagled, on his haunches inside his tent, which was erected just outside the huge circle of sand within the stadium. It was within this circle that the matches of the Ibuthodili had been held since its beginning.

His entourage danced in a circle around the tent softly chanting "Ko-la...Ku-jo...Ogun Ye-O! Ko-la...Ku-jo...Ogun Ye-O!" – *"Kola Kujo; Ogun lives!"*

Jomoke handed Kola Kujo half of a large young coconut. Kujo dipped his hand into the cool coconut water and then rubbed the back of his neck with it.

"Now, hydrate," Jomoke said.

"This is the third agbon I have drunk from today," Kola Kujo sighed. "I am going to turn into an agbon if I drink one more of these."

"Water constitutes about sixty-six percent of muscle tissue, twenty-five percent of fatty tissue, and acts within each cell of your body to transport nutrients and dispel waste," Jomoke said. "In each match – taking into account the heat in the auditorium and the intensity of the fights, you are losing more than a quart of water; so, you must hydrate."

"Okay, okay, I will drink it," Kola Kujo said. "Of course, after I have felled my last opponent and taken this championship, you will bring me a cask of that famed Sati Baa wine, in celebration of today's victories."

"Of course." Jomoke replied with a slight bow.

"Gods!"

Kola Kujo looked toward the source of the voice. Tifase, one of the bearers of Kola Kujo's litter, stared, wide-eyed, at the circle of sand.

Kola Kujo crept behind Tifase. He peered over the litter bearer's shoulder and then focused on the circle.

A rail thin wrestler, who stood nearly eight feet tall, was ripping away at his opponent with lightning fast elbows, knees and kicks. His opponent, a stocky man, with leathery skin, grabbed the thin man's arms in desperation. With blinding speed, the thin man broke out of the leather-skinned man's grip and then yanked the man's head under his armpit.

The thin man wrapped his arm around his opponent's neck, which trapped the man's head against the thin man's ribs. The thin man then pulled his wrist up into the leather-skinned man's throat, strangling him with a tight guillotine choke. After a second, the man tapped the thin man's arm in submission.

"Who is that?" Kola Kujo inquired.

"He calls himself *The Ghoul*," Jomoke said, peeking out of the tent. "He won't tell anyone his real name. I did not know he was in this tournament. I thought they had banned him from the circles of sand throughout all Ki Khanga."

Banned him?" Kola Kujo said. "Why?"

"Because he finished his opponents too quickly, from what I heard" Jomoke replied. Spectators felt they were not getting their money's worth. Also, his gaunt appearance sickens many."

"Well, ghoul, goblin, or whatever he calls himself, I am putting him to sleep."

"Well, it looks like you are about to get your chance,"

Jomoke said, pointing toward the circle, from where they were removing the Ghoul's opponent. Yigo strode toward Kola Kujo's tent.

"Let's go, *champion*," Yigo said with a smirk. "The Ghoul awaits you."

"You lied to me, trainer," Kola Kujo said, springing to his feet. "You promised that I would have the first victory of the tournament."

I promised you the first match," Yigo spat.

Kola Kujo waved his hand as if he was swatting a horsefly. "Match…victory…they are one and the same for Kola Kujo.

"And I did not lie; that unlucky fool was just The Ghoul's warm-up," Yigo said. "You are, indeed, the first match of the day."

Kola Kujo began dancing before Yigo, swaying from side to side and hunching his shoulders an inch below the trainer's chin.

"Good, the heat seems to have sapped the energy of the spectators, bearing witness to my skills will lift their spirits," Kola Kujo said. "Now, go, trainer! It is time to bless the circle of sand with my presence."

The drums thundered as the chant of Kola Kujo's entourage grew louder.

Yigo stormed off.

Kola Kujo danced out of the tent. Jomoke, Tifase and the rest of his litter bearers followed closely behind him, matching the wrestler's steps. The entourage joined him, the dancers and drummers smiling and waving at the spectators in the packed stadium, encouraging them to join in.

And they did, shaking the arena with their chanting.

"Ko-la…Ku-jo…Ogun Ye-O!"

****

"…hailing from Oyo and weighing in at two-hundred and sixteen pounds…Kola Kujo!"

Bunseki, the announcer and referee, shouted, his voice echoing throughout the stadium.

A thunderous cheer rose from the crowd.

Kola Kujo shook his shoulders up and down to the rapid fire rhythm of his drummers and then, in time with the boom of a big bass drum, he stomped the sand with his right heel.

The crowd roared again.

"And on this side," Bunseki began, pointing his fingers at the Ghoul, who stood perfectly still, staring at Kola Kujo with a twisted grin stretch across his face. "Hailing from parts unknown... standing a staggering seven-feet eight inches tall and weighing one hundred and sixty-one pounds...join me in welcoming the return to the circle of sand of the enigmatic and oh, so dangerous fighter known only as...*The Ghoul!*"

A weak applause followed Bunseki's introduction, as *The Ghoul* raised a long willowy arm skyward and wiggled his long, crooked fingers.

Bunseki called the fighters to the center of the ring. Kola Kujo sprinted to his place. The Ghoul shambled toward the Bunseki, the bottoms of his feet making scraping noises with each slow step.

"Gentlemen, I want a good, clean fight," Bunseki said. "Obey my commands at all times. Defend yourselves at all times. Now, touch fists and return to your sides."

The Ghoul ran his grayish-pink tongue over his scarred and calloused knuckles and then extended his fist. Kola Kujo ignored the Ghoul's gesture and backed away to his corner.

"Fight!" Bunseki shouted.

Kola Kujo strode to the center of the ring.

The Ghoul circled him, switching between left and right fighting stances with blistering speed.

Kola Kujo rushed forward with two brisk jabs, followed by a powerful shin kick toward the Ghoul's inner thigh.

The Ghoul parried the punches with two quick flicks of his wrist and then blocked the shin kick with a spear-like right knee strike.

A sharp pain spread up and across Kola Kujo's shin. He felt like he had slammed it into a steel post.

The Ghoul countered with a devastating punch, kicking his

right leg behind him as he skipped forward with a heavy right cross. The pulverizing blow caught Kola Kujo square on his nose.

A blanket of darkness fell over Kola Kujo, smothering him. He collapsed onto his back, succumbing to its warmth and comfort. A screeching voice pierced the darkness, shredding it. *Get up, Champion-of-champions!* He realized the voice was his own. The darkness dissolved just as Kola Kujo felt a weight fall upon him. He instinctively shifted his head toward his right shoulder. The Ghoul's fist rocketed past him and crashed into the sand, leaving a small crater in its wake.

Kola Kujo exploded upward with his hips driving the Ghoul, who had straddled him, off balance.

The Ghoul reached out with both hands, protecting his forehead from colliding with the sand, which was an automatic loss.

Kola Kujo reached up, wrapping both arms around the Ghoul's right arm. He pulled the arm to his chest, holding tight. He then trapped the Ghoul's right foot in place with his left foot. He exploded upward with his hips again and rolled to his left, slamming the Ghoul onto his back.

The Ghoul wrapped his skeletal legs around Kola Kujo's waist, crossing his ankles at the middle of Kola Kujo's back.

Kola Kujo scooped his left arm under the Ghoul's right leg and straightened his back, breaking the Ghoul's grip.

The Ghoul followed Kola Kujo's momentum, driving his hips high onto Kola Kujo's chest as he threw his right leg onto the back of Kola Kujo's neck. The man-monster then pulled Kola Kujo's right arm across his body as he kicked his left leg over his right shin.

Kola Kujo was now trapped in a tight triangle choke that felt like a garrote around his neck. He felt as if his eyes would pop out of their sockets. He knew he would be unconscious soon if he did not escape. He hugged Ghoul's thigh to his chest with both arms and then leaned forward, pushing Ghoul's knee into his own chest and rolling the Ghoul's shoulder onto the single velvet sand flea left in the sand after the stadium's cleaning crew had purged it a week before the tournament. The flea bit the ghoul on the back of his neck, right in the irritating sunburn he had suffered earlier that morning while swimming in the Sati Baa River.

The Ghoul wailed in agony. He released his choke on Kola Kujo and then leapt to his feet.

Kola Kujo hopped into his fighting stance and then burst forward with a sharp front knee that caught the Ghoul in his side.

A loud crunch could be heard above the cheering of the crowd.

The Ghoul dropped his left elbow to his side to protect his shattered rib from anymore damage.

Taking advantage of the Ghoul's lowered guard, Kola Kujo hammered a devastating right hook into his jaw.

The emaciated man's spindly legs buckled and he collapsed onto his right knee.

The Ghoul struggled to return to his feet.

Kola Kujo skipped forward and whipped a high shin kick toward him. The pulverizing kick slammed into the side of the Ghoul's neck.

The Ghoul's body tensed and he toppled, like a tree fallen victim to a woodsman's axe.

Kola Kujo pounced, but he was pushed back by Bunseki.

Bunseki knelt down beside the Ghoul and laid a firm hand on his chest. The Ghoul's eyes opened, but were still unfocused. Bunseki stood up and waved his arms, signaling Ghoul would not be able to continue the fight.

Kola Kujo shuffled around the ring, peacocking for the crowd, who cheered him on with whistles, claps, stomps and the chanting of his name. "Ko-la…Ku-jo…Ogun Ye-O! Ko-la…Ku-jo…Ogun Ye-O!"

Jomoke and Kola Kujo's entourage rushed into the ring, joining Kola Kujo in his victory dance.

The referee grabbed Kola Kujo's wrist and coaxed him to the center of the ring.

"The winner," Bunseki began. "And the first to move on to the semi-finals is Kola Kujo!"

Bunseki raised Kola Kujo's hand in victory.

Standing at the side of the circle, Yigo fumed.

Kola Kujo's smiled at the trainer as he danced back to his tent.

****

Kola Kujo sauntered down the walkway leading to the circle, moving in time with the rhythm of his theme music.

His dancers somersaulted, leapt and shimmied on either side of him as he strutted. Jomoke walked closely behind him with his hands on each of the wrestler's shoulders.

The thunderous cheer from the spectators in the stadium was deafening.

"Sati Baa…it's time," Bunseki's voice was unnaturally powerful, resounding over the music and the roar of the crowd. Kola Kujo figured the referee used some spell to enhance the volume of his voice. "The semi-final battle you have been waiting for. Yes, this Ibuthodili has been shorter than most – due to an unforeseen mishap that made half of our fighters ill – but it has been more spectacular than ever!"

The spectators cheered.

Kola Kujo sauntered into the circle. He knelt in the traditional salute of Oyo, facing the North, the South, the West and the East and then slapped the ground four times, alternating between his palm and the back of his hand, signaling that all on Earth and in the very Heavens above, would witness him bury his opponent, Yoro Ida.

Kola Kujo intended to end Yoro's career because Yoro happened to be Yigo's eldest son.

He stood and danced to his side of the circle. Jomoke whispered in Kola Kujo's ear as he massaged his neck and shoulders.

"Stay alert," Jomoke said. "The Ghoul hit you with some very hard blows, but this Yoro is even stronger. We know you will win, but we don't want you to get hurt doing it."

"See, this is why you had to be so great at the spiritual practices," Kola Kujo said. "You just don't understand how wrestling works. If I win too easily; too quickly, like the Ghoul, I will not be invited to any other matches. Great champions are as much entertainer as warrior."

"So, you wanted the Ghoul to knock you on your back. I understand, now." Jomoke said with a smirk.

"It was not a conscious decision," Kola Kujo said. "At my level of skill, such things are beyond thought; they are purely instinct and would amaze even me if anyone else was to achieve such wondrous feats."

Yoro Ida sprinted down the walkway. His djeli sprinted behind him, holding an ornate golden sword with a jewel encrusted handle high above his head.

He jumped into the circle and then performed a brief, but complex shadowboxing combination of kicks, punches, sprawls and rolls.

The crowd roared in approval.

"They love me!" Yoro shouted, shuffling backward toward his corner. "They love me!"

Bunseki raised his hands high above his head and shouted, "Let's get ready to wrestle!"

The spectators clapped, screamed, stomped and whistled with zeal.

"On this side of the circle," Bunseki said, pointing at Kola Kujo. "Hailing from Oyo…standing six feet, two inches tall and weighing in at two-hundred and sixteen pounds…Kola Kujo!"

More cheering rose from the crowd.

"And on this side," Bunseki said, pointing toward Yoro Ida. "He hails from right here in Sati Baa…"

The spectators erupted in applause.

"He stands six feet four and weighed in at two-hundred and four pounds," Bunseki continued. "With a professional record of fifteen wins and no losses…the undisputed, undefeated, champion of Sati Baa…Yoro…Ida!"

Bunseki walked to the center of the cage and then waved for both fighters to join him.

Kola Kujo walked toward Bunseki, stopping an inch from

the extended fingertips of the color commentator's left hand.

Yoro sprinted toward the center of the cage, coming to rest with his chest pressed against Bunseki's right fingertips.

"Gentlemen, I expect a good, clean fight tonight," Bunseki said. "Listen to and obey my commands at all times. Defend yourselves to the best of your ability at all times. And give these good people a match to remember! Now, touch fists and go back to your respective sides."

Kola Kujo and Yoro touched fists and then backed away from each other.

Bunseki looked toward Kola Kujo. "Are you ready?"

Kola Kujo thrust his thumb forward and nodded in affirmation.

"Are you ready?" Bunseki asked Yoro.

"Ready to destroy!" Yoro answered.

"Then, fight!" Bunseki shouted as he backed away from the center of the circle.

Kola Kujo and Yoro charged each other.

Kola Kujo let fly a jab, cross, lead low hook, rear uppercut combination.

Yoro deftly parried the jab, parried the cross, blocked the low hook with a descending elbow and then rocked backward, evading the uppercut.

Yoro countered with a blistering lead uppercut, followed by a robust rear uppercut.

Kola Kujo dodged the strikes and exploded forward, lowering his stance until his knees nearly scraped the mat.

Yoro took a step backward in an attempt to evade Kola Kujo's charge, but his ankle twisted, throwing him a little off-balance.

Kola Kujo grabbed Yoro's forward leg with both arms. He then exploded upward with his hips, hoisting Yoro's left foot high off the ground.

Yoro drove his weight downward onto Kola Kujo's right arm stuffing the throw. He then grabbed Kola Kujo's wrist with his one hand as he snaked the other over Kola Kujo's triceps. The champion of Sati Baa grabbed his own wrist with his hand, trapping Kola Kujo's arm in a tight *figure-four* grip. He then rolled backward, kicking his right foot upward between Kola Kujo's legs.

Kola Kujo staggered forward and then fell, rolling headlong, onto the sandy floor of the circle.

Yoro held on to Kola Kujo's arm and used the combined momentum of Kola Kujo's forward roll and his own backward roll to tumble over into a side-mount position with his chest atop – and perpendicular to – Kola Kujo's chest. He then cranked Kola Kujo's right arm behind his back, forcing Kujo's wrist upward toward his head.

A terrible pain ripped across Kola Kujo's shoulder. He sat bolt upright to relieve the tremendous pressure on his shoulder and then rolled forward onto his knees to escape the torturous lock.

Yoro clung to Kola Kujo like glue, rolling onto Kola Kujo's back. He released his grip on Kola Kujo's arm and began hammering the sides of Kola Kujo's face with heavy hook punches.

Kola Kujo grabbed Yoro's wrist with both hands and then rolled sideways as he jerked Yoro's arm downward.

Yoro flew over Kola Kujo, his back crashing into the sand.

Kola Kujo shifted his hips, bringing himself into a pushup position and then drew his legs in toward his chest, propelling himself into a standing position.

Yoro rolled over backward into a kneeling position and began to rise to his feet.

Kola Kujo skipped forward driving his knee into Yoro's solar plexus before he could stand.

Yoro grimaced as the air flew out of his lungs. He stumbled backward, landing on his haunches.

Kola Kujo charged toward the downed Yoro.

Yoro lay flat on the sand.

Kola Kujo pounced, his fist poised overhead to deliver a powerful hammer-fist strike.

Yoro drove his hips upward and shot his foot out, slamming it into Kola Kujo's cheek.

Kola Kujo blinked rapidly to regain his focus. His face

felt as if it was falling apart and his shoulder throbbed terribly. He peered over at Yoro, who was struggling to stand.

Kola Kujo leapt to his feet, ignoring the ache in his shoulder and charged toward the center of the cage.

Yoro Ida also darted toward the center of the cage, his eyes locked on Kola Kujo's eyes.

The combatants circled each other, their hands moving elliptically as their eyes sought an opening.

Yoro slid his thumb across his throat, signaling he would give the fans the excitement of taking Kola Kujo's life.

Kola Kujo waved to Yoro to "bring it on."

The stadium shook from the rousing applause rising from the stands.

Kola Kujo stomped the mat with his right foot and lurched forward with his right shoulder, feigning a high attack.

Yoro threw up his hands in defense, but no punches came.

Instead, Kola Kujo whipped a rear-leg shin kick into the outside of Yoro's thigh, which he followed with a lead-leg shin kick to the inside of the same thigh.

Yoro winced. His damaged leg buckled. He shifted his back leg forward to remove his bruised leg out of the line of fire.

Kola Kujo hammered two lightning-fast rear shin kicks into the outside of Yoro's other thigh.

Yoro staggered to the side. He shifted his rear leg back to the forward position.

Yoro lurched forward, firing a weak jab, cross combination at Kola Kujo's nose.

Kola Kujo raised his rear, then front elbow, simultaneously defending his face as he attacked Yoro's fists.

Yoro grimaced as the small bones in his fists collided with the points of Kola Kujo's elbows.

Kola Kujo countered with a powerful punch aimed at Yoro's jaw.

Yoro ducked the blow and then exploded forward, wrapping his arms around Kola Kujo's waist before Kujo could regain his balance. Yoro drove his hips into Kujo's thigh as he yanked Kijo's waist upward.

Kola Kujo's eyes grew wide as dinner plates as his feet flew high above his head.

Yoro held Kola Kujo high above his head.

Too high. The blazing sun's rays speared into Yoro's eyes, blinding him.

The blindness and the rubbery feeling in his knees caused Yoro to lose his balance and he collapsed.

Yoro's head hit the mat first, the top of his skull slamming into the floor with a loud thud. His back crashed into the mat a moment later with Kola Kujo still on top of him.

Kola Kujo slithered up the stunned Yoro's body, taking a dominant straddled position on top of him.

Yoro's arms fell limply at his sides and his legs convulsed once, twice, and then went still.

Kola Kujo sat upright, bearing his weight on Yoro's chest and raised his right elbow, ready to deliver a pulverizing finishing strike.

Bunseki charged toward Kola Kujo and pushed him off of Yoro just before his elbow struck.

Kola Kujo was sent tumbling backward.

Bunseki knelt to inspect the unconscious champion of Sati Baa. He waved his arms, signaling the end of the fight.

Kola Kujo leapt to his feet, holding his fist high. He danced around the ring as the crowd exploded into his chant.

Jomoke ran into the circle and then ran to Kola Kujo, embracing him.

Bunseki tapped Kola Kujo on the back. "It's time."

Kola Kujo followed Bunseki to the center of the circle. Silence fell over the arena.

Bunseki grabbed Kola Kujo's wrist and then raised his hand high.

"The winner, first finalist and new champion of Sati Baa... Kola Kujo!"

The spectators leapt to their feet, cheering and clapping joyously.

Four healers rolled Yoro Ida onto a blanket and carried him out of the circle.

Kola Kujo's dancers were in a frenzy as they danced around their master. Kola Kujo and Jomoke joined the dance. They whirled and gyrated around the circle of sand and then continued up the walkway and back to the tent.

Kola Kujo squatted down and then danced into his tent as his entourage cheered him on. Jomoke followed him inside.

"Seal the flaps, Jomoke," Kola Kujo said.

Jomoke pressed the flaps together and then tied the five straps that ran from top to bottom on each flap.

When the interior of the tent was completely concealed from outside eyes, Kola Kujo collapsed onto his haunches.

"Tired?"

Kola Kujo nodded.

Jomoke grabbed a coconut from his bag along with a short, broad ada. The short sword sliced through the top of the coconut with one cut. He thrust the coconut toward Kola Kujo's face. "Hydrate!"

Kola Kujo took it and drained the coconut of its sweet, cool contents.

His heavy breathing ceased and the aches in his muscles faded away.

"Congratulations!" Jomoke said. "You are now champion of Oyo and of Sati Baa!"

"And after this next match, I will be champion of the greatest tournament in the world, affirming to all of Ki Khanga what Oyo has long known...I am the greatest wrestler of all time!"

****

Kola Kujo looked up from his seat at the side of the circle of sand. Thousands of fans sat in the stands, screaming and stomping in a show of their approval for all the fighters – the victorious and the defeated – who had come from every corner of Ki Khanga and now stood in the circle, demonstrating flashy, acrobatic dances, jaw-dropping feats of strength and powerful self-defense techniques in honor of the two warriors who would soon battle for the title of Champion of the Ibuthodili.

Jomoke, who sat beside Kola Kujo, was dressed in sky blue, traditional lace garb: *shokoto*; *dashiki*, *fila* and *agbada* – trousers, and matching shirt, hat and a flowing, wide-sleeved robe.

Kola Kujo's entourage stood behind him, sporting traditional indigo cotton dashiki and shokoto.

Kola Kujo wore only an indigo cloth tied around his waist and between his legs to conceal and protect his groin and the organs in his lower torso.

After the performances, the beautiful and fierce hero of Kamit, Amuntat Hutip – famed throughout Ki Khanga for defeating the mad giant, Udoo – entered the ring, her white dress swaying, accentuating her sensuous curves, with each step. "Are you ready, Sati Baa?" She shouted.

The crowd replied with whistles, claps, stomps and shouts of approval.

"To my left," Amuntat said, pointing toward Kola Kujo. "Is the current champion of Sati Baa! Weighing in at two hundred and sixteen pounds and standing six feet, two inches tall … representing the beautiful lands of Oyo…show your appreciation for Kola Kujo!"

Kola Kujo leapt to his feet as his entourage and the spectators chanted his name:

"Ko-la…Ku-jo…Ogun Ye-O! Ko-la…Ku-jo…Ogun Ye-O!"

Kola Kujo danced into the ring in a low crouch, his shoulders hunching up and down to the rhythm, his feet hammering into the sand. He danced around the circumference of the ring and then circled the lovely Amuntat, increasing his pace as the speed of the rhythm sped up. Amuntat joined him in the dance and the crowd went wild. Suddenly the music – and Kola Kujo – stopped. The crowd roared once more in approval.

Amuntat wiped her brow and then flicked the sweat into the sand at her feet. "Whew! You might have to ride in my litter after the fight Kola Kujo – if you're still any good after it, that is."

The crowd laughed.

Kola Kujo lowered his gaze and smiled as his cheeks turned a deep maroon.

"And now, without further ado," Amuntat shouted. "He hails from Mali. Standing seven feet, two inches tall and weighing in at three hundred and seventy pounds…the undefeated, undisputed, three-time champion of the Ibuthodili…Kankan Musa!"

The crowd rose to their feet and, in unison, began to sing the Sati Baa National Anthem:

"Arise, Oh, compatriots,
Sati Baa's call, obey
To serve our Motherland
With love and strength and faith.
The labor of our heroes past
Shall never be in vain,
To serve with heart and might
'Til only freedom, peace and unity reign.
Oh this world, watch and listen:
The enemy came coveting my position,
We shall fight with Truth and defenses
And if I die, I'll take him with me!
Say it with me, say it with me:
Sati Baa is greatest!
Sati Baa is greatest!"

Thunderous applause rose from the dense crowd. The people parted, revealing a hulking figure sitting upon an iron throne, carved in the shape of a leopard resting on its haunches.

Kankan Musa rose from the throne, looming above the crowd like a statue carved from onyx stone. His forearms were as thick as an average man's thigh and appeared to be as hard as the throne he had just risen from. He slammed his cantaloupe-sized fist into his chest and the crowd roared. He sprinted into the circle, charging directly toward Kola Kujo.

Kola Kujo stood his ground as the human locomotive called

Kankan Musa sped toward him.

The colossus stopped just inches in front of Kola Kujo, his massive chest almost touching Kola Kujo's nose.

The giant stood still and in silence.

"Are you ready, Kola Kujo?" Amuntat asked.

Kola Kujo nodded.

"Are you ready, Kankan Musa?"

Kankan Musa tapped his chest twice with his fist.

Amuntat slid her arm between the fighters. "Then, fighters, take your places."

Kola Kujo shuffled backward to his place at the edge of the ring. Kankan Musa shambled backward to his place, his unblinking gaze locked on Kola Kujo's throat.

"And now …" Amuntat raised her hand high above her head, her fingers pointing toward the clear noonday sky. After a long pause, she brought her arm down sharply, slicing the air with her well-manicure fingers. "Fight!"

Kankan Musa lurched forward. Kola Kujo charged forward to meet him.

Kola Kujo hammered into Kankan Musa's ribs with a volley of heavy right and left hooks. Kankan Musa staggered backward.

Kola Kujo shuffled forward with a lead-hand hook toward Kankan Musa's chin.

The giant leaned back. The punch shot past his face. He then countered with a fierce cross, catching Kola Kujo square on the jaw.

Kola Kujo collapsed to his knees. He shook off the pain and exploded back to his feet.

His feet had barely touched the earth when he was lifted high into the air by the giant, who had grabbed him from behind in a tight bear-hug.

Kola Kujo thrust his leg to the outside of Kankan Musa's thigh, hooking his foot behind the giant's knee. With the throw now blocked, Kola Kujo bent at the waist as he threw his palms toward the ground, breaking free of Kankan Musa's grip.

Kola Kujo thrust back and upward with his left foot, driving his heel into Kankan Musa's solar plexus. The giant doubled over in pain.

Kola Kujo whirled toward Kankan Musa, slamming a crushing shin kick into the outside of his thigh. Kankan Musa's leg buckled.

Kola Kujo followed with a second shin kick to the inner thigh of the same leg. Kankan Musa's leg quivered and he switched feet, bringing his left leg forward to protect his right leg from further onslaught.

Kola Kujo burst forward, wrapping his arms around Kankan Musa's waist and pulling him close. The giant thrust his massive right arm between his hips and Kola Kujo's to partially break his grip.

The men mirrored each other, both holding the other's triceps with one hand and his waist with the other hand. They then fought for superior position, snaking their arms over and under each other in an attempt to grasp the other around the waist with both hands.

Kola Kujo proved to be a bit faster, lithely coiling his arms deep under Kankan Musa's armpits and then digging his fingers into the colossus' sinewy shoulders.

Kankan Musa shook furiously, but could not free himself from Kola Kujo's boa constrictor-like control of his upper torso.

Kola Kujo thrust his hips forward and pressed on the middle of his back in an attempt to bend him back and throw him to the ground, but the giant was too strong.

Kola Kujo tried again, straining against Kankan Musa's rigid core. The force of the strain transferred to Kola Kujo's legs and his feet slipped from beneath him. Kola Kujo punched his arms skyward in an effort to catch his balance, but they were trapped under Kankan Musa's armpits.

The force of Kola Kujo's legs slipping forward, combined with the upward snap of his arms sent Kankan Musa flying high into the air.

The giant's eyes widened.

A hush fell over the crowd.

Kola Kujo torqued his hips as he arched backward, increasing the momentum of the throw.

Both men struck the ground with a thunderous din. A cloud of sand billowed up from the circle.

The cloud dissipated. Sand rained down upon the wrestlers.

Kankan Musa lay on his back, writhing in pain.

Atop him was Kola Kujo, who held up a fist in victory.

The crowd clapped and stomped as they chanted "Ko-la... Ku-jo!"

Kola Kujo leapt to his feet as unconsciousness overtook Kankan Musa.

Jomoke and the other members of his entourage stormed the ring. Kola Kujo pulled Jomoke close and hugged him.

After a few moments, he released the djeli and then he strutted around the ring, waving to the adoring crowd.

"The winner," Amuntat shouted. "And new Ibuthodili champion – Kola Kujo!"

Kola Kujo approached the center of the ring. Four men of Sati Baa carried the heavy iron leopard throne into the ring. They placed the throne behind Kola Kujo.

"Take your seat, champion," Amuntat shouted. "For a while, at least, you are king of the Ibuthodili!"

Kola Kujo sat upon the throne and the crowd went wild again. His entourage surrounded him. His litter bearers lifted the throne by the iron bars at its base and then the entourage danced out of the circle.

"Hail to the king!" Jomoke shouted.

Kola Kujo, the spectators and even many of his fellow wrestlers raised their fists high into the air. "Hail to the king!"

Kola Kujo closed his eyes and inhaled. The smell of barbecued goat, pepper, honey and palm oil greeted him.

The scent of Sati Baa, Kola Kujo thought. *My kingdom!*

The Bene's Daughter

By Milton Davis

"I am not a thief. I am not a thief." Omolewa repeated the words in her head as she waited in the dark alley between compounds, her eyes focused on the harbor across the walkway. A massive dhow rested among its smaller merchant brethren, a beauty of a vessel with clean white sails and a towering crow's nest that peered down on the humble harbor. Why it had come to their modest Kiswala mooring of Nacala rather than the much larger harbor of Baseemah was a mystery. Omolewa did not dwell on the reasons; she only cursed the consequences. She waited for a man that carried the key to her family's freedom, a simple scroll that once in the hands of those who held them hostage would end her family's terror and bring her life back to normal. At least she hoped it would.

Pik-Pik clawed her shoulder as she chattered into her ear, the ferret just as nervous as she.

"Calm down!" she whispered sternly. "You'll give us away."

Omolewa sunk deeper into the corner. Hiding made her think of the games she played with her friends when she was younger, but this was far from a game. The men who held her family hostage made that clear.

"Bring us the scroll or they all die," the leader of the ruffians ordered her. His face stood out in her mind not only because of the missing eye, but because his skin was dark like her. He was the first such person she'd come face to face with in her life, the first person she'd met that resembled her in any way. There was no doubt he'd arrived on the large clipper resting in the harbor, for it hailed from

Zimbabwa, the land of the Blameless Ones, the home of people like her.

Omolewa wiped his foul visage from her mind as she focused on her task. She closed her eyes and slipped into her second sight. Pik-Pik went rigid and ceased chattering. She did not understand what affect her powers had on her pet, but she knew her skills were heightened by its presence. She extended her sight around the corners of her lair then above the people traversing the road. She sought a man like herself, dressed in fine leather carrying a gilded satchel over his shoulder. He possessed what the ruffians sought. He was the key to saving her family.

She found the man strolling among the throng, ignoring the admiring looks and whispers of Kiswala folks. Omolewa changed her view of him, seeing him as if she faced him. He was handsome; deep brown flawless skin with a broad nose and captivating amber eyes. A thin mustache graced his full lips, joining with the tuft of hair on his chin. The way he stared made her think he could see her; the slight smile that came to his lips startled her. Did he know he was being watched? She pulled away. Of course he didn't know. How could he?

She readied herself as he neared the alleyway. She focused on his satchel, delicately unbuckling it and raising the top slowly. As he passed the alley entrance she raised the top completely. The scroll rose from the satchel and sped to her waiting hands.

"Come Pik-Pik," she said urgently. "It's time to go home."

She hurried to the other end of the alley and melded into the market crowd. Not that she could meld. Omolewa was well aware of her story. Her father, a former Mikijen, found her as a babe on a campaign in Zimbabwa. Kiswala allied itself with the Blameless Ones against a threat from the Haiset, sending in their elite mercenaries to project Kiswala interests. Baba found her in a village that had been overrun by Haisetti hordes and, captivated by her strength and beauty, hired a wet nurse for her with his meager earnings. After the war he brought her back to Kiswala. Mama readily accepted her; she was a Blameless One and nothing but good fortune would come to them with her as part of their family.

Up until this day, good fortune had been their lot.

Omolewa worked her way toward the Backwater, the tattered working district where she lived. Her nerves frayed as she approached her home, her eyes darting about to see is she had been seen or followed. Pik-Pik chattered and darted from shoulder to shoulder, her restlessness reflecting Omolewa's mood.

She finally stood before the wooden door to her family's cabin. She knocked twice as the one eyed man instructed her to do. The door cracked opened, revealing his vile face. He snatched the door open, grabbed her wrist and dragged her inside. She ignored his brutality, her desperate eyes scanning the main room of the cabin. Momma and Papa sat at the meal table, hands and legs bound and mouths gagged. Her siblings were crowded in a corner at the rear of the one room house, bound and gagged as well. Two men stood beside her parents, daggers in their hands. Their pale hands revealed them as Kiswali despite their covered faces. The men guarding her siblings were Kiswali as well. All were apparently hired by the one-eyed man.

He gripped her chin, turning her face to his.

"Where is it?" he demanded.

Omolewa took the scroll from her pocket and handed it to him.

"Here. Now let us go," she said.

The man grinned as he placed the scroll in his shoulder pouch.

"A change of plans, darling," he said. "You're coming with us."

He looked at his henchmen. "Kill them all."

"No!" she screamed.

Pik-Pik leaped from her shoulders, landing on the one-eyed man's chest. She sank her teeth into his nose.

"Aahhh!"

The man let go of her wrist. He stumbled away, pulling at Pik-Pik on his face. The others laughed briefly, giving Omolewa the time she needed. She thrust her hands toward the daggers at her parents' throats and they flew from the ruffians' hands. She jerked her hands back and thrust again. The men guarding her siblings winched and doubled over holding their guts. Omolewa tried to run to her parent but jerked back, almost falling on her back. The one eyed man gripped her by the hair, his cheeks and nose bloodied.

"Don't make me hurt you, girl!" he shouted. "You're worth more alive than dead."

He dragged her toward the door. Omolewa tried to struggle but she was exhausted from her efforts. Tears streamed from her eyes as the men picked up their knives and returned to her parents.

"Finish this so we can go," the one-eyed man ordered.

A booming sound filled Omolewa's ears. She fell onto her back then watched incredulously as the one-eyed man sailed over her. A pair of boots appeared beside her, stopping briefly then proceeding in the direction of the table. She struggled upright and stared into the back of the man from whom she'd stolen the scroll. With the flick of his hands the men beside her parents flew left and right, each smashing into the walls with a crunching finality. He extended his hands and the men threatening her siblings jerked into the air then slammed into the ceiling. He dropped his arms and they fell to the floor.

The one-eyed man lay before him. The man knelt to his side and grasped his face. He jerked the man's head and snapped his neck. The interloper stood and went to her parents.

Omolewa reached out with the last of her strength. The interloper slowed; he turned to her with a smile on his face.

"Don't hurt them, please," she begged.

"I won't," he replied.

He untied her parents then removed their gags.

"Creator bless you!" Baba exclaimed. Both baba and mama ran to the back of the cabin to free her siblings. The interloper approached Omolewa and knelt before her.

"You are a terrible thief," he commented.

He touched her and she felt a surge of strength.

He stood and stepped away. She was suddenly engulfed by her family, submerged by hugs and tears. Eventually they relented, allowing the mysterious man through. He carried Pik-Pik on his shoulder. Her furry familiar jumped from her perch and into Omolewa's arms.

"Thank you for saving us," she said.

The man nodded. "You've grown into a beautiful woman."

His statement made Omolewa curious and nervous.

"Do you know me?" she asked.

The interloper smiled. "I do know you, in a way."

Omolewa looked to baba. He nodded.

"It's okay. I knew this day would come."

Omolewa was perplexed. "How? I was brought here as a baby. That's what baba told me."

"That's what my baba told me, too," he said.

"I ask you again, sir. Who are you?"

The man knelt before her. "I'm your brother."

Omolewa stared blankly at the interloper. "Brother? I have only one brother. Papa told me my family was dead."

She looked at baba. "Tell him."

Baba looked at her, his eyes downcast.

Omolewa's hands began to tremble. "Baba, tell him!"

"He told you what he was instructed," the man claiming to be her brother said. "The world was not safe for you then. There were ... forces that would have brought you harm if you were found. Our homeland was not safe for you, so you were sent here."

Omolewa's didn't want to believe what she was hearing. This man, apparently a powerful sorcerer, claimed to be her brother. Baba knew him and had lied to her about her origins. She was about to asked more questions when the room echoed with urgent knocking.

"Hello! Hello? Is everything alright in there?"

Baba went to the door and opened it. Three constables rushed in with short swords drawn. They looked at the bodies strewn on the floor then looked to Baba.

"They attacked my family," Baba said. "They wanted something from this man and they forced my daughter to take it."

One of the constables knelt beside the body of the ringleader. He looked at the interloper expecting an explanation.

"He is of my homeland, but I am not familiar with him," the interloper said. "I will handle him."

"I know these two," another interloper said. "They're always causing trouble on the wharf."

The head constable joined the others. "Doesn't look like they'll do that anymore. Let's get them out of here."

The constables dragged the dead Kiswali outside.

"Are you sure you'll deal with this one?" the head constable asked. The interloper nodded his head.

"Then we will bid you farewell."

The constables left with their grim cargo.

Baba let out a breath. "That was too easy. They'll be back."

"Yes they will," the interloper said. "But you will not be here when they return."

His words sounded ominous to Omolewa. Baba pulled her close.

"What are you talking about?" he said.

"My sister…your daughter must come with us, but it would be unrealistic for her to come with us alone. Although I am her blood family, you are her family in every other way. So you must come with us."

Baba opened his mouth to answer but was interrupted by another door knock. This time the interloper opened it.

The men that entered looked similar to the interloper, black skinned and handsome wearing robes that fell to the ankles of their studded leather boots. The interloper gestured with his head and the men went to the body of their nefarious brethren. One of them dug his fingers through the man's hair as if searching for something hidden. His search stopped abruptly and he looked up with a concerned look on his face.

The interloper knelt beside him as the man pushed the hair away. Omolewa felt a sudden urge and broke away from her baba's grip. The other man moved to block her way but the interloper waved him off.

"She should see this. She needs to know her enemy."

The interloper took the other man's place. He pushed the

hair aside, revealing a small curled horn on the side of the man's head. Omolewa's eyes went wide.

"Is that real?" she asked timidly.

"Yes it is."

"Who is he?"

The interloper grimaced. "Joka Watu."

Omolewa waited for an explanation from the interloper but received none. Instead he stepped away from the body then pulled Omolewa aside. His brethren lifted the body then left the house.

"I urge you all to come with us," he said. "I know this is sudden, but all of your lives are in danger, as you can see. We will be here for three more days. I will station my men around your house during that time but once we leave we cannot insure your safety."

He placed his hand on Omolewa's shoulder and she felt familiarity with his touch.

"You know I speak the truth to you, Omolewa," he said.

Omolewa grabbed his hand to remove it from her shoulder but held it instead. It was true that his touch made her feel safer than mama's embrace, but she was no fool.

"You are a sorcerer, sir," she replied. "I cannot be sure of anything."

The man smiled. "Very good sister, but think on this. Your family is not safe if you stay. This is not their choice. It is yours."

The man removed his hand from her shoulder and fear flooded her mind again. The interloper nodded slightly then strode for the door.

"You ask much of us, sir," baba said. "Yet we know not who you are."

"I am Kulal Chihota, son of Bene Chadamunda, brother of Omolewa."

Kulal smiled then exited. Omolewa and her family immediately converged, hugging and kissing and crying.

"You are safe!" mama exclaimed.

"We all are," her father added.

Omolewa picked up Diwani and rubbed Kazija's head that

clung to her leg.

"You are a hero, Lewa!" her brother said.

Omolewa's joy was brief. The revelations of the past few moments settled on her mind.

"Baba," she said. "What is going on? Are the words of Kulal true? Why did you not tell me these things?"

Mama took Diwani from her and pulled Kazija away as well. She looked at baba with the same questioning look. Omolewa realized that mama did not know as well.

"I did not tell you the truth, for I didn't know until the moment Kulal stepped through our door," baba confessed.

The family sat around the table, looking at baba with a mix of expressions.

"How could you not know, Tayari?" mama asked. "We have been married for thirteen years and you never told me these things."

"I promise you, Jamela, I did not know." Baba finally sat with them.

"When Kulal walked into our home it was as if the sun emerged from behind a dark cloud. Images came to me that I knew was my true life."

"His...my family are people of nyama," Omolewa said. "They must have done this to you."

"Why would they do such a thing?" mama asked.

"To make sure Omolewa was safe," baba answered. "I could not tell what I did not know."

Baba closed his eyes for a moment then opened them. His expression was solemn as he looked at each of them, finally resting his eyes on Omolewa. The clarity in them confirmed the truth he was about to share.

"I was a Mikijen," he said. "A civil war raged in Zimbabwa, a war that threatened Kiswala interests in the region. My unit was ordered into the interior to protect a group of villages that supplied our ships with yams and sorghum."

"Did you fight for Kulal's family?" her brother asked.

Baba smiled. "No. The Kiswala do not take sides in local conflicts. The Mikijin only protect our interests. We were marching into the valley when we came across a Zimbabwa army retreating from the north. To say they were in dire straits would be an understatement. We gave them food and tended their wounds. Their commander sought me out and asked for our help. They planned to return to battle, but of course we could not assist them. The commander understood, but then asked me to come with them. That's when I met you."

Baba's smile made Omolewa's cheeks warm and she smiled back.

"They took me to a man and woman whose dress told me they were people of great importance. The man stood before the woman and extended his hands to her. She looked at him with worry then looked at me with sympathy. Then she handed him the child. He came to me directly."

"There is much turmoil in our land," he said. "Too much for our daughter to remain."

Zimbabwa has always been a volatile mix," I remember saying. "It will pass."

"There is a deeper evil afoot," he said. "One that comes from beyond our borders. I cannot take any chances."

He gave you to me.

"Take my daughter with you. Her name is Omolewa. We will come for her when the time comes, hopefully."

I took you in my arms dumbfounded.

"I can't," I said.

The man's eyes took on a strange look, as if the storms of times resided in them.

"You can, and you will," he said.

Baba leaned back in his chair. "From that moment I believed the story I told you before. He must have cast some type of spell on me then. If I did not know the truth, I could not tell it if the wrong people found me."

Baba reached toward Omolewa and she fell into his comforting arms. She snuggled close to him, wishing she could stay this close to him forever.

"Today has been a trying day for us all, but for you especially," he said. "A great burden has been revealed to you."

"It's not fair," she said. "I did not ask for this."

"No one asks for the life they are given," baba replied. "We open our eyes and it is there. All we can do is live it in the best way."

"Enough of this," mama interjected. "You can't make any decisions on an empty stomach. I'll make us stew and we will talk of this later. We have been through enough this day."

Mama sent everyone into a whirlwind of chores, trying her best to get everything back to normal. Omolewa was grateful for the distraction, but she couldn't forget for one moment the decision looming in her immediate future. She didn't want to go anywhere. Tilamel was her home despite what this man claiming to be her brother claimed. A journey to Zimbabwa would be a journey to a foreign land. But the man said her decision would save many lives, and after what occurred she knew her life and that of her family were in danger.

They did not talk again of the incident and of her decision for there was nothing to discuss. As Omolewa prepared her siblings and then herself for bed he caught glimpses of baba and mama packing clothes and other items in a pair of wooden chests that served as tables. So they were going. That night as she lay in her bed, she stroked Pik Pik's soft fur and thought of this new adventure about to take place in her life.

She woke to pounding on their door an images of the ruffians flooded her mind. She searched about for something to defend herself. She would not be taken unaware this time. Baba rose from the bed and went to the door.

"Baba, no!" Omolewa shouted.

Baba looked at her and smiled, his eyes confident and assured.

"It's okay, Lewa," he whispered.

Baba opened the door, revealing Kulal's smiling visage.

"Good morning!" he said. "I pray I'm not too early."

"No," baba replied. "This is a late morning for us. I think everyone needed a bit more rest after yesterday."

Kulal nodded. "I understand. May I come in?"

Baba stepped aside and her new found brother entered. He walked directly to her and knelt.

"Good morning, sister," he greeted her.

"Don't call me that," Omolewa replied. "It doesn't feel right...yet."

Kulal's eyes revealed his disappointment but he smiled regardless.

"It is a strange thing for me to say as well, but I decided the sooner I began the faster I'd get used to it."

He left her side to address her father.

"My men are coming for your things," he said. "Do you have any outstanding debts?"

Baba seemed surprised at Kulal's question.

"If a man his breathing he had debts," he replied.

"Make me a list of whom you owe and where they are located," Kulal instructed.
"Your debts will be settled immediately."

Baba's eyes bulged. "You will do this for us?"

Kulal looked at Omolewa. "You are family."

Baba turned to mama. "Jamela did you hear?"

Tears welled in Jamela's eyes. "Yes I did."

She rushed by Baba and hugged Kulal

"Thank you! You were sent by the Creator, you were!"

Kulal hugged her back. "Save your joy. You may think otherwise later."

Omolewa's reservations diminished seeing the joy in her parents' faces. Kulal seemed a very good person. The feeling of future dread did not leave her completely, but she knew that whatever lay ahead Kulal would be steadfast.

Kulal's men entered and gathered her family's belongings. They carried them to a large wagon waiting in front of their home. A crowd gathered as the wagon was loaded, curious neighbors and passersby looking enviously at the apparent good fortune that had fallen on her family. As she looked into the eyes of strangers she realized how few friends they really had. Another revelation came to her which filled her with guilt. Her father had deliberately distanced them from everyone in order to keep her secret. With the exception of mama's family, they had no friends. With Omolewa the isolation extended to her friends. She had none. Her beauty was as ostracizing as it was attractive.

Kulal led them to a noble's coach hitched to six horses draped in gold stitched and cowrie trimmed finery. A warrior opened the door.

"You will ride with me," Kulal said.

Her brother and sister needed no urging; they giggled as they ran to the coach and clambered inside. Omolewa walked slowly with her parents in wonder.

"This is too much,' her mother whispered. "Too much."

Kulal shook his head as he accompanied them. "If Omolewa lives up to her potential there will never be enough to thank you."

The words fell on her shoulders like a sack of sorghum. She searched her brother's smiling face and discovered another emotion lurking behind his joy; hope.

Their procession caused a stir throughout the town. By the time they reached the docks an enormous crowd had gathered, ululations rising and scarves waving. When Omolewa and her family emerged from Kulal's coach the crowd roared in approval. They walked single file behind him, waving to the crowd like dignitaries. Omolewa's brother and sister were especially enthusiastic, blowing kisses as well. Omolewa tried to smile but it would not come. Her life would change forever once she set foot on the long black ship with the towering sails, a ship that would take her to a home she'd never known. As she scanned the vessel from bow to stern, a person caught her eye. He stood by the central mast draped in a white robe accented with golden thread about the raised collar. His skin was a darker brown than the Kiswala, but not as deep as the Zimbabwans scurrying about the deck preparing to set sail. A golden cap rimmed by cowries sat snug on his head. His white eyebrows matched his short white beard; there was no other hair on his handsome face. He stared at her with eyes that reflected intelligence, wisdom…and nyama.

Omolewa tugged on Kulal's shirt.

"What is it, sister?" he asked.

"Who is he?" she said, nodding her head toward the mysterious man.

Kulal grinned. "He will introduce himself soon enough."

She looked at the man and he smiled. Omolewa looked away, embarrassed.

As they proceeded up the gangplank the man approached them. Kulal greeted him with a respectful bow. The man returned the bow them came directly to Omolewa. Her baba came quickly to her side.

"Who are you?" he asked. His voice was stern, but Omolewa detected fear in her baba's voice as well.

"I bear you daughter no harm, Tayari," he said. His voice was deep, resonant and comforting.

"How do you know me?" Baba asked.

"Who would not know the guardian of such a treasure," he replied. "Welcome to my ship, Omolewa. I am Kashta."

Kashta extended his hand just as Kulal approached. Omolewa took his hand and was suddenly overcome by images. See saw an island split by a wide river, desert north of the waterway, forest to the south. She saw proud brown people who lived in towering stone homes and who practiced nyama and other mysterious skills. Her mental vision finally focused on a boy, a bright child whose life sped across her mind until she stared into the face of the man standing before her. It was a moment before she realized the face she gazed upon was before her and not in her mind.

"Now you know me as well," he said.

"Yes, I do," Omolewa replied.

Kashta turned to Kulal. "Please take Lewa and her family to their cabins. We'll be leaving immediately."

Omolewa's eyes widened. "How did you know my little name?"

Kashta grinned. "I told you, we know each other very well now."

Omolewa looked at her father and he shrugged. She looked

back at Kashta as he marched across the deck shouting orders. He was right when he said she felt as if she had known him all her life. He was the most fascinating person she'd ever met, and he was to be her teacher. The journey to Zimbabwa could not get under way fast enough for her.

They followed Kulal below deck to the stern. The narrow hallway ended at an ebony double door carved with patterns and shapes that were strange yet beautiful to Omolewa's eyes.

"Is this our room?" she asked.

"No, this is Teacher Kahsta's cabin. Your cabin is here." He pointed to a gilded door to the left of Kashta's cabin. My cabin is across the hall."

Baba opened the door to the cabin and mama gasped.

"This cabin is bigger that our home!" mama exclaimed.

Her family rushed into the room but Omolewa didn't follow.

"I want to go back on deck," she said.

Baba looked at her from the sumptuous room. "You should see this room!"

"I've never been on a ship before, baba. I want to see."

Baba and mama looked at each other then back to Omolewa.

"I'm an old Mikijen," baba finally said. "I've seen enough of the sea. I would be at ease if Kulal joined you."

Mama nodded in agreement. Her brother and sister were oblivious to the conversation, their attention absorbed by their comfortable beds and big pillows.

"Thank you for trusting her with me," Kulal said. "Come, sister!"

He grabbed her hand and they hurried to the deck. Kashta stood by the helm, his hands grasped behind his back. He looked at them as if expecting them.

"You two look as if you grew up together," he commented.

Omolewa looked at Kulal and they smiled. The apprehension she felt diminished with every moment. Kashta seemed like a favorite uncle, and the ship's crew like friends. She couldn't explain what was happening but she was happy to be surrounded by so many people that seem to have her interest at heart.

The anchor rose with a loud clatter and the mooring ropes tossed onto the deck. The sails were lowered and they immediately filled with a strong wind. The helmsman, a broad shouldered Zimbabwan, steered the ship into the open harbor and they sped by the other ships. People waved goodbye as children followed them as far as they could along the dock, yelling and laughing along the way. Omolewa looked overhead, watching the seagulls flying along with them. As the ship entered open water she looked to stern, watching the only home she'd ever know diminish into the horizon.

Another muscled Zimbabwan came to Kashta.

"When do we raise the stacks," he asked.

Kashta glanced to stern. "Not yet. We must be sure we're clear their field of vision."

The burly man walked away. Omolewa was not about to let this mystery slip away.

"What are stacks?" she asked.

"You'll see soon enough," Kashta assured her. "Meantime you should return below. Your family misses you."

Omalewa nodded then hurried back to the cabin. Baba and mother had soothed but her siblings were far from over. Baba looked almost relieved to see her.

"You have come back," he said.

"Yes baba. This is a wonderful vessel."

"That it is," baba replied. "I've spent much of my life sliding across slick decks. To call this lovely thing a ship is an insult."

She was about to answer baba when a shrill whistle interrupted the. Omalewa hurried back to the deck just in time to learn the meaning of the work stacks. The sails had been furled and stored away. The masts were bare; a situation that even she knew was not good. Kashta stood with the others, their eyes on two square boxes that she hadn't noticed earlier.

"Open them up!" Kashta shouted.

A crew of men pulled at a series of ropes and pulleys, lifting thick wooden tops from the squares. Once the tops were clear Kashta shouted again.

"Okay, raised the stacks!"

A shudder gripped the ship. Omolewa grabbed Kulal and he laughed.

"It will be over soon, and then you will see a Kamite wonder."

The ship continued to shudder as two wide metal tubes rose from the boxes. By the time they finished rising her parents and siblings were standing beside her.

"It can't be," baba whispered.

The tubes began to hum and white smoke belched from the tops. Baba ran to the stern then peered over the bulwark. Omolewa joined him. The water was churning beside the boat with a slow rhythm that slowly increased. As it increased the ship began to move forward; slowly at first, then faster and faster. Soon they were travelling faster than the wind.

"It's amazing!" baba shouted.

"No, it's nyama," Kashta replied. "A special type that is within the grasp of men."

He placed his hand on Omolewa's shoulder. "I will teach you this, and so much more."

"What is it?" she asked.

"It is a device that runs on steam. It is driving the ship."

Omolewa beamed. "It's wonderful!"

Kulal laughed. "The Kamites possess many wonderful things. They have come to share with us all."

Omolewa's joy dimmed. "Why?"

Kashta nodded. "That is a good question, Lewa."

He patted her shoulder and walked away.

"Come on, Lewa," Kulal said. She liked the way he said her little name. "Spend time with your family. Once we reach Zimbabwa your time will by occupied. You'll grow tired of Kashta's face."

"I don't think that's possible," Omolewa replied.

Kulal laughed. "Believe me, it is."

She went to her mama and baba and hugged them both.

"This is amazing!" mama said.

"Yes it is, but I feel all this will become more serious once we land in Zimbabwa."

"I think you are right, baba," Omolewa said.

"Lewa! Come run with us!"

Her siblings grabbed her hands and tugged her away from her parents. And thus they spent the next few days, walking the fast moving ship and exploring ever inch they were allowed to. The crew was tolerable the entire time and Kashta kept a watchful eye on Omolewa. Baba and mama spent much time locked behind the cabin door, much to the frustration of her siblings but to the amusement of Omolewa. She was old enough to know what they were doing, and they were doing it much more than they had in months. She wouldn't be surprised if her next brother or sister would be born in Zimbabwa.

Her siblings finally tired of the new adventure, worn down by repetition and sea sickness. Omolewa seemed immune to it, walking the deck like a seasoned sailor. She rose early one morning, donning her clothes and sneaking out of the room. To her surprise she met Kulal and Kashta in the hall. Both men had serious looks on their faces; Kashta looked concerned, Kulal worried. Kashta looked into her eyes and his concern transferred to her.

"Follow me," he said.

The trio marched to the upper deck. The Zimbabwans went about their work, but their faces were tight, their motions stiff. Omolewa noticed them glancing into the sky as if looking for something.

"Can you feel it?" Kulal whispered.

"Feel what?" Omolewa whispered back.

Kulal glanced up into the sky and Omolewa was puzzled. What was she missing?

She followed Kashta to the helm. He stood by the steersman, the chugging of the mysterious engine driving the ship matching the rhythm of her heart. He circled, his eyes searching the far horizons. As he looked starboard he stopped the pointed.

"There," he said. "They are following us."

Omolewa looked into the distance confused. She saw no other ships on the horizon.

"You are looking in the wrong direction," Kashta said.

"Look higher."

Omolewa jerked her head up. "Into the sky?"

Kashta nodded.

Omolewa and Kulal looked into the blue grey sky. She was something, a speck floating high above the undulating sea.

"It is a cloud," she said instinctively. Kashta's looked told her she was wrong.

"Joka Watu!" Kulal exclaimed.

The deck exploded in activity. The sailors rushed to wooden chests on the deck, extracting bows and lances. Some climbed up the masts, positioning themselves will full quivers.

Omolewa shook with fear when Kashta's fell on her.

"Come with me," he ordered. She and Kulal followed the Kamite below deck to his cabin. They were about to enter when her family emerged, her father's face more serious than she'd ever seen.

"Are we under attack?" he asked.

"Yes," Kashta replied.

"I'm a former Mikijen. What can I do?"

"How are you with a bow?" Kashta asked.

Baba's eyes narrowed. "Better than average."

"Good. We can use you."

Baba grasped Omolewa's shoulders. "Go below deck with your mother and siblings."

"No," Kashta said. "We need her on deck."

Baba frowned at the Kamite. "I know she had special abilities, but she is just a girl. Her eyes should not see what is about to take place."

"I cannot stop what is pursuing us without her," Kashta replied calmly. He then looked Omolewa.

"This why we came for you," he said. "I'm sorry you had to learn the truth so soon."

Omolewa looked at baba, then Kashta, then back to baba.

"What must I do?" she said.

Kashta opened the door to this cabin. Omolewa expected an opulent scene, but was instead greeted by a sparse room with a simple bed, table and chair. The only other object in the room was a large ebony wood chest standing beside the bed. Kashta went directly to the chest and threw the doors open.

"Here," he said to Omolewa.

Kashta handed her a bow. She'd seen few weapons in her life; her father owned a sword and a few knives from his Mikijen days. The bow was heavy; it was strung with a material she could not recognize.

Kashta handed her a quiver of fletchless arrows as well. She took it as if it was some strange thing.

"It goes around your waist like this." Kulal took the quiver and fastened it around her narrow hips.

"I…I don't know how to use this," she protested.

"Today it doesn't matter," Kashta replied. "Consider this intense training."

Omolewa looked at baba and he knelt before her.

"Stay close to Kashta and me," he said. "You'll be fine."

Omolewa saw the worry in his eyes but nodded anyway.

"Come," Kashta said. "We must hurry."

They ran to the deck. The flurry that filled the deck when they went below had transformed into nervous stillness. The seamen stood along the bulwark, against the mast, or perched on the sails armed with lances, swords and bows. All eyes gazed at the object in the sky which had grown from a speck to a discernible threat. It flew almost like a bird, its appendages moving up and down but not as fluid as the birds she knew. There was something else as well, a long white trail of smoke rising from the rear of the object resembling a translucent tail. She looked at the smoke rising from the ship's stack and immediately saw the connection.

"These are your people," she said to Kashta. "Why are they pursuing us?"

For the first time Omolewa saw anger flash across Kashta's face.

"They are not my people!" he snapped.

He closed his eyes briefly. When he opened them he seemed to have regained his composure.

"As your brother said, they are the Joka Watu. Although we share knowledge, we discovered it by different means. They are the reason why I came for you."

"They mean us harm," Omolewa concluded.

"They mean the world harm," Kashta replied.

Omolewa could not conceive her actions protecting the entire world, but she could understand the threat to her baba, mama and her siblings. She would do whatever she could to prevent that from happening.

She lifted her bow. "I am ready."

The thing in the sky gained on them despite their speed. An eerie silence commanded the ship; Omolewa stood between her baba and Kashta, her trembling hands holding the bow.

"The trick is to use your nyama as well as your hands to pull back the bowstring," Kashta instructed. "Follow me."

Omolewa and Kulal followed the Kamite to the rear of the ship.

"Raise your bows," he commanded.

Omolewa looked puzzled. "But I must load an arrow!"

Kashta gave her his familiar smile. "Trust me. Raise your bows"

Omolewa peeked at Kulal and he calmed her doubts with a brotherly nod. She raised her bow.

"Now pull back the bowstring with your hand and your head," Kashta instructed.

Omolewa watched as Kashta and Kulal drew their bowstrings with ease. Omolewa imitated their moves. Her bowstring did not budge.

"You're not using your head," Kashta commented. "Pull the string like you attacked the men who invaded your home."

Omolewa closed her eyes. The bowstring pulled easily, coming back to touch her cheek. She opened her eyes with disappointment.

"There still is no arrow," she said.

Kashta grinned. "There will be. Now focus on the Joka.

Release on the count of three."

Omolewa nodded slightly as she struggled to keep her concentration.

"One…Two…Three!"

The bowstring twanged as she released it. She looked ahead and sighed. There was no arrow; neither were there arrows from Kashta and Kulal. She glanced at Kulal.

"Keep looking,' he mouthed.

Halfway between the ship and the Joka three bright, slim images appeared. They streaked fast toward the flying craft, emitting a shrill sound. The images began to separate; the center streak continuing directly at the joka, the streak to the right of it veering slightly toward the 'wing' and the third wavering as it dropped toward the sea.

That's mine, Omolewa thought.

The center bolt, Kashta's arrow, smashed into the joka's head. The craft wavered; Kulal's arrow grazed the right wing and the joka slowed. Omolewa's arrow grazed the joka's bottom. The craft did not move.

The joka slowed but continued to gain on the ship.

"Everyone find cover, now!" Kashta yelled. Zimbabwans scrambled for shelter, some hiding behind boxes and barrels on deck while others filed below. Kashta pulled Omolewa down behind the bulwark.

"I missed," she said.

"Yes you did," Kashta replied. "But you did very well. I didn't think you would be able to shoot it. You are turning out to be what we all imagined."

Kashta's words made her both proud and nervous. She didn't have long to think of her feelings. The Joka's shadow filled the deck, followed by the whistles of hundreds of bolts released from its underside. The bolts clattered against the deck, the rattling mixed with the cries of men. One bolt struck the deck only a few inches from Omolewa. The bone white projectile seemed almost to glow. She reached out to touch it but Kashta grabbed her hand.

"No!" he barked.

He let go of her hand as he stood. The Joka was in front of them. It tilted to the left then began to turn.

"It's coming back," Kulal said

"Of course," Kashta answered. "This time it will be worse."

Kashta stood tall. "Everyone below deck now!"

There was no hesitation to his command. Omolewa found her father then gasped. A bolt protruded from his shoulder. Despite the wound he smiled when he saw her

He cut a glance at the wound. "Don't worry, Lewa. I'm a former Mikijen. I've suffered much worse and lived."

He grabbed her hand. "Come on; let's go below as the mage ordered. He seems to know this thing and what it might do."

Omolewa lingered on the deck as the massive joka wheeled about in the sky. Sailors rushed by her, seeking safety below deck. Kashta walked along the deck, following the joka's movements. Kulal followed him, his eyes darting between the joka and the deck.

She removed her father's hand. "No baba, I must be with them."

Baba's grasped her shoulder again. This time his grip was tighter.

"Lewa, come below."

"Baba, please let me go," she insisted. "I have to go to Kashta. I must learn."

Baba's eyes sagged and his grip loosened. "You are right. You must learn. But you be careful and trust your feelings. Kashta is a learned man, but all men make mistakes."

Omolewa kissed baba's cheek, which seemed to ease his fear.

"I will baba."

She scampered across the littered deck to Kashta and Kulal, her bow tight in her hand.

"It's a fascinating machine," Kashta commented absently. "Steam powered mostly, but some other source as well."

"Vipande?" Kulal asked.

Kashta nodded. "Probably. But how to they contain it without hurting themselves? Or do they need to contain it?"

Omolewa had no idea what they were talking about.

"They may not need to," Kulal said.

Kashta's head snapped toward Kulal and a proud smile split his face. "Very true. If their origin is where we suspect, vipande may be to them like blood is to us."

He shared his smile with Omolewa. "You do not understand of what we speak, but you will. It is essential that you do."

He turned his attention back to the joka then pointed at the rear of the machine.

"Can you see the smoke?" he asked.

Omolewa squinted. A thin trail of smoke emerged from the rear of the joka.

"I see it!" she exclaimed.

"That is our target. We'll wait until it passed then shoot at it. That is if we survive its next pass."

There was no emotion in Kashta's voice but his words raised fear in Omolewa. These people meant to kill them. She knew this, but the weight of it finally settled on her young mind. She decided that she would not let them.

The joka was completely turned about hand heading at them from starboard.

"Come quickly," Kashta said. "We must hide."

The trio ducked under deck. Moments later there was a large whoosh immediately followed by intense heat.

"The ship is on fire!" someone yelled.

"No it's not," Kashta replied. He waited for a few moments then opened the hatch then stepped back on deck. Omolewa followed behind. The deck was wet, as if a sudden squall had spent itself over the ship. Vapor rose like ghosts into the sails. The heat felt through the deck lingered.

"Steam," Kashta commented. "It is as I suspected."

Omolewa did not understand what happened, but she understood the joka would return. She did not want that to happen.

Once again Kashta seemed to read her thoughts.

"Come, this is our chance!" he shouted.

They ran starboard to the bulwark. Kashta raised his bow;

Kulal and Omolewa did the same.

"Aim for the base of the columns," he instructed.

Omolewa nodded then released her bowstring in time with her companions. The glowing bolts streaked toward the joka as it began to turn. Kashta and Kulal's bolts struck true. Smoke and steam erupted from the joka's rear and it shuddered. Omolewa's bolt reached the thing a moment later. It struck nearby as the joka flanked. The joka boomed like thunder then a fireball rose from the rear. The joka fell flat onto the sea, breaking into sections. Omolewa spied people emerging from the wreckage as a cheer rose from the ship.

"There were people inside it!" she exclaimed.

Kashta only nodded.

Omolewa looked at her new mentor. "We must save them!"

"They stay where they are. If they are lucky the Creator will be merciful and end their lives quickly."

He looked at Omolewa. "It is more than they would do for us."

He took her bow. "You did well, Lewa. Go and see to your family. I promise you I will explain everything soon."

Kashta and Kulal walked away, Kulal turning back to share a smile and a head nod. Her family rushed by him then fell on her with hugs and kisses.

"Thank the Creator you are alright!" mama exclaimed.

Omolewa melted into their affection. Was she okay? She wasn't so sure.

The ship arrived in the Zimbabwa port three weeks after leaving Kiswala. Omolewa stood on deck with her family as they docked. Zimbabwa was a green land, with high hills rising beyond the city. There were other ships docked nearby, ships with columns replacing masts. They spewed the same smoke like their ship and the joka. Her thoughts went back to the joka and the people they left behind in the sea. She shuddered then hugged herself.

Kashta approached them, wearing a wide smile that complemented his elegant robes. Kulal was with him as always.

Her new found brother wore a loose green robe, a golden necklace and a cap studded with golden buttons.

"Welcome home, Omolewa," he said. "I know it is unfamiliar and strange to you, but you will soon see that this is where you belong."

She looked at the land then to her family surrounding her.

"Home is here with me," she said.

Kashta smiled. "You are wise beyond your years."

A commotion on the dock drew their attention. Wagons approached, drawn by creatures Omolewa had never seen. They resembled horses, yet they were smaller and their hind quarters were striped.

"Our parents have sent for us," Kulal said.

Kulal went to the game plank, gesturing for everyone to follow. Everyone did except Kashta. Omolewa looked back at him with questioning eyes.

"I'll be along," he said. "There are things I must tend to."

She felt baba's hand on her shoulder.

"Come Lewa. We'll be fine."

Omolewa walked with her family to the awaiting carriages. She had no idea of the path that lay before her, but she knew as long as she was with family everything would be fine. At least that is what she hoped.

The Deal

By Balogun Ojetade

Tears cascaded down Zurah's cocoa cheeks, soaking the collar of her tunic. A moist lump in Uqmal's throat choked his words.

"It *will* happen, Zurah."

"When," Zurah cried. "When will I be blessed to hold our baby in my arms? To feel it suckle from my breasts? *When*, Uqmal?

"Soon," Uqmal croaked.

"You have told me that every season, for the past three sun cycles," Zurah hissed. "It is time to *make* it happen!"

"How?" Uqmal inquired. "Our magic has been unsuccessful."

"A baby is spirit in flesh," Zurah replied. "Magic cannot manipulate spirit; only Divine Power can."

Uqmal grabbed his wife's arm and pulled her away from the midwives' tent.

"Have you lost your mind?" He whispered. "The Al-Askari will have our heads for even *thinking* about submitting ourselves to the Divine!"

"You know you don't have to tell *me*," Zurah said. "My father...my siblings...*all* Al-Askari. However, preservation of the bloodline is the one thing my family holds dearer than the protection of Fez. They *will* support me."

"You're serious?" Uqmal asked.

"I have already spoken to Zaakah," Zurah replied. "She has agreed to accompany you to Targa, which should not raise any suspicion, as she travels with you on your expeditions all the time."

"You want me to ask High Priest Yabo'Daan to intervene?" Uqmal asked, shaking his head. "Those Sand Elves can be a tricky lot."

"The Shadi-Khain only uses chicanery for their protection, or to teach life-lessons," Zurah replied. "They are not rogues like their Kel-Tamajaq neighbors."

"How you lived amongst those dune dwellers for so long without losing your mind, or your virtue, is beyond me," Uqmal said, his nose wrinkling in disgust.

"Had you not swept me off my feet, I would still be ambassador to Targa," Zurah said. "The dunes are never dull."

"One does not taste stew with another's tongue," Uqmal said with a shrug.

"So, will you go?" Zurah asked.

"Of course," Uqmal sighed. "Anything for you, my love."

Zurah clapped her hands and then leapt into Uqmal's arms. They embraced and shared a kiss as torrid as the Fezzan plain.

****

Uqmal sat beside his sister-in-law, Zaakah and perused the colorful artwork etched into her copper skin. The tattoo of a dove flittered from one side of her neck to the other and then disappeared under the collar of her tunic. The tattoo of a spider on her right cheek fed on the tattoo of a horsefly.

"How long before we arrive at the oasis of the Shadi-Khain?" Zaakah inquired, massaging the fresh tattoo of a great-spear on the middle finger of her left hand.

Uqmal closed his eyes and inhaled, allowing his mind to become one with the residue of consciousness that fueled the oga'koi-koi – the "Sand Creeper" – whose corpse had served as Uqmal's transport on his many hunts for magic relics throughout the lands of Ki-Khanga.

"We should arrive by tomorrow morning. However, we will surface in an hour or so to fill the oga'koi-koi with fresh air."

"Good," Zaakah said. "My companions are restless. They

long for the sun upon my skin."

"The Al-Askari have strange and fearsome magic," Uqmal said. "But much appreciated."

Zaakah responded with a slight bow of her head.

A rhythmic swishing sound echoed throughout the Sand Creeper as it darted beneath the surface of the desert. Uqmal patted Zaakah on her knee.

"We will surface shortly. If you need to move for any reason, do it now."

"I'm fine", Zaakah said.

Uqmal closed his eyes and raised his palms before his face, as if he was offering a platter of fruit to a guest. His chair turned soft, molding itself around Uqmal's waist and thighs, locking him in its warm embrace. The wizard's back sank deeper into the seat as the oga'koi-koi shot upward. The transport broke the surface, its massive, crimson head spearing through the sand. The creature slithered forth, sending a cloud of sand into the afternoon sky. Uqmal willed the mouth of the oga'koi-koi to open and then he stepped out, squinting as his eyes adjusted to the sunlight reflecting off the surface of the sand.

Zaakah stood at Uqmal's flank. A sigh escaped her lips. Uqmal peered over his shoulder. The exposed tattoos on Zaakah's face, neck and arms raced across her flesh.

"Your companions seem even more agitated than before," Uqmal said.

"While the sun satiates them, a fight is coming," Zaakah replied. "My companions become rather…excited at the prospect of battle."

"A fight?" Uqmal gasped. "When? Why?"

"Now," Zaakah answered. "As to 'why'? You should probably direct your question to *them*."

Uqmal followed Zaakah's finger to a cloud of sand rolling toward them from over a distant sand hill. He could make out the silhouette of five men on camelback.

"Those are Blue-Men," Zaakah said. "Kel-Tamajaq."

"The Sharks of the Sands," Uqmal spat. "Thieves and

cutthroats, all of them."

"Exceptional warriors, too," Zaakah said. "May I suggest we take to higher ground?"

"Understood," Uqmal replied.

He closed his eyes and mouthed a low, hissing chant. The sand under their feet shook violently and then swelled. A moment later, a large, rectangular column of sand rose from beneath them, carrying Uqmal, Zaakah and the oga'koi-koi skyward. Uqmal peered down at the party of Kel-Tamajaq, who, from so high up, looked like a swarm of blue beetles scurrying about. The camel-riders – all of them covered from their head-wraps to their feet in dark blue, cotton clothing – crept toward the column of sand.

"Ho, strong warriors of the Kel-Tamajaq," Uqmal called down to the Blue-Men. "How might we be of service?"

One of the Kel-Tamajaq rode out in front of his brethren, staring skyward. "Ho, friend. What business do you have in Targa?"

"None," Uqmal lied. "We are simply passing through on our way to Oyo for their Odunde Festival."

"Have you paid your toll, yet?" The leader of the Blue-Men asked.

"We weren't aware of a toll, friend," Uqmal replied. "How much cowry or iron is required?

"Such trinkets are no good in these parts," the leader of the Blue-Men answered.

"What, then?" Uqmal inquired.

"The woman," the leader inquired.

"I'm not for sale, *Targareg*," Zaakah hissed, calling the Blue-Man the Shadi-Khain word of insult for the Kel-Tamajaq.

"Then, you will spend the rest of your lives on this piece of sand," the leader said, patting the column.

Zaakah yanked her scarf over her face. "Stay put." She then leapt from the column.

"And so, it begins," Uqmal sighed as he pressed his palms toward the floor of the sand column.

Zaakah landed with a loud thud. A cloud of sand billowed up from the earth, swallowing her and the Kel-Tamajaq. Shrill cries rent the dense cloud. Uqmal could just make out the silhouette of a person flitting about the sand cloud like a butterfly darting from flower to flower to drink of their sweet nectar.

The sand settled. The Kel-Tamajaq all lay dead, their bodies twisted, torn and broken.

"A deadly butterfly, indeed," Uqmal whispered.

Zaakah pulled the scarf from her neck and wiped Kel-Tamajaq blood and flesh from her fingers. Her tattoos were now still. "We should leave this place. This was just a scouting party. More will come."

"The oga'koi-koi should have enough air to reach the Shadi-Khain oasis," Uqmal said. "When we arrive, I will buy us some of that scorpion stew you like."

"And some pineapple bread," Zaakah said, stepping into the oga'koi-koi's mouth.

Uqmal perused the carnage that lay upon the reddening sand behind him. "O…okay…anything you want."

****

The oga'koi-koi burst through the sand, coming to rest a few yards from a line of palm trees. Uqmal stepped out of the mouth of the crimson worm with Zaakah close behind him. They both took a knee and bowed their heads. A moment later, a cool breeze washed over them. A pair of massive talons landed before Uqmal.

"*You may stand, friends,*" A rich, alto voice said.

Uqmal and Zaakah rose and stood face-to-chest with a giant, alabaster eagle – *kulutasege*, the Shadi-Khain called them – which nodded its head in greeting. Sitting upon the bird, in a saddle cast from fine gold, was a Shadi-Khain scout. Her sand-brown dreadlocks danced on her shoulders as she leapt from the gargantuan bird's back.

"Menan'Jo," Uqmal said, extending his hand. "Long time."

"Too long, Uqmal of Fez," Menan'Jo said, pressing her inner wrist to Uqmal's in the customary Shadi-Khain greeting.

The Sand Elf turned her attention to Zaakah. "My warrior

sister; good to see you, again."

"Likewise," Zaakah said, extending her hand.

Menan'Jo pressed her outer wrist to Zaakah's outer wrist in the traditional greeting between warriors.

"So, what business do you have in Shadi-Shan?" Menan'Jo inquired.

"We seek counsel with Chief Priest Yabo'Daan," Uqmal replied.

"A Fezzan? Seeking the divine wisdom of Yabo'Daan?" Menan'Jo gasped. "That is heresy and high treason, is it not?"

"Only if we're caught," Uqmal replied. "We have worked hard to maintain discretion."

"Perhaps you should have chosen a transport not so…*red* if discretion was of importance to you," Menan'Jo said.

"The oga'koi-koi is the perfect vehicle for relic hunters such as me," Uqmal said. "Unfortunately, I killed this one during its mating season, when the Sand Creeper changes from sandy-brown to a deep crimson."

"Well, may you not hang, Uqmal of Fez," Menan'Jo said, pointing toward the sandy trail leading to Shadi-Shan.

"Umm…thank?" Uqmal whispered as he walked past the Sand Elf and her kulutasege.

Zaakah tapped her chest with her fist. Menan'Jo returned the salute.

The mage and the warrior were met by a cooling breeze and the smell of fresh grass and sweet watermelon. Men and women bustled from gazebo to gazebo, haggling with vendors and purchasing their goods and services. Although Uqmal hated the dunes of Targa, he loved Shadi-Shan, for it was much more than the home of the Shadi-Khain; it was also the largest open air market in the world and carried the highest quality magic decoctions and spell-scrolls in all Ki-Khanga.

"The Chief Priest is *this* way," Uqmal said, pointing up the winding cobblestone road that ran the length of the oasis. He and Zaakah strolled up the road until they came to a small tent.

"Yabo'Daan," Uqmal called. "Please, master, we are in

need of your assistance."

"Come in," a soothing voice replied.

Uqmal and Zaakah crouched down a bit and then stepped through the slit in the white, cotton cloth that covered the entrance. Sitting before them, on a traditional sand-chair, constructed from camel hide stuffed with sand, was a bronze-colored man, lean in stature, with the face of a man in his late teens. His eyes, however, revealed a wisdom possessed only by a venerable elder.

"Master Yabo'Daan," Uqmal said, prostrating at Yabo'Daan's feet. "Abuyu; abuye."

"Agbu adu," Yabo'Daan replied as he patted Uqmal between his shoulder-blades, signaling him to rise.

Zaakah dropped to one knee and tapped her chest with her fist. "Abuyu; abuye."

"Agbu adu," Yabo'Daan replied, tapping his left palm with the back of his right hand. "How may I help you, friends form Fez?"

"I am in need of your divinely guided assistance, Great Father," Uqmal replied. "My wife and I are desperate to have a child, but, despite our efforts, we have been unable to conceive."

"And you dare come to me, Fezzan?" Yabo'Daan inquired. "Are you not at risk of hanging for this heresy?"

"The blessing of a child is well worth the risk," Uqmal replied.

"I can help you acquire what you seek," Yabo'Daan said. The price, however, is quite steep."

"I will give anything," Uqmal said. "Name your price, Great Father."

"Have you heard of the joka?" Yabo'Daan asked.

"The winged terrors that inhabit The Cleave," Uqmal replied. "I have heard them spoken of in fearful whispers."

"Their masters, the Joka Watu, have terrorized us for the past two seasons," Yabo'Daan said. "They use their monstrosities to attack our kulutasege, stinging them with their tails, which carry a powerful magic. The sting paralyzes our steeds in mid-flight, causing the birds – and their riders – to plummet to their deaths." Yabo'Daan rose from his sand-chair and paced back and forth before Uqmal and Zaakah. "Bring me the tail of a joka and I assure you that what you want will be yours."

Uqmal shot a glance at Zaakah. Zaakah nodded and then patted her chest twice with her open palm. Uqmal returned the nod. "You have a deal, Great Father"

"Good," Yabo'Daan said. "When will you set out for The Cleave?"

Uqmal sprang to his feet. "Now!"

****

A hissing din rose from the earth. The stone ground buckled and then gnarled, rolling in upon itself. The large circle of stone melted away, leaving a massive hole. A moment later, the oga'koi-koi slithered to the surface. Uqmal and Zaakah crept out of the worm's maw, crouching in the shadow of the mountain at their backs.

Uqmal perused his surroundings. Colossal iron spires rose high into the night sky, their summits belching gray smoke. A vast field of black grass, with tips the hue of tarnished silver, lay before them and the fetid stench of burnt metal and rancid meat pervaded the air. His heart raced and a chill crept up the back of his neck. The Cleave was even more grave and menacing than the tales the old wizards would tell around the communal fires when he was a boy. He glanced toward Zaakah. Her tattoos scurried about, dodging and chasing each other.

The Al-Askari pointed toward the ebon tract. Uqmal snapped his head in the direction of her finger. Lying in the black grass was a gargantuan, winged beast. The creature was covered in a purplish-gray chitin; even its wings – each the span of three men lying head-to-foot – were armored. Its tail, as long and sharp as a great-spear, emitted a fluorescent blue glow.

The tattoo of an owl soared from under Zaakah's tunic and perched on her collarbone. Zaakah stared into the darkness, craning her neck toward the field where the creature lay. "Two men sleep beneath the wing of the joka. It would appear the joka is asleep, too.

It is hard to determine, since the creature has no eyes, but it lies as still as the grave."

"Perfect," Uqmal whispered. "The oga'koi-koi should get us within striking distance without raising any alarm."

Zaakah nodded.

The pair crept back into the mouth of the worm. The oga'koi-koi then slithered back into the cavity in the earth. A few minutes later, the oga'koi-koi emerged no more than spitting distance from the joka. The crimson worm spasmed and then oily, yellow sputum erupted from its maw. The vomit rained down upon the Joka Watu and the joka. Silence escaped the men's mouths as their seared vocal cords seized their screams of agony. Within moments, the men were nothing more than pools of steaming, brown and yellow sludge upon the black grass. A large, crescent-shaped wound was carved into the joka's wing. The joka, however, did not scream; nor did it even move.

"Strange," Uqmal whispered. "The creature remains still."

"Shall we investigate?" Zaakah asked.

Uqmal replied with a nod as he stepped out of the oga'koi-koi's mouth. Zaakah followed. The grass vibrated gently beneath Uqmal's feet, massaging his soles and soothing him.

"This must be how they keep the monstrosities in this place from tearing them apart," he mused.

Zaakah approached the joka from its rear flank, her fists at the ready. She crouched beside the creature's tail and examined its hind parts.

"What?" She gasped.

"What is it?" Uqmal inquired as he knelt beside her.

"Look," Zaakah replied.

Uqmal leaned sideways, pressing his head against Zaakah's shoulder. His mouth fell open and his eyes grew into twin full moons. "Daarila's beard!" He crawled under the rigid, chitinous tail of the joka toward a circular iron door. A soft blue light escaped from the slightly open portal. Uqmal opened the door and crawled into a small cabin that was bathed in blue light generated by a network of glass veins that ran the length of the walls and ceiling.

The veins terminated at the joka's tail. In the floor were two beds of stuffed ram hide, held in place with leather straps. At the head of each bed were two smooth, iron levers that protruded from domes in the floor.

Uqmal crawled out of the cabin. "Help me," he said, placing his palm on the joka's tail.

Uqmal and Zaakah yanked at the tail, but it did not budge.

"Let's try to turn it," Uqmal said. "Toward me."

Zaakah pushed; Uqmal pulled. A low "click" came from the base of the spear-like tail. A quick twist and the chitinous covering slid off, revealing a long glass spike. Inside the spike was a clear liquid, with flickers of fluorescent blue light swirling about.

"It is said that the Sea of Tyrak shimmers in such a way," Zaakah said.

"The water is infused with vipande," Uqmal said. "It seems to be fuel for the joka."

"And this material," Zaakah said running her hands along the length of the joka's tail. "It looks like glass, but feels denser."

"It is called *glassteel*," Uqmal replied. "A material created by our Sultan ages ago, but abandoned because it was too costly to maintain production of it."

Uqmal stared at Zaakah's hands as they glided across the rigid glassteel and they aroused him. He snapped his head away and lowered his gaze. Something warm and soft brushed against the back of his hand. He peered toward the sensation. Zaakah was touching him, tracing the veins in his hand with her fingertips. Uqmal took a deep breath in an effort to calm his racing heart. Zaakah leaned toward him a bit. Uqmal rushed to meet her. Their mouths pressed together and with the tip of his tongue, Uqmal drew a wet circle around Zaakah's full lips.

They frantically unscrewed the joka's tail. Zaakah pressed it to her chest and then sauntered toward the waiting mouth of the oga'koi-koi. She shot a quick glance over her shoulder at Uqmal as she entered the crimson worm. Uqmal strutted behind her, admiring Zaakah's athletic body. The joka's tail glowed brighter and pulsed against Zaakah's sweating palms.

****

Uqmal leapt from his bed, fumbling for his clothing. He slipped on his trousers, tunic and sandals and then headed toward the galley, which smelled pleasantly of vanilla, nutmeg and sweet cream. Zaakah was there, fixing two cups of tea.

"Good morning," Uqmal croaked.

Zaakah did not meet his gaze. "Good morning."

"It was the vipande, Zaakah," Uqmal said. It bewitched us."

"How do you know?" Zaakah asked.

"Because, despite how wrong it is…despite the fact that being with you can mean the end of us both…I want you; now, even more than last night."

"I fear that if I look into your eyes, I will take you, right here, in this galley," Zaakah said.

"You had better not look, then," Uqmal said, taking a step toward her.

Zaakah looked up into Uqmal's eyes. She sat her cup on the countertop and rushed into his arms. They kissed passionately, their tongues fighting to become one.

The oga'koi-koi lurched upward, sending the couple staggering across the galley.

Zaakah pushed Uqmal away. "We're surfacing."

"We must be near the Shadi-Shan," Uqmal said. "To our seats!"

They ran to their seats, which immediately turned gel-like and sucked them in, locking them safely in place. The worm surfaced a few yards from the oasis. Zaakah grabbed a long leather sack that rested against a wall and slung it over her back. The mage and the warrior then exited the oga'koi-koi and took a knee.

"Go right ahead," Menan'Jo shouted from far above them. "Yabo'Daan is waiting for you."

Uqmal and Zaakah sprinted toward the oasis. Upon reaching it, they dashed up the cobblestone street, weaving their way through the hurrying crowd. The old Sand Elf stood before the entrance to his tent, eating chunks of watermelon from a calabash.

"Do you have it?"

Zaakah unstrapped the sack and placed it on the ground. Yabo'Daan opened it and peeked inside. A smile spread across his face. He closed the sack and slid it into his tent.

"Come inside."

Uqmal and Zaakah followed Yabo'Daan into his tent.

"We have upheld our end of the bargain," Uqmal said. "We trust you will uphold your end soon?"

"I already have," Yabo'Daan replied.

"You have?" Uqmal gasped. "Zurah is with child?"

"Zurah is forever barren," Yabo'Daan replied. "*Zaakah* is the one who carries your seed."

"This cannot be!" Uqmal cried. "My wife…"

"Is to be Zaakah," Yabo'Daan said. "Zurah could not – and never will – conceive because *I* placed a curse on her three sun cycles ago. A curse paid for by the wife of the man with whom she had an affair on your wedding day."

"You lie!" Uqmal hissed.

"He speaks the truth," Zaakah sighed.

"Are…are you sure?" Uqmal asked as he brushed a tear from his cheek.

"I caught them," Zaakah said. "My big sister…and my husband."

"Kaleeq?" Uqmal gasped. "Did you…?"

"Yes," Zaakah replied. "He did not die at the hands of any robbers. But I could not kill my sister, so I took other measures."

"Zurah will expose us as heretics when she finds out about us," Uqmal said.

"That she will," Yabo'Daan said.

"They will hang us for conceiving a child through the machinations of a priest," Uqmal cried.

"That, they will," Yabo'Daan said, "*If* you return to Fez."

"What do you suggest?" Zaakah asked.

"Stay here and work for me," Yabo'Daan replied. "Take the joka's tail to Kamit. They will use it to develop a weapon to crush those mechanical monstrosities once and for all. I will pay you handsomely for that."

"So, you already knew that the joka are machines," Zaakah said.

"I have known for quite some time," Yabo'Daan replied. "I also know that vipande heightens emotion a hundred-fold."

"You set this whole thing up," Uqmal said, shaking his head.

"I merely moved destiny along a bit faster and in the direction we all needed it to go," Yabo'Daan said.

Uqmal shot a glance at Zaakah. She nodded and then picked up the sack that housed the joka's tail.

"Prepare that handsome pay you spoke of, Great Father" Uqmal said, placing a hand on Yabo'Daan's shoulder. "We leave for Kamit tonight!"

Simple Math

By Milton Davis

Omari Ket stood on the hill overlooking the Kiswala port of Bashaba, fighting to hold back tears. At that moment he was the happiest man in Kenja, if not all of Ki-Khanga. For weeks he'd trudged across the Kenja savanna hounded by Nubia's militias and harassed by the local fauna that viewed him as an easier meal than the thousands of herd animals whose shit his feet had an uncanny ability to find. He wiped away the tear trails with his grimy hands, and then raised them high in celestial praise.

"I don't always believe in you, Creator," he croaked. "But today I do!"

He stumbled down the sandy slope onto the nearest road. A group of farmers with donkeys loaded with grain quickly distanced themselves from him, their pinched faces making their reason obvious. Under any other circumstances Omari would have either beat them up, robbed them, or beat them up and robbed them. But on that day he had neither the energy nor the inclination. All he wanted was a bath.

He made a quick trip to the local brothel. It wasn't hard to find for all Kiswala ports were laid out basically the same no matter where they were located. Two guards flanked the tall wooden doors, their bulk and turbans marking them as Zimbabwans. They snarled at his approach then held their noses.

"On your way," one of them snapped. "Monafiki only services Kiswala and Mikijen."

Omari lifted the tattered sleeve covering his left bicep,

revealing the Kraken tattoo.

"What about a Mikijen with gold dust?" he patted the leather back strapped to his waist.

The guards pushed the doors open then stepped aside. Omari stepped into the brothel as if he was entering the gates of a palace. The building was empty, as it should have been early in the day. The Kiswala were handling their business and the Mikijen were busy protecting them. He would have the place to himself for at least half a day. No sooner had his foot touched wood did a tall woman emerge from a room opposite him, her shapely body wrapped tight in a yellow kanga. She approached Omari with a suggestive smile and only flinched briefly when close enough to smell him.

"You are quite the handsome man," she said. "Apparently you've spent some time on the road."

Omari's spirits were rising. "Longer than I'd like to remember. I need a bath, and maybe some other things."

He winked and the woman smiled. "All things are possible with the proper motivation."

Omari was not the show off type, at least when it came to his money but he deserved some pampering after all he'd been through in Kenja. His chest was still sore from his encounter with the short people, and his ego was still bruised from Kadira's rebuffs. He took his bag from his belt and opened it enough for the woman to see. Her eyes went wide.

"I'd like exclusive use of your hospitality for the day," he said. "I think I have enough to make it possible."

"For that bag I will tend to you myself," the woman replied.

"That won't happen," Omari said. "Give me what a pinch of this bag will pay for."

The woman snarled. "You Mikijen are all the same!"

"Thank you," he replied. "Now where's my room?"

"Wait here,' the matron said. 'I'll have a bath prepared for you."

"Thank you," Omari said.

"Don't thank me. It's for our sake. You smell like shit."

Omari shrugged; it was a fair assessment. He plopped down at the nearest table then stripped off his ragged boots. A quick whiff and he put them back on. He'd wait for his bath before taking off anything else.

A woman appeared from a hidden door carrying a simmering bowl. She was pretty despite her unkempt appearance; her kanga barely held her womanly assets. Omari winked at her as she placed his bowl and spoon before him.

"A wonderful meal served by a beautiful woman," he said. "The Creator has blessed me today."

The woman smiled as she turned her head away. She lingered as Omari gulped down a spoonful of stew then moaned.

"Tasty indeed," he lied. "I wonder what else here is just as good?"

"Do not toy with me, stranger," she said. "I'm no village girl."

"Oh, I never play with certain subjects," Omari replied. "And let's not be strangers. I'm Omari."

"Kapera," the woman replied.

"Well, Kapera, you seem to be the only person that doesn't mind that I smell like a rutting camel."

"I tend the livestock. I'm used to it."

Omari frowned. "Maybe after my bath we can discover what other things you do well..."

"Don't mess with anything you didn't pay for, Mikijen!"

The matron stormed into the room. "Get out of here, Kapera. You have no business with this man."

Kapera scurried from the room. The matron glared at Omari.

"Your bath is ready. Follow me."

The matron led him to the back of the brothel. It was the worst room in the building, Omari suspected. Inside was a shallow tub filled with dingy water.

"This is it?" Omari said.

"You get what you pay for," the matron replied.

Omari began taking off his clothes. The matron stood

before him until he was fully undressed.

"Now you own me," Omari said.

The matron struggled not to smile. "Let me know when you're done."

She walked out the room. Omari waited.

"Creator! He's fabulous!"

Omari grinned. He settled into the lukewarm water and fatigue overwhelmed him. He closed his eyes and was asleep in seconds, drifting slowly into what he hoped was a peaceful slumber. Instead he fell, spinning downward at a speed that made him nauseous and dizzy. He knew he would vomit in moments but mercifully the falling ceased. Light invaded his darkness, illuminating a scene that played out in his life months ago. He was at the temple again in Wadantu standing beside Kadira. Sebe held the strange idol and the men who called themselves Caretakers stood before him with their staffs. Omari was raising his hand cannon when he felt a searing pain in his chest.

"By the Creator!" he exclaimed. He bolted up in the washtub and the sword point touching his old wound broke his skin. The brothel door guards hovered over him, one larger one holding his tarnished sword against his chest. The matron peered over his shoulder.

"Don't kill him!" she exclaimed. "The Haiseti will pay well for him. He'd make an excellent pleasure slave."

Omari's eyes narrowed. "Think carefully about what you do. I'm Mikijen. We take care of our own."

The big guard laughed. "You were Mikijen. You haven't reported. As far as they are concerned you're still dead."

"So how will you explain a certain tattoo on my arm?" Omari asked.

The guard looked skeptical.

"Don't listen to him!" the matron barked. "The Haiseti won't care and if they do, we'll peel it off. It will reduce his value, but gold is gold."

The matron grinned. "Speaking of gold, search his clothes. I believe we have another bonus waiting."

The other guard went to the pile of odoriferous garments then shifted through it with his sword tip.

"It's not here," he grumbled.

"Here it is." Omari stood in his naked glory. The gold bag rested against his hip, held in place by a thin leather cord.

"Get it!" the matron ordered.

While the life of a Haiseti pleasure slave was not the worst fate for anyone, Omari had no intentions of crossing Wadantu again. He twisted to his left, slapping the blade against his chest with the flat of his hand and wincing as it cut his chest again. He pounced from the washtub, driving his right fist into the man's throat then catching his sword as the big man went limp. The matron tried to run but Omari swept her feet. She fell hard, her head slamming the floor boards. He turned to face the other guard. The man hesitated, looking at his choking comrade and his dazed boss.

"Looks like you have a decision to make," Omari said.

The guard attacked. Omari parried the clumsy thrust then drove his sword into the man's abdomen. The guard collapsed into the washtub.

Omari looked at the mess around him.

"This was unnecessary," he murmured.

He stripped the big guard of his clothes and donned them. The matron moaned and he hit her on the head with the sword hilt. Omari searched her pockets and found his gold dust in addition to a handful of cowries. He grinned; he'd taken a bath and made a profit. Not bad for a day's work. He decided to go immediately to the Mikijen post. He wasn't sure if the matron was dead or not, but he was sure that if she wasn't she would report him. Once he rejoined he would be immune to her charges. He stepped over the bodies then sauntered downstairs. As he left the brothel Kapera appeared. She looked at him puzzled and Omari winked.

"There's a mess for you to clean up," he said. He walked up to her, pulled her to him, kissed her deep then gave her the cowries.

"You should visit," he whispered.

"I will," she replied.

Omari patted her butt then strolled out the door and into the streets of Biswana, ignoring the curious glances at his makeshift outfit. He'd done worse; he grinned as the memory of Ile-Kanta came to mind. He'd been caught in a compromising position with the head elder's daughter, an embarrassment to the local Mikijen garrison and a blow to the young woman's loloba. He was forced to strip naked in the middle of the village to walk a gauntlet of the village men, but the protests and attention of the village women forced the men to give up the gauntlet idea. They dressed him and gave him a head start to run for his life instead. Luckily for him the village women provided a reasonable obstacle to their jealous men.

As he reached the docks he felt a pressure in his chest. Omari rubbed it, noticing it was the spot where he received his Wadantu wound.

"I'll have to get a medicine-priest to look at this," he mused.

He massaged the wound as he walked along the mooring. Fishing dhows tainted the sea air with their pungent cargo. A few merchant dhows rested on the calm sea, while further out Mikijen war dhows guarded the harbor entrance. A flood of bittersweet memories invaded his head; Omari began to question why he had returned. But there really was no choice. He was technically broke. True, he could live well for quite some time with the gold dust in his pouch but he had no intentions of doing so. Omari was a planning man; he envisioned a small tavern in a quaint town where he would live out his old age charming the locals with stories of his travels and keeping the old widows company.

He finally came to the building flying the Kraken banner. He walked in and was greeted by a sleeping mercenary, his snores echoing through the small, dingy room. Omari grinned; he walked up to the table then slammed his hand on the table. The mercenary's eyes popped open.

"What in the Cleave?" he shouted.

Omari folded his arms across his chest. "I've come to reenlist and it looks like I'm just in time."

The man scowled at Omari. "You're former Mikijen?"

Omari turned and revealed his tattoo.

The man stood, walking to a wall of scrolls divided alphabetically. "What's your name?"

"Omari Ket."

The man stopped then turned. "You're Omari Ket?"

Omari grinned. "You've heard of me, I see."

The man nodded. "Yeah, I've heard of you. Decent fighter; ladies man."

He looked Omari up and down. "You don't look that good to me."

"I'm glad I don't. You're not my type. Too much between your legs."

The man grinned. "Smart mouth. I heard that, too."

The man pulled out Omari's scroll. The Kiswala kept meticulous records. Once a person entered their employ he or she was forever in their archives. He opened the scroll then went directly to the bottom. He went into his table drawer, taking out a quill and an ink vial. With the dip of the quill and a quick scribble Omari was active again.

"You'll come in as you went out, third rank. You'll be paid accordingly."

"And how soon will that be?" Omari asked.

"Next week."

Omari frowned. "I could use an advance."

"You won't get it. This is Biswana, not Kiswala."

The man sat, rubbing his chin. "There is an opportunity to make a little extra coin."

Omari eyes brightened. "How little?"

"Twenty nari," the man said.

Not a bad amount, Omari thought. "I'm in."

The man smiled. "Give me a minute."

He went into the back room then returned with a lance and a bow, a quiver of arrows on his hip.

"Haisetti?" Omari guessed.

The man nodded then extended his hand. "I'm Zenawi."

Omari grasped his hand. "Hello Zenawi. Let's get on with it."

He followed Zenawi into the street then waited as he locked up the office.

"This way," Zenawi motioned.

Omari grinned. Now this was more like it.

Omari forced Zenawi to stop at the nearby vendor then feasted on boiled rice and shrimp. He was wiping his face when he heard a familiar voice calling him.

"Mikijen! Mikijen!"

He looked toward the voice and grimaced. It was the young maid from the brothel. She ran toward him, waving her hands as if greeting a long lost friend.

"How long have you been here exactly?" Zenawi asked.

"One night too long," Omari said under his breath. He forced a smile on his face as he sauntered to meet the woman.

"Well, well, you found me! Why so much joy?"

"I left the brothel!" she said. "I have come to live with you!"

Omari looked at the woman stunned.

"Ah...Uh..."

"Kapera," she said sweetly. "My name is Kapera."

"Jambo, Kapera," Zenawi said. "It is good to have you. Our post has been too long without a woman's warmth."

"Wait a minute! What in the Seven Winds are you doing?"

Omari's outburst seemed to wound Kapera. She lowered her head and turned away.

Zenawi cut Omari a mean glance. "Here, take this key. We will be back in a few days."

Kapera head jerked up, her eyes glowing. "Thank you, bwana!"

She winked at Omari and ran off to the post.

Omari was furious. He grasped Zewani's shoulders before he could walk away and spun him around.

"What in the Cleave was that? Why did you send her to the post? This is my business!"

Zenawi removed his hands. "The mistress kicked her out. No one quits the brothel. She has no work and would be in the streets otherwise. Whatever business you have you can sort out when we return."

Zenai turned and walked away. Omari considered stabbing him in the back but he needed the money. He shrugged and followed. If he was the cause of the woman's firing he would give her a few coins and send her on her way.

They spent the remainder of the day walking along the coast, the ocean a constant companion. Toward nightfall a large structure loomed in the distance, rising over the swaying palms.

"What is this?" Omar said. "I don't remember a Kiswala fort this far south."

"It's not Kiswala," Zenawi replied. "It belongs to Enzi Chande. He was just a local fisherman five years ago before he built a dhow and began trading with the villages to the south. Now he claims to be a bwana."

"I'm sure the Kiswala are not happy with him," Omari replied.

Zenawi nodded. "A Mikijen force from the north came a few weeks ago to deal with him. They did not return."

Omari stopped walking. "What happened to them?"

Zenawi shrugged. "I assumed they dealt with Enzi then sailed home."

"You assume wrong," Omari said. "They were either paid to join Enzi or they were wiped out. Either situation is not good for us."

"You assume too much," Zewani suggested.

"I'm alive today because I assume too much," Omari replied. "So I guess your plan was to walk right up to the gate and ask if anyone is home."

Zenawi shuffled about and Omari spat.

"We'll wait until nightfall then have a good look at that fort."

Zenawi frowned. "That is the coward's way. We are Mikijen."

"We walk up to that fort in the open and we'll be crab food. I'm waiting until nightfall. You can do what you wish."

Omari dropped his gear and sat. He took out his dagger and began cleaning his fingernails. Zenawi glared at him then sat beside him.

Omari stood beside Kadira. Three elderly women faced them, staffs in their withered hands. He said something to Kadira then attacked the women. One of them stepped forward, stabbing him with her staff. Then he was on his back, looking up at the three women as they lifted a carved head from his aching chest.

"Wake up and serve," the women said.

Omari remained on his back, trying to understand what had just happened to him.

"Wake up!"

Omari sat up suddenly, gripping his shirt over his heart. It was dark, the night sky spotted with dense stars. Zenawi knelt before him, his face curious.

"Are you okay?"

Omari ignored Zenawi. He poked and felt about his chest with both hands before opening his shirt. A ragged scar rested over his heart.

"   What in the Creator's name is this?" he said aloud.

"Omari, what is going on?"

Omari finally looked at Zenawi then remembered where he was. He closed his shirt.

"Nothing. Just a bad dream."

He stood then proceeded toward the fort.

"Wait!" Zenawi called. "We need a torch."

Omari blew out an exasperated breath. "No, Zenawi, we do not need a torch. If we light a torch they will see us."

Zenawi looked puzzled. "'We don't want to be seen?"

"Not yet," Omari answered. "It will ruin the effect."

Omari put the strange dream and wound behind him. First things first. He moved with care through the dark woods, thankful for a full moon. He stopped at the forest's edge, signaling for Zenawi to do the same. On a closer inspection the fort was in a sorry state. The pockmarked walls showed signs of wear, and in certain section hole punctured the stone.

"This fort is old, probably as old as the Kamit temples," Omari whispered.

"You've been to Kamit?" Zewani's voice shook with excitement.

"Shut up," Omari barked. There were no guards to be seen, but a soft glow stealing through the wall breaches indicated activity inside. Omari looked about then smiled as he located Enzi's dhows.

"Now you can make your torch," he said.

Zenawi went to work, locating two thick branches then wrapping the ends with palm fronds. Omari inspected them then took them from Zenawi.

"Follow me."

They crept to the dhows. Omari took out his flint then lit the torches. He climbed aboard the first dhow, sword in one hand, torch in the other. Once he located the pitch barrels on deck he set in on fire. He rushed out of the first dhow then did the same to the second.

"Come on!" he ordered.

He ran to the wood's edge then watched gleefully as the dhow burned. Raised voices came from the fort; moments later a dozen men rushed to the dhows. Omari jumped to his feet, sprinting into the fort through a wall breach. The fort courtyard was empty as he hoped. It didn't take him long to locate Enzi's lair, a large stone room at the rear of the fort. He took a glance behind him; Zenawi was just entering the breach, his face still confused.

"Keep up, damn it!" Omari shouted at him. He ran to the stone room, stopping only to gingerly open the door. Enzi laid sleep in an elaborate bed, his snores filling the opulent room. Omari took out his dagger.

"What are you doing?" Zenawi whispered.

"Eliminating the competition," Omari replied.

"You can't do that! It is not honorable!"

Omari stopped and glared at Zenawi. "You have a lot to learn about being a Mikijen."

Omari went to Enzi's bedside. He raised his dagger and then blinding pain struck his chest.

"What the..."

The pain flared again. Omari fell to his knees, dropping the dagger. The blade rattled against the stone floor. Enzi sat upright.

"What is it? What's going on?"

Omari looked into the merchant's eyes, grimacing with pain. Zenawi stood at the door dumbfounded.

"Assassins!" Enzi shouted. "Assassins!"

Omari felt hands slip under his arms. He was lifted to his feet and dragged away from the screaming Enzi.

"No!" he groaned. "I'm not finished!"

"We must flee!" Zenawi countered. "The other will hear him!"

Omari fought past the pain, managing to pull his wrist knife free. He took his best aim then threw it at Enzi. The blade whizzed by the merchant's ear then stuck into the wall behind him. Enzi yelped then flattened against the bed.

"You've been warned, fisherman!" Omari croaked.

Zenawi continued to drag him until they were outside Enzi's room. The pain in his chest subsided; Omari jerked away from Zenawi and stood.

"What is wrong with you?" Zenawi asked.

Omari rubbed his chest. "I don't know."

Zenawi dropped him then pointed ahead. "There they are!"

Omari and Zenawi both looked across the courtyard. Enzi's guards ran toward them, swords drawn and lances lowered. Omari's pain diminished rapidly as they closed in.

"I think it's time you used some of that Nuba skill with the bow," he said to Zenawi.

Zenawi hesitated. "Shouldn't we wait to discern their intentions? These men are former Mikijen. They might..."

"Take that damn bow and shoot somebody!" Omari yelled.

Zenawi notched an arrow then let it fly. The projectile sank into the throat of the closest man. Before he could hit the ground Zenawi let two more arrows fly. Two more men fell, another with an arrow to the neck, one with an arrow to the knee. Omari smiled. He was good.

The other guards scattered for cover. Omari scanned the courtyard, spotting the nearest gap in the wall.

"Let's go!"

Omari ran, Zenawi close behind. He was halfway to escape when a guard jumped in his path, sword drawn. Omari didn't slow his pace. He feinted, raising his sword over his head as delivering an overhead blow. The guard raised his sword to block then Omari lowered his body, ramming his shoulder into the guard's gut. The guard huffed as he doubled over onto Omari. Omari straightened and threw the guard over his shoulder. The guard slammed into the ground; Zewani leaped over him to avoid falling over him.

They were well into the woods before the guards decided to pursue. They stumbled about in the dark, but without torches the guards couldn't spot them. Enzi's men gave up the chase after a time, hurling curses at Omari and Zewani before returning to the dilapidated fort.

"We'll stay here until dawn," Omari said. "As long as we're on the way back before daylight we should be fine."

"I am not happy with your idea," Zenawi said. "What you attempted to do was an affront to the reputation of the Mikijen."

Omari had to put his hand over his mouth to keep from laughing out loud. "I think you need to take a second look at what you signed up for. We're mercenaries. We do anything we get paid to do. Anything. The Kiswala pay us well for this. I'm assuming that you've came straight from your backwoods home to Bashaba."

Zewani swallowed. "I did."

Omari shook his head. "Go to sleep. I'll take first watch."

Zewani found a soft spot then quickly fell asleep. Omari shook his head again. Times must be hard if the Mikijen recruited men and women like Zewani. He was a good man, and good men had no place in the Mikijen. He sat, leaning against a palm, and then examined his chest. The pain was completely gone. He rubbed the scar, trying to remember if it was there when he left Kenja. His mind went hazy as he tried to think, so he decided to forget it. He'd find a healer and get his opinion.

He woke Zewani for his shift then fell immediately asleep. It was a deep dreamless sleep; when Zewani woke him he was angry.

"What? What?"

Zewani didn't answer. Omari rubbed his eyes before opening them. Zewani stood before him flanked by Enzi's guards.

"Is this the one?" one of the guards asked.

Zewani nodded.

"So you're Omari Ket." The man looked Omari up and down as Omari stood. There was no reason for him to go for his weapons for he was too close and too outnumbered.

"I am. Who are you?"

"Gerial Badogo. We served together in Kiswala."

Omari didn't remember him but thought it prudent to act otherwise.

"Of course. So Gerial, do you plan to kill us?"

Gerial rubbed his chin. "We should. You robbed us of a generous employer."

"That was my plan, but I remember that I didn't kill him."

"You might as well have. The man was so frightened we couldn't get him out of the bed. I tried to convince him that he could have other dhows made and he almost died again. He ran into the night. He could have at least told us where he kept his cowries."

Omari put his hands on his waist. "So what now?"

Gerial folded his arms across his chest. "We become Mikijen again. You'll speak for us because we didn't kill you and your friend."

"Sounds fair," Omari agreed. "There will be no revenge killing? No blood feud?"

Gerial smiled. "The men you killed were our comrades, not our family. If they were family you'd have never awakened."

"Wait!" Zenawi shouted. "They are traitors! We cannot speak for them!"

Gerial glared at the Nuba, his hand finding his sword hilt. Omari raised his left hand, his other hand on his sword hilt.

"He means no harm. Let's not have anyone lose their life over a misunderstanding."

Zenawi was about to speak again but was silenced by Omari's stare. Once Zenawi was silenced Omari turned to Gerial with a bright smile.

"The day gets away from us. Shall we go?"

"Of course."

What began as a two man task was now a twelve man return. Omari kept smiling while inside he cursed. They would have to split the money with Gerial and his cohorts. This had not turned out the way he hoped. At least Kapera waited on his return. He'd have to thank Zenawi for that, at least. But first he would see a healer. It was time he learned what was causing him so much pain.

Omari never imagined himself happy to see a backwater like Bashaba, but he never imagined being in the company of such annoying people. Zenawi whined the entire trek back, wondering how he was going to feed all his new Mikijen friends. Enzi's former cohorts were equally annoying, constantly bickering and complaining about various aches and pains and threatening to make him and Zenawi pay for ruining their good work. Omari was about to call them on their threats when the palm tree thicket cleared and the city came into view.

"Zenawi, can you take our new army to the barracks?" Omari asked.

"Me? I thought you were coming!"

Omari rubbed his chest, remembering the pain inflicted on him in Enzi's bedroom.

"I'll be along. I'm going to see a healer."

Zewani hurried to his side.

"I don't know what to do with them!" he whispered. "These are dangerous men!"

"Feed them," Omari replied. "That should hold them until I return. Besides, you'll have help. Kapera is there, remember?"

Zewani's eye lit. "Yes, Kapera is there!" His face settled into worry again. "Kapera is there!"

Omari rested his hand on Zewani's shoulder. "I know what you're thinking. Kapera can handle herself. She worked in a brothel."

"I don't know, Omari. This is not a good situation."

Omari shrugged. "We'll handle it the best we can. Once we start assigning duties things will calm down. If it doesn't, I'll pick a few fights and lighten the load."

Zewani's brows clinched. "You are not a good man, Omari."

"I never claimed to be. Now who's the best healer?"

"Abasi, without a doubt," Zewani replied. "His stall is behind the cow stables."

Omari's nose crinkled. "The cow stables?"

"He doesn't need to hawk his skills and the smell keeps the casual shopper away. But he is the best by far."

Omari shrugged. "I'll return soon."

He made his way to the marketplace, watching his step as he worked his way behind the cow stalls. Abasi the healer sat before a plain kanga, his healing tools and concoctions displayed on cloth. He wore a red shirt and pants with charms on his neck and bracelets on his wrists. He appeared too young to be a learned healer but Omari knew that a healers looks were deceiving.

"Go away," Abasi said.

"Zenawi told me you could help me," Omari replied.

Abasi studied him for a moment then signaled him to sit. Omari check to make sure the ground was dung free before sitting.

"What ails you?" Abasi asked.

"I had a terrible chest pain," Omari replied. "I have no idea what caused it."

"Open your shirt."

Omari opened his shirt, revealing his mysterious wound. Abasi's eyes went wide. He reached out, touching the wound delicately.

"I can't help you," he said.

Omari pushed his hand away. "You haven't even examined me."

"I don't have to. That is not a wound. It is a mark. What affects you is beyond my skills. It's beyond anyone's skills."

Omari jumped to his feet. "This isn't a mark, it's a wound! I was stabbed by..."

Abasi titled his head. "By what?"

"By a staff."

"And who wielded this staff?"

"A priestess."

"And why did she stab you?"

"Because we were violating a temple"

"And where was this temple?"

"In Wadantu."

Abasi folded his arms across his chest. "So you were stabbed by a priestess because you violated a temple in a land where no one has ever entered and returned."

Omari nodded.

"Like I said, I cannot help you. She will make herself known when it is time."

"She?"

Abasi looked beyond Omari. He turned to see a young woman holding her wrist.

"Go," Abasi said. "There are people that I can heal that need my help."

"But..."

"Go!"

Omari trudged away. What did the healer mean by a mark? He recalled the dream he had nights ago and a shudder gripped his body. This was not mark; it was a wound was beyond the healer's skill so he made up this mark thing to save face. By the time he reached the post he was already angry. What he saw before him made him boil. Zenawi laid again the wall, trying to stop the bleeding from a chest wound. One of his 'cohorts' was trying pull

Kapera out of the post, a rope tied around her wrists. The other men were ransacking the place. Gerial sat behind the desk, a smug look on his face.

"What in the Cleave is this?" Omari growled.

"We're just collecting our payment," Gerial replied.

Omari unsheathed his sword and dagger. It was time to pick a fight.

Gerial ducked behind the desk as Omari raised his dagger, but he was not the target. Instead the blade found the back of the man holding Kapera. The man collapsed to his knees, reaching in vain for the blade. Kapera screamed then kicked him onto his side, anger clear in her face.

Omari was ready when the first man attacked. He sidestepped his charge then severed his spine as he barreled by. The second man swung his blade at Omari's neck but cleave only air as the agile Mikijen ducked the blade. He drove his sword into the man's as he rose then kicked him free of his blade. Omari sprinted toward the desk where Gerial cowered, determined to finish him before him before the others reached him. His reason was practical; if any of them was any type of a skilled sword fighter it would be Gerial. He wanted to rid himself of the most skilled before he wasted his energy on the others. That way he might just live through this debacle.

Kapera reached Gerial first. Omari watched as the woman snatched the dagger from her former captives back then plunge behind the desk. Her hand rose and fell, each time the blade covered with more blood. Then she was airborne, apparently shoved away by Gerial. He stood, his chest and arms bleeding. He looked at Omari, then his eyes lost focus and he fell behind the desk, never to rise again.

Omari smirked as he turned to face the other false Mikijen. Kapera came to his side, gripping the bloody dagger in her hand. Gerial men halted, each looking at the other to determine who would lead them against this formidable swordsman and the crazed woman. The man in the rear fled first; the others soon followed. Kapera relaxed with a gasp, dropping the knife then sitting on the floor before cradling her face in her bloody hands and crying. But Omari was not done. He went to Zewani's side. The man was still breathing but barely. He picked up Zewani's sword.

"Tend to him," he said to Kapera. He ran out the door.

Omari was not about to leave enemies alive. Unfortunately the interlopers decided to stay together as they fled. They'd underestimated Omari's speed and his intentions. He jumped among them like a leopard on a flock of sheep. In minutes they all lay at his feet in the throes of death. Omari lingered to make sure his work was done before trotting back to the outpost. Kapera sat beside Zewani, pressing bandages against his chest. He sheathed his sword then knelt beside Zewani.

"Hang in there, Mikijen," he whispered. "Maybe that healer will work better for you than he did for me."

As he lifted Zewani he felt pleasant warmth spread from his chest wound throughout his body, easing his fatigue. He shrugged then ran as fast as he could to the healer, Kapera close on his heels.

Omari carried Zewani through the streets to the healer's lair. The healer immediately cleared a space before him and cut Zewani's clothes away to reveal the wound. He reached to his left, grabbing a large gourd then scooped out a handful of a clear cream-like substance. Zewani yelped when the healer applied the cream to his wound.

"   Did you do this?" the healer asked.

"No!" The question angered Omari. "Why would you think that?"

"How do you feel?" the healer asked.

"I feel...rather good, actually."

The healer nodded. "Open your shirt."

Omari opened his shirt. The scar was barely visible, much as it had been when he first arrived.

"What it going on?" he whispered.

"As I said, only She can tell you, and She has not chosen to yet."

Omari wasn't about to get into another argument with the

healer. He massaged his chest then changed the subject.

"How is he?"

"He'll live, but he'll need lots of rest."

The healer was interrupted by Kenja's arrival. She scrambled to Zewani's side, scooting by the healer the cradling Zewani's head. Omari smirked; he'd seen that look before. Kenja was lost to him. Her feelings were now centered on Zewani.

"What can I do?" she said.

"Nothing for now. My paste will cleanse the wound. After tomorrow I'll sew him up. He won't' be fit to work for a few weeks."

"I'll take care of him," Kenja said quickly.

"Looks like I'll be running the business for a while," Omari groaned.

For the next two weeks Omari suffered through the daily routine of a Mikijen clerk. He received the goods from the local farmers and paid them in Kiswala currency. In the evenings he armed himself and strolled through the streets, fulfilling his other responsibility of enforcer and peacekeeper. His public display with the former Mikijen made the latter roles easy. No one would come near him and everyone bowed to him when he walked by. Omari was utterly and painfully bored. If it wasn't for the fact that Zewani was recuperating he would pack his things and head north. But he would stay at least until the man was back on his feet.

A week later his prayers were answered. A large Kiswala dhow arrived, flying the Mikijen banner. When the word reached Omari he almost hurt himself running to the harbor. A relieved laugh escaped his lips and a boat filled with Mikijen was lowered into the calm waters. As the boat neared Omari realized he knew the man commanding this dhow.

"Sonnai Maduo!" he shouted.

"Omari Ket?" Sonnai Maduo shielded his eyes with his ring encrusted hand.

The boat eased onto the beach and the Mikijen waded to shore. Omari greeted each of his brothers with a handshake, but for Sonnai he added a hug and a solid back pat. Sonnai was one of a few Kiswala that served in the Mikijen, for the role of a mercenary was considered beneath the merchants. But Sonnai had the soul of a fighter despite wearing the turban of a merchant.

"I heard you were dead," Sonnai said.

"I was, a couple of time, but the Cleave keeps spitting me back out."

Sonnai chuckled. "Still blasphemous, I see. Anything good to drink in this hole?"

"Of course not, but we'll drink it anyway."

The two walked side by side to the streets.

"So is this a relief visit?" Omari asked.

"No," Sonnai said. "We came to collect you and any other Mikijen in the area. The Kiswala are going to war."

Omari felt a warm rush. "Who this time?"

"Axum."

Omari almost giggled. When Kiswala went to war against Axum they spared no expense. There was nothing like war between relatives.

"I have to admit I'm disappointed," Sonnai commented. "I expected more Mikijen here. The census count put you at twenty."

"There were at least 13 until recently," Omari said.

"What happened to the others?" Sonnai asked.

Omari smirked. "I killed them."

Sonnai stopped in his tracks. "Why did you do that?"

"It's a long story."

Sonnai shrugged. "Then my trip here would be a waste if you weren't here."

Omari was flattered. "Thank you."

"You're the perfect man to command my special warriors."

Omari's rush faded. "Your special warriors?"

It was Sonnai's turn to smirk. "There's a mission within this war that requires special handling, an assassination actually. It pays an astronomical sum and required a unique individual to lead it."

Omari closed his eyes. He knew what was coming.

"Who are these special warriors?"

Sonnai smiled. "Ndoko."

"Shit."

Omari led the other Mikijen to the outpost. They stashed their gear while he checked on Zewani and Kapera. Zewani smiled weakly when he entered the room. Kapera studied him with suspicious eyes.

"Who is out there?" she asked.

"Mikijen."

Her hand went to the knife lying beside her.

"Calm down, these are real Mikijen. They've come to gather us for a military operation."

Zewani tried to sit up. "I must get ready."

"Stay where you are, Zewani. You're in no shape to go anywhere. You've done a fine job here and with Kapera's help you'll do even better."

Zewani frowned. "I'm a Mikijen! It's my duty to answer the call!"

Omari rolled his eyes. "It's your duty to get paid as much as possible without getting killed. That's our way. Now relax and get well."

Omari and the others strolled to the tavern, Sonnai catching Omari up on Kiswala business since his departure. They stood before the tavern entrance when Omari remembered his last incident beyond those doors.

"I can't go in there,' he said.

Sonnai sighed. "Another long story?"

Omari nodded.

Sonnai patted his shoulder. "Come on. We'll straighten things out."

Heads turned as they made their way to a table.

"No!" a shrill voice screeched.

Omari dropped his head. "Here we go."

"Get out of my place now!" The matron screamed at him. She charged the table followed by two large brutes with studded orinkas in their large hands. Sonnai stood between the woman and the table.

"Is there a problem?" he asked.

The matron jabbed her finger at Omari. "He's the problem! He killed two of my best men and stole the best worker I ever had."

"You're upset, and I understand," Sonnai said calmly. "My friends and I have traveled far and don't wish any trouble. We are hungry and very thirsty. Maybe our patronage will make up for his transgressions."

The matron stood nose to nose with Sonnai.

"Maybe on the day the Cleave becomes Paradise, but not today."

Sonnai gripped the woman's arms then lifted her off her feet as his men stood, their hands on their swords.

"Here's another option. I'll break your arms then we'll kill the rest of your men and burn down this place. I'm sure the next matron will be more pleasant than you."

The brutes slowly turned and shuffled away. Sonnai place the woman down.

"Now please be kind to bring us some food and that swill you call beer."

The matron cut a mean glance at Omari then stalked away rubbing her arms. Moments later servants appeared with large pots of sorghum beer, chaff bowls and drinking reeds. Sonnai took a sip then blew the chaff into a bowl.

"This is bad," he commented.

Omari sipped and agreed. "So tell me about this war."

"Kiswala established trade with Mugadi a few years back. Not long afterwards Kiswali were setting up villages outside the city. The Auxites turned a blind eye to it until some of the settlers started ranting about divine redemption and final homecoming stuff."

"Damn fools," Omari commented.

Sonnai nodded. "Next thing you know an army swooped in from Adisha. They killed every Kiswali and razed their villages. They spared Mugadi with a stern warning."

"So now the Kiswala want revenge."

Sonnai took another sip of the beer then shoved his pot away. "How can you drink this crap?"

Omari shrugged. "You get used to it. Besides, sometimes you just need to get drunk."

Sonnai broke his reed. "Anyway, the plan is to launch an attack on Mugadi. It's actually a diversion. The true objective is to assassinate Adisha's Ras. That's the task of the Ndoko...and you."

Omari took a long sip of beer, swallowing the chaff.

"We're talking 30 stacks for the team," Sonnai added, "and an extra ten if you bring back his head. And you know the stacks are split among the survivors."

Omar cringed. "I know."

"So what do you say?"

"Shit."

Sonnai laughed. "You're the only person I know who speaks KaNdoka. You can do this."

Omari was torn. The pay would make up for the Kashite disaster and then some. But dealing with the Ndoko?"

Omari drained the beer pot. "Get me another beer. If you get me drunk enough I might say yes."

Sonnai raised his hand. "Another beer pot!"

He smacked his hand on Omari's back. "You won't regret this, brother."

"Yes I will."

Omari didn't remember leaving the tavern. He awoke at the Mikijen post, smelling of fish and vomit. Sunlight stabbed his eyes like knives and he fell back to his cot for another two hours, whether asleep or unconscious he didn't know nor care. His second attempt to wake went much better. He craned his neck to the right and saw the bucket of water resting beside him. His clothes were ruined so he tore them off then tossed them as far away as possible. Whoever brought him the water left a cloth and a ball of fat soap. He cleaned up then changed clothes, ignoring the snickers of his fellow Mikijen as he took his clothes behind the post and burned them. Sonnai waited for him when he returned.

"You won't regret it."

Omari grunted and his head ached.

"I already do. When do we leave?"

"Tomorrow."

Omari struggled to his feet. "I'll be back."

He trudged through town to the healer. The man looked at him, shaking his head.

"You drink too much," he said.

"I'm not here for that," Omari replied. "What do you have for pain?"

"I told you I can do nothing..."

"I'm not talking about my damn chest!" Omari shouted. "I'm talking about body aches."

The healer rummaged through his concoctions then pulled out a small green pouch. He set it before Omari.

"Do you have any numbing cream?"

The healer tilted his head, then went through his gourds then gave Omari a wide mouth gourd sealed with a thick cotton cloth.

"Are you in pain elsewhere?" the healer asked.

"No, but I will be."

Omari paid the man then returned to the post. The Mikijen were gone apparently back at the dhow. Zewani and Kapera waited for him, their faces drawn.

"So you are leaving," Zewani said.

"Yes. It's time to move on. There's a war, and war means profit."

Kapera rushed him, throwing her arms around his neck then burying her head in his chest.

"You'll be killed!"

"That's not very optimistic." Omari pushed her back at arm's length.

"I'm very hard to kill."

She looked at him, sorrow clear in her eyes. If Omari didn't know better he'd think she still had feelings for him.

"You and Zewani will be fine. Sonnai has a special task

that only I can perform."

Zewani moved Kapera aside then shook Omari's hand.

"It was an honor to serve with you."

Omari did his best not to laugh out loud.

"No, the honor was mine. You have proven yourself a fine Mikijen. We are better because of you."

Zewani smiled, his eyes glistening.

"Be well, Mikijen!"

Omari patted Zewani's shoulder. "Be well, Mikijen!"

He quickly gathered his other things then headed for the dock. It was a good thing Zewani was hurt. He wouldn't last the journey to Kiswala, let alone a war. He was good where he was. As he neared the docks his mind shifted to other matters. The Ndoko waited for him in Kiswala. Sometimes he wished he's never saved Tundu's life then helped him gain dominance of his clan. If not for that he would know nothing of the Ndoko or their strange language. Things always went bad for him personally when he did good for someone else. By the time he reached the docks he was in a sour mood. Sonnai waited with his ever-present smile, which depressed him even more.

"They're on the ship, aren't they?"

Sonnai nodded.

"Let's get his over with then."

Omari handed his items to Sonnai then took off his shirt. He swallowed the entire pouch of painkiller then washed it down with water. He then took the numbing cream and spread it over his torso and face. He waited for a few minutes then pinched himself. He felt nothing.

"I'm ready. Take me to them."

Sonnai led him on board then below deck. They walked to the back of the ship to the hold for animals.

"It's not right for them to be there," Omari commented. "They are not animals."

"It wasn't meant that way," Sonnai answered. "It was the only place left on the dhow. You know they won't share with us."

Omari grunted his disapproval. He grasped the door handle.

"Good luck," Sonnai said.

"Luck had nothing to do with it," Omari answered. He snatched the door open then stormed inside. The Ndoko sat huddled around a communal eating pot enjoying their evening meal. Omari grunted and the clan leader sprang to his feet. His proportions resemble that of a man, except for the hair that covered his entire body. His face was like that of the Old Men, though the Ndoko were as far from those powerful yet gentle creatures. Omari and the clan leader ran at each other, slamming their chest together. Omari staggered back but regained his feet, surviving the first challenge. They approached each other again. Omari raised his arms, slamming both fists on the clan leader's shoulders. The leader did not budge. The leader the same to Omari and he staggered, but again he did not fall. They circled again, eyes locked. Then the leader's eyes glanced at Omari's chest. He stopped pacing.

"That is a killing wound," he said.

The other Ndoko came to their feet, all of them advancing on Omari.

"Where did you get it?" he asked.

"In Wadantu."

His eyes widened then his body posture relaxed. He gestured toward the food pot.

"Come eat with us, brother," he said. He returned to the pot and ate, the others following.

Omari looked at the faint scar and smiled.

"This gets more interesting every moment," he whispered.

He joined his new clan and shared their meal.

Omari sat among his new clan and began eating with his hands as was Ndoko tradition. He kept his eyes down, waiting for clan leader's signal for introductions. It came with a slight shove to his shoulder. Omari looked up and into the clan leader's black eyes.

"Pomu," he said. He looked to his left where his second sat.

"Reth," he said. His brows narrowed as he looked at

Omari, letting him know he was not welcomed. Omari returned the gesture, meaning he didn't care. Reth glanced to his left and the others shared their names.

"Agu."

"Bem"

"Senwe"

"Cheelo."

"Fahru."

"Tumo."

"Vembe."

They all looked at him. Omari took a swallow, preparing himself for the worst.

"Ngozi mtu."

The room exploded with shouts. Reth jumped to his feet, swaying from side to side. Omari sprang to his feet as well, repeating the gesture. He looked at the other clansmen. Thought their eyes were angry, they kept their place. Omari finally looked at Pomu. The elder Ndoko looked at him with a smirk on his face. He stood slowly then put his hand on Reth's shoulder. Reth shrugged it away. Pomu slapped it down his shoulder, pushing Reth to his knees. Reth stayed down.

"So you are Ngozi mtu?"

Omari stopped swaying then nodded.

He stood before Omari.

"Dumi is dead."

"I know," Omari replied.

"You should have died with him!" Reth spat.

"I know," Omari said. He fought hard to keep the emotion from his voice.

Pomu looked at the others. "He is marked by Her, so he is under her eye. I have accepted him in our clan and I do not take back my word."

The others shifted about. Omari could tell they were not happy with Pomu's decision but they would abide by it.

"Come," Pomu said. "We'll play."

Omari nodded but on the inside he cringed. He might just

not survive this after all.

He and the others followed Pomu to the deck. The Mikijen sailors looked stunned for a moment then quickly cleared the deck. Pomu lead Omari to a crude circle painted into the floor planks. He nodded and Omari entered the circle.

Agu was first. He and Omari swayed from side to side in synch as the Ndoko struck the deck in a familiar rhythm. The game began. Agu was unskilled; Omari swept his feet; Agu crashed onto his back, the momentum sending him tumbling out of the circle. Senwe replaced him quickly, cartwheeling into the circle then falling in time with Omari's movements. Omari played through them all, struggling to raise his 'play' with each one. Then Reth back flipped into the circle and the game became deadly. They spun, somersaulted and dodged, landing hard blows with each move. Somehow Omari landed a kick in Reth's chest that sent him sprawling outside the circle. He yelled then rushed back to the circle but Pomu shoved him aside, entering himself. It was then the game went beyond Omari's skills. Try as he might, he was just too rusty to keep up with the clan leader. A few quick blows and Omari tumbled from the circle.

Pomu appeared over him, his hand extended. Omari grabbed his hand and the Ndoko lifted him to his feet. He heard clapping; the crew was apparently impressed with his skills.

"I see why Dumi chose you," Pomu said. "You will sit beside Reth."

Reth grunted then stomped away. Omari nodded.

"Come, we go back down."

Omari took a step then swayed. His concoctions were wearing off. He crashed into a wall of pain then passed out.

****

Omari opened his eyes to Sonnai's face. He immediately tried to sit up but Sonnai pushed him back down.

"You're not going anywhere," he said.

"I have to get back," Omari said.

"No you don't. Those monkey men beat the Cleave out of you. Maybe this was a bad idea."

Omari tried to sit up again. Sonnai attempted to push him down again but Omari shoved his hands away.

"It's part of the process," Omari said. "If you want me to lead them I have to become part of the clan. Playing the game is part of it."

"You call that a game?"

"It is for them."

Omari swung his legs off the table he'd been placed on. He ached everywhere. Even his hair hurt. The first thing he would do once they reached shore was get more painkillers.
Sonnai folded his arms across his chest.

"You're no good to me dead, you know."

"I'm no good to myself, either," Omari cracked. "I'll be fine."

"I'll have to admit, you held your own. That second to last guy has it out for you, though."

Omari smirked. "Yes he does. I figure his clan must have been on the wrong side of Dumi."

Sonnai's eyes widened. "You knew Dumi?"

Omari nodded. "I was his second."

Sonnai laughed until he saw that Omari was serious.

"That was you? You were The Skin Man?"

Omari frowned. "I always hated that name."

"Toss me in the Cleave! Omari Ket was the Skin Man! I'm surprised they all didn't beat you to death."

Omari stood. His legs were a bit wobbly but he could walk.

"Dumi was a lot of things to a lot of people, but to me he was a friend," Omari said. "At first I fought with him because he let me live when he didn't have to. After a while I found myself believing in him."

"Well, I'm glad he failed." Sonnai rubbed his chin. "Could you imagine the Ndoko as a kingdom?"

"Dumi did. He almost succeeded."

"But then the Skin Man disappeared." Sonnai looked at

him as if expecting an explanation. He wouldn't get one. There were some stories Omari would not tell, some stories he'd rather forget.

He staggered to the cabin door.

"Omari, be careful," Sonnai called out. "You're my friend, too."

Omari turned to Sonnai. "Quit it with the sweet stuff. You need me alive so I can carry out the assassination."

Sonnai chuckled. "That, too."

Omari spent the rest of the voyage submerged with the Ndoko. Every day they played the game and every day Reth tried his best to kill him. But Omari's old skills gradually resurfaced, making it easier to deal with Reth. He was beginning to give Pomu a challenge as well, but he decided to hold back. The time to confront him had not come yet. He needed to be sure the others were fully dominated before he made that move. Pomu was skilled, but he was no Dumi.

Two weeks after setting sail from Bashaba they arrived in Kiswala. If Omari had any doubts the Kiswala were going to war they were dashed by the huge dhow fleet assembled in Zanabar Harbor. He stood on deck with his clan, gazing into the city teeming with Mikijen. Omari's mind was on other matters. He looked at Pomu and the Ndoko grunted.

"Go," he said. "I know your needs."

Omari held back a grin until his feet his solid ground. He placed his hands on his hips, his legs spread wide. Sonnai stood beside him.

"So where do we begin?" Omari said.

"At the bath house," Sonnai answered. "You reek."

Omari sniffed at Sonnai. "And you smell like rainy season flowers."

They laughed and exchanged jabs.

"How many days do we have before we challenge fate?" Omari asked.

"Three."

"Then let's make the best of them!" Omari shouted. They

ran into Zanabar like boys.

Omari was very familiar with the pleasures of the city. No sooner did they disembark did he stride purposely toward the hostel district with Sonnai and his cohorts in tow.

"This is the wrong direction," Sonnai commented.

"No it's not," Omari replied.

"Yes it is," Sonnai argued. "It's not like this is my first time to Zanabar. I know this city."

"But you don't know it like I do. Just be quiet and follow me. You won't regret it."

They reached the hostel district, rows of stone buildings that served as respite for visiting merchants. The buildings were separated by walls and designated by origin, with each merchant folk claiming their own section. They passed through the hostel district to free lodging, an area set aside for those with no particular origin or profession. It was a rundown district, an area where one would not wish to be alone day or night. But it was the next district which was Omari's destination. It was called the Hole, an area where if one fell in, he did not return. Sonnai and his men stopped following Omari.

"No," Sonnai said. "We're not going in there."

Omari shrugged. "Suit yourself. I have a bath waiting for me."

He walked on alone. Sonnai and his men fidgeted, looking at each other as they silently debated whether to follow him.

"I promise you, Omari, if I get killed I'll never forgive you!"

Sonnai and the others ran and caught up to him.

They could feel eyes upon them, but Omari was familiar with those eyes. Long ago his were among them, another beggar boy preying on the helpless and naïve. His face and his reputation was his passport through the dangerous streets and anyone with him was allowed safe passage. He continued until they reached a battered looking building at the end of an alley, the only redeeming quality a beautifully carved door accented with gold and precious gems.

Omari turned to his friends, his arms spread wide.

"Bwanas, welcome to paradise," he announced.

He approached the doors, which swung wide before he could knock. An elderly man appeared with a smile on his wrinkled face.

"Omari Ket," he said, his voice almost a whisper. "They said you were dead."

"They always say that until I return."

The old man laughed silently. "There are quite a few that will be disappointed that you're not."

"Nothing has changed then. Bilal, these are my friends. We require food and baths."

Bilal held out his hand. Omari took a gold pouch from his belt. He gazed at it longingly, kissed it then tossed it to Bilal.

The old man caught it then tossed it up again, testing the weight again. His eyes widened.

"I know this pains you greatly," he said.

"Yes it does," Omari said. "Please, put it away before I change my mind."

Bilal tucked the bag away then opened the doors.

"Bwanas, you may enter. But I warn you, you may never wish to leave."

The interior of Paradise lived up to its name. A wide corridor extended before them, the floor covered with luxurious rugs from Asanteman. Lovely figures of men and women decorated the marble walls, each shaped carved into the stone by skilled hands. Two guards stood by the entrance, their stoic faces and broad blades making their purpose clear. Omari and the others followed Bilal down the corridor to a wide rotunda. In the center was a towering statue of the Creator raising his celestial axe, about to deliver the blow that defined Ki-Khanga. Omari wiped a tear from his eye as he gazed upon the magnificent sculpture.

"Are you crying?" Sonnai asked.

"No! Of course not!" Omari replied.

"I wonder about you sometimes," Sonnai said.

On the opposite side of the rotunda were twelve doors.

"Bwanas, choose a door and enter. It does not matter which you choose, for in Paradise all is equally satisfying."

Omari walked to the door in the center and entered the room. A porcelain bath resting on squat gilded legs greeted, herb-scented mist rising from inside. A man and woman stood on either side of the bath. Omari stripped then eased into the warm water, his tension dissipating with each inch of his body submerged. By the time he was completely immersed he was asleep, a relaxed smile on his face. He was awakened by another person entering his bath. He opened his eyes to the woman. Her male companion was gone.

"I didn't pay for this," Omari said with a grin.

The woman smiled. "No one will know if you don't tell."

"My lips are sealed," Omari said.

The others were waiting when Omari emerged from the room. They all looked refreshed, clean and happy. Sonnai sported a wide grin which gradually faded as Omari came closer.

"You didn't!" he said.

Omari smirked. "What can I say? I'm irresistible."

"Damn it to the Cleave! You were to take us to Matalai Shamsi!"

"I will, I will," Omari assured them. "There is no way I can come to Zanabar and not visit the Jewel. Come, we waste time."

A pair of wagons waited for them when they exited the bath house.

"My compliments," Bilal said. "It is not often that our patrons make our staff as happy as we make them."

Bilal and Omari winked at each other. The Mikijen climbed in then were on their way to the Jewel. The city district which held the pleasure house was the complete opposite of the Hole. Tall white washed villas with elegant verandas lined the wide paved streets. Lush fruit gardens divide the villas, the trees pregnant with bananas, oranges and other sweet fruits. Matalai Shamsi rested on the corner of the wide avenue, a tall arch heralding the entrance. Omari was barely out of the wagon when he heard a squeal.

"Omari! Omari!"

A beautiful pair ran to him, a woman with a cloud of hair bouncing over her head and a man with tight red beaded braids. They hugged him like a long lost brother, which in some ways he was.

"Isabis! Iridis! It is good to see you!"

"Come, come," they said in unison. "Makadisa will be so happy to see you!"

They dragged Omari through the arch and the lush veranda to the gilded doors. The guards opened the doors, winking and smiling at Omari and his companions. The Matalai Shamsi foyer teemed with men and women, the patrons indistinguishable from the servers.

"Everyone look!" Iridisi shouted. "Omari Ket is here!"

All heads turned to the entrance and Omari struck a victorious pose. The foyer erupted in a cheer; somewhere a chorus of drums fell into a vigorous rhythm and everyone broke into dance.

"Now this is a homecoming!" Sonnai shouted.

"Yes it is!" Omari replied.

A vision of beauty emerged from the opposite side of the foyer. The celebrants paused momentarily as she sashayed through, each person acknowledging her with a slight nod before continuing to dance. Omari waited patiently as she made her way to him. She halted before him, her flawless ebony skin and amber eyes glittering with anticipation.

"Welcome home, Omari," she said.

"My beautiful Makadisha," Omari whispered.

"Come, we have much to share." She extended her jeweled hand. Omari took it, his smile radiating his anticipation.

"How many days do we have before departure again?" he asked Sonnai without taking his eyes off Makadisha.

"Three days."

He looked at his friend then grinned. "I'll see you in three days."

****

Three days later Omari was awaken by gentle kisses on his eyelids. When he finally opened his eyes Makadisha hovered over him, her dazzling smile brighter than any sunshine he'd ever witnessed. She was the only woman who rivaled Kadira. Although Kadira was not as beautiful as Makadisha, her martial talents and spirit made her just as attractive.

"You must leave me today," she whispered.

"It's probably best," Omari replied. "Otherwise I'd die in bed."

"And what's wrong with that?"

Omari gently pushed Makadisha away and rolled out of her plush bed. He picked up his clothes from the floor where he dropped them three days ago. He dressed slowly, giving Makadisha the last look he knew she wanted. She in turned continue to walk about nude, returning the favor.

"You said you will quit the Mikijen and open a drinking house."

"I will," he replied.

"You said that three years ago," she frowned.

"And if my last commission had gone as it should, that day would have been today." Omari gritted his teeth as he remembered the Wadantu fiasco.

"So will this new commission help?"

Omari finished dressing then pulled Makadisha to him and kissed her hard.

"If it does you'll be the first to know. For now, it's time to serve."

Makadisha threw on a thick silk robe then walked out the room at his side.

"You know I love you," she said.

"And I love you," he replied reflexively.

"No you don't. You love yourself. You love the idea of loving me."

Omari didn't reply. That was what he didn't like about

Makadisha. She knew him too well. There was nothing he could get past her. But she wasn't exactly right. If he did finally fall in love, it would surely be her, especially since Kadira was taken. But of course that could change. There were always other possibilities.

"Makadisha, I…"

She put her fingers to his lips.

"Don't say anything you don't mean, Omari. Go and be safe. We'll talk more if you return."

"When I return," he said.

She kissed his cheek. "Goodbye, Omari."

Omari looked back at Makadisha as he met his companions. There was something in her eyes that bothered him. It continued to do so as they returned to the dhow.

"That was amazing!" Sonnai said.

Sonnai's words broke his musing. "Thank you."

"A man would do well to be your companion," Sonnai continued.

"Most of those who chose to be my companions are dead," he said. "I'm not good luck."

They were about to board the dhow when Sonnai raised his hand.

"Your journey with us is over, Omari. Another dhow will take you to Aux."

Omari's stomach tightened. "You didn't tell me about this."

Sonnai smiled. "Don't' worry. You'll be in better hands. Take care of yourself, my friend. Don't die."

Omari grasped Sonnai's extended hand then pulled him into a hug.

"I don't plan to. May the Creator keep you and your sword never breaks."

He heard commotion on the deck and looked up. The Ndoko ambled across the deck single file, the other crew members giving them a wide berth. They walked down to the gangplank and directly to Omari, ignoring Sonnai.

"Did you have…fun, Ngozi mtu?" Pomu asked.

"Yes," Omari replied.

"Good. We must serve the Goddess now. Come."

Pomu continued past him. Reth tossed him his gear, a scowl on his face.

"Get behind me," he said.

Omari did as he was told. The respite was officially done. In his absence his rank had been decided; he was third, ranked behind Reth. Pomu was a smart leader. Omari's performance in the game had earned him second status but ranking him such would cause a challenge from Reth that would only be decide by the death of one of them. Pomu needed every one for the task ahead; he couldn't afford to lose anyone yet. Besides, Omari had not been blooded with them yet. Sure, he was Pomu's second and his reputation was undeniable, but reputation did not supersede experience. Omari didn't protest. If he survived the mission his association with the Ndoko would be done. He'd collect his pay and be on his way.

Curious and fearful stares followed them across the harbor to a large dhow docked a good distance from the other craft. Omari's eyes widened in wonder. There was very little in Duniyaa the traveling mercenary had not seen or experienced, but what lay before him was such a thing. The Tyrak war galley loomed over the nearby dhows, a terrible and beautiful craft. He was aware the Kiswali traded with the mysterious guardians of the Cleave, but as far as he knew their ships never ventured away from their martial vigil. His curious eyes swept across every detail, the almost organic design of the dhow, the way it drifted on the waves as if it lived, as if the bones and hide of the indigo joka from which it was constructed pulsed with blood. Sharp bolt tips from the loaded onagers protruded over the deck edge. Tyrak baharia inspected the sails and maintained the decks, oblivious to the file of Ndoko approaching their mooring. They were black skinned, powerfully built men and women, their heads bare and bald. Intricate ivory tattoos covered their heads instead. Both men and women wore no clothing above the waist, their lower bodies covered by *kangas* which stopped short of their knees, revealing their muscle corded legs. What stood out most were their wide chests and backs. These people were swimmers, a folk who though graceful and sure on land obviously spent much, if not most of their time in the cold waters of their homeland. Maybe the other stories were true as well, Omari thought. He hoped he wouldn't find out.

A female Tyrak broke away from the others and approached them, her only distinguishing feature a small medallion hanging by a leather cord around her neck. She walked directly to Pomu

"Our cargo has arrived,' she said.

She clasped Pomu's bicep in traditional Ndoko greeting to outsiders and he grasped hers as well. Omari wasn't sure, but he thought he saw the Ndoko smile. That would be two miracles in one day.

"It's been a long time, Narsus," he said.

"It has," she replied. "Eda had kept you well, I see."

"As she has you," Pomu replied.

Narsus looked from Pomu to Omari. Omari flashed his smile and Narsus's face became stern. Her eyes narrowed as the look of recognition came to her face. Pomu nodded to her, giving her permission to speak to him.

She advanced on him quickly.

"Omari Ket," she said. "Or should I call you Ngozi mtu?"

"It is Ngozi mtu among my brothers," he replied.

"You are new to Edu's embrace," she said. "We who serve Her are closer than most. Pomu trust you. Do not let them down as you did Dumi. If you do, you will answer to me."

Omari felt her threat in his bones. He was not a man easily intimidated but the stories he'd heard of the Tyrak nahoda gave him pause.

"I have no intentions of letting anyone down," Omari replied. "Pomu knows this."

Narsus's eyes lingered on his face for a moment then went to his chest. She grabbed his shirt then opened it, revealing the faint scar. Her touch was rough like sand.

"Eda had marked you," she said with a grin. "My mind is at ease now. You will serve her well. You have no choice."

Narsus walked away and the Ndoko followed her onto the warship. The other Tyrak ignored the new passengers, staying focused on their duties. Narsus led them below deck. The innards of the Tyrak dhow were much more spacious, a requirement because of the Tyraks' bulk. They were led to a space which was obviously a cargo hold, the only space on a dhow that accommodated the Ndoko communal living style.

"We have made arrangements for you specific needs," Narsus said. "We weren't aware Omari would be with you, but I think we can provide for him as well."

"How long will our journey take?" Pomu asked.

"All the fleets are launching today," Narsus replied. "The Kiswala say they will reclaim Bashaba in two weeks' time but they are always optimistic. We will reach our destination in one week."

"One week?" Omari blurted. "From here to Aux?"

Narsus smiled. "Our dhows are very fast."

Omari and the Ndoko secured their gear then left the room to roam the dhow. Omari went immediately to the deck. The docks were filled with well-wishers waving, ululating and shouting words of encouragement to the fleets. Omari spotted his people as well, the brightly colored and beautiful workers from Matalai Shamsi resembling a flock of birds as they waved scarves at random. Omari whistled and they turned to the Tyrak dhow. A cheer went up among them; Omari was leaving in style. A few folk from the Hole dared to emerge to wish him well briefly then went to work silently robbing the crowd. The Tyrak paid no attention to the celebrants, their efforts focused on getting the dhow under way. If the Kiswali were masters of the sea, the Tyrak were their gods. Omari had never in his life experienced such a fast dhow. He'd heard rumors of Kamite craft so fast they seemed to glide in the air, but people were always saying such things about the Kamites. He'd yet to see any of it proven.

The Tryak warship raced out of the harbor and into open sea. Narsus had not boasted when she spoke of the ship's speed. Omari was very familiar with dhows as all Mikijen were, and he was impressed. The Tyrak worked the sails with amazing precision, capturing every gust of wind like stingy Kiswali merchants after wealth. He watched the crew for hours, fascinated by their coordination. His time on deck let him witness another skill of theirs; their swimming prowess. A team of Tyrak stripped naked then took up spears, tridents and nets. They dove into the water then disappeared into the clear blue depth faster than Omari thought possible. Minutes later they returned to the surface with the ocean's bounty, easily swimming alongside the ship then climbing back on deck on the cargo nets lowered over the side.

"I take it you like seafood?"

Omari looked to see Narsus standing beside him. Despite her bulk she was able to approach unnoticed. Omari studied her instinctively. It wasn't taking him long to appreciate Tyrak female attributes. A smirk came to Narsus's face.

"You're living up to your reputation," she commented.

Omari flashed a seductive grin. "I'm a man of wide appetites."

"Well, curb your appetites here. I doubt any of my crew would be interested in such a slight man as you."

"We'll see," Omari said with a wink. "And of course I love seafood. I'm Mikijen, aren't I?"

"Your companions prefer land fare. We've made accommodations for them."

Narsus reached into her lap pouch and extracted a scroll.

"Take this to Pomu. It's the map for your mission."

Omari took the map. "I'll deliver it now."

"Please do. You're becoming a distraction. Some of my crew is pairs and the men are becoming angry at your lingering eyes."

"I thought you said I was too slight," Omari replied.

"Tyraks can be curious as well."

Omari chuckled as he headed below deck. As he strolled to their room his mercenary mind began its simple math. With each of them offered 30 stacks for the mission, his payday would rival what he lost in Kenja. He doubted they all would not make it back and the Kiswali would honor the payment with those who remained. He felt somewhat bad about losing a few of the Ndoko, but war is war. He might as well make the best of the situation. When he opened his drinking house we would have a drink in their honor.

His chest tightened, a pricking pain rising around his scar. He rubbed it until the pain subsided.

"Got to do something about 'Edu's mark," he said before entering the Ndoko lair.

His clan gathered in a circle as if expecting him. He approached Pomu, map held high.

"A gift from Narsus," he said.

Pomu took the scroll then spread it out. It was a map of Aux, with major roads and cities highlighted.

"We will land here," Pomu said, pointing at an obscure harbor. "We will travel at night. Once we get to Esmeera we'll follow the main road to Qwera. It is their Kandak who led the attack on Bashaba. It is he who is our target."

Pomu looked at Omari. "You will lead us into Qwera."

The others nodded with Pomu. Omari nodded back but was slightly surprised. He knew Aux but not well enough to lead an assassination into the city. But the clan leader had made the decision and he could not refuse. Pomu rolled up the map then handed it back to Omari.

"We will trust you," he said.

Omari nodded again, absently rubbing the scar as it ached.

****

The Tyrak dhow eased close to the Auxite coast on a humid, moonless night. Omari stood on the deck with his clan, straining his eyes to see where the ocean ended and the shore began. His efforts were in vain. It was a dangerous night to attempt a landing, but a perfect night to begin a mission. Omari took inventory, patting his body as he counted his weapons. His hand ended on the etched metal of his hand cannon. He opted to bring the weapon at the last minute. It was cumbersome, loud and inaccurate, but if their task was discovered and their situation desperate it would be a powerful distraction.

The Tyrak lowered their boat over the side then climbed down and entered the warm water. Pomu patted each of them on the shoulder, lingering for a moment before Omari.

"Eda deliver us, either to our home or to her bosom," he said.

Omari and the clan repeated his words. It was a morbid thing to say before going on a mission, but it was the Ndoko way. They followed the Tyrak over the side, lowering themselves into the waiting boat on thick ropes. There were no oars; the Tyrak decided to tow the boat to avoid the noise of oars against the waters. The guardians of the Cleave prove themselves more than capable. Omari had to grip the side of the boat to keep from toppling backwards when the Tyrak swimmers swam toward the shore. In moment they slipped into shallow water, the Tyrak standing on their broad feet as they pulled the boat close to shore. Omari eased into the water then waded to the rocky shore. The Tyrak offered them no words as they trotted to the sparse brush; by the time they settled their deliverers had melded into darkness.

"Ngozi mtu," Pomu said. "Lead us."

Omari trotted into the darkness. Though the details were obscure he'd memorized the map. They traveled the entire night then found shelter among a stand of prickly shrubs during the day. It was their pattern for the next week. They covered the miles at a pace that would have worn down the strongest man except the exceptionally long winded Kenjans. Omari would have been included with those incapable if not for his constant playing with his clan members. That was the true purpose of the game; to build endurance and strength for missions such as this. They avoided cities and settlements except when food and water was needed. Omari's body remembered what his mind had forgotten; by the time the Qweran citadel loomed before them he was primed for action.

The fort loomed over the sparsely forested valley from

atop a slab of granite extending from the nearby mountain like an open hand. One narrow road undulated from the cluster of villages along the river to the peak. The road was easily defended. Its narrowness prevented mass attack and the fort's position gave its occupants plenty of opportunity to shower death on attacking hordes. Omari chewed on a kola nut as he and the others waited for darkness, ruminating on the citadel's interior details. A servant had been bribed into providing the details and Omari committed them to memory as he had the route to Qwera. The Ndoko sat motionless, holding their infamous serrated edge scimitars in each hand. The sight of them made him reach absently for his left side. Long ago he'd been on the wrong end of one of those blades and almost died. He didn't envy the Auxites they would encounter soon. Pomu watched the sun slowly settle behind the horizon with intense eyes. As soon as the last portion of light disappeared under the horizon he looked at Omari then nodded.

Omari sprang to his feet the sprinted full speed to the citadel walls, his clan brothers close behind. There was no hesitation, for Qwera was far in the interior of its province and feared no attacks from its enemies and local villagers. When they reached the base of the walls they took the ropes and grappling hooks from around their waists then threw them up into the ramparts. Omari stepped aside as the Ndoko sped up the ropes. No matter how much he'd trained he couldn't match their natural abilities. He waited until the last Ndoko was on his way up before he climbed. His progress was amazing for a man, but slow compared to his clan. When he reached the top his brothers feigned sleep. It always amazed him how the Ndoko always chose to display their limited sense of humor in the most dangerous situations.

"It is good you decided to join us," Pomu said to him. "Can we continue now?"

Omari grinned then led the Ndoko down the ramparts to the citadel entrance. According to his internal map the hallway behind the door led to the main corridor which in turn led to the kandak.

"Intruders! To the Kandak! Hurry!"

The urgent voices came from behind them. Omari looked at the door to the ramparts then to the gilded portals of the kandak's chamber.

"Go,' Pomu said. "It only takes one Ndoko. We will hold here."

The rampart door crashed open and Auxite soldiers spilled in like water from a failed dam. The Ndoko twisted, somersaulted and leapt into the mass, striking like sharp fists. Omari sprinted to the kandak's chamber. He smashed his shoulder against the door but it did not budge.

"Damn it to the Cleave!" he hissed.

He swung his hand cannon from his back the loaded the weapon with a double charge. He braced it against his chest, not knowing exactly what would happen. He discovered the answer moment later. The charge exploded; Omari sailed through the air then landed hard at the heels of his fighting comrades. He stumbled to his feet then ran back to the kandak's chamber. The doors were open, a splintered hole where his shot struck. Five bodyguards sprawled on the marble. Three were definitely dead, the others too wounded to stop him. The five remaining guards stood before the smirking kandak, blades drawn and spears lowered.

"Sonnai sends his greetings," the kandak said.

"Can't trust a mercenary," Omari whispered as he attacked. He threw his hand cannon at the guards as he sprinted, slowing them down just enough to gain more speed. As the warriors converged, Omari jumped. He cleared them then tucked his body and flipped twice before landing on his feet before the startled kandak. His sword was in and out of the man's throat before he recovered.

The guards had failed but they were determined to avenge their kandak. Their fury made them clumsy; Omari deftly worked through them with sword and dagger, staying close to take away the spearmen advantage. He kicked the last man off his sword then looked into the hallway. The Ndoko still held the soldiers back, though not without a price. Two lay dead on the stone.

Omari looked about the room and found the window. He began unraveling the rope around his waist as he sauntered to the opening. This was even better than he imagined. He could escape alone, leaving the Ndoko to die the noble death. As the only survivor with confirmation that the kandak was dead he's be the wealthiest merchant in Sati-Baa. Forget a drinking house; he'd purchase a mooring, a warehouse and a couple of dhows. He was part Kiswala after all. Trading was in his blood.

The pain struck suddenly. He clutched at his chest as he fell to his knees, overwhelmed by the excruciating sensation. Omari tried to stand but the pain increased. It surged through him, taking away his sight, his feeling and his voice. The kandak's chamber faded into an empty darkness.

"You would leave my children?" a female voice asked.

A female form emerged from the dark. Amber eyes opened before him, followed by a solemn smile. There was no doubt that this was the most beautiful woman Omari had seen. But then she was not a woman.

"Eda?" he managed to say.

Her smile removed his pain and filled him with joy.

"You belong to me, Omari Ket," she said. "You became mine in Wadantu."

"How?" Omari rose from where he lay to his knees.

"When I gave life back to you."

He remembered everything. Three old women stood between him, Sebe and Kadira. He drew his sword to kill them and Kadira tried to stop him. Then one of the women stabbed him with her staff. The next thing he remembered he laid at their feet, the woman holding the idol they sought.

"So I was dead."

"Yes," Eda answered.

"You gave me my life back," Omari said. "Why?"

"Kadira asked me."

"Kadira belongs to you, too?"

"Yes, although she is not aware of it."

Omari stood. He didn't like belonging to anyone or anything, not even a beautiful goddess.

"Would you prefer I rescind my gift?" she asked.

"No, no!" Omari said. He was trapped. There was no way out of this one.

He sighed. "So what must I do?"

"Save my children, then wait for me to come to you again."

Omari dropped his head. "So be it."

Light flooded the room. Omari stood by the dead kandak, his sword and dagger in his hands. He sheathed them then collected the kandak's golden cap, medallion and one ear to prove the deed was done. He jammed the items in a pouch then secured it to his waist, his anger rising with each second. He didn't ask to be saved in Wadantu. He didn't ask for this mission. He didn't ask to be bound to a goddess. He picked up his hand cannon, reloaded it with a handful of shot then stomped his way to the melee at the end of the hall. By the time he was in the hand cannon's effective range he was furious.

He lit the hand cannon fuse.

"Get out of the way!" he shouted in baNdoko. The Ndoko somersaulted away from the Auxites, coming to rest behind him just in time. Omari braced himself as the fuse disappeared. The corridor echoed with the blast; he saw scores of Auxites fall before smoke filled his view.

Omari turned then stomped away.

"Follow me," he said.

They hurried to the throne room window. Omari uncoiled the rope around his waist, secured it to a column then lowered it to the ground below. He stepped aside and the Ndoko climbed down. They carried their dead brothers on their shoulders as they descended; Bem, Fahru and Reth. Omari's gaze lingered a moment on Reth's glazed eyes. At least the bothersome Ndoko would trouble him no longer.

Omari was the last to descend. They set off on a run that continued without rest for three days, each one taking his turn to carry their fallen comrade. The Ndoko was silently surprised that Omari kept the pace and did not ask for rest. The truth was that Omari's stamina was fueled by his anger. His fatigue did not emerge until they were on the Tyrak dhow and well on their way to Kiswala. He slept the entire journey, too tired to be angry. When Pomu awoke him they were moored in Zanabar harbor. He rubbed his eyes clear to a comforting sight. His Ndoko brothers sat in a semi-circle, each with the promised stacks before them. Omari's stack sat before him as well. Then a surprising thing occurred. His brothers, one by one, added their stack to Omari's.

"What is this?" Omari said.

"You saved our lives," Pomu answered. "Besides, we have no use for this."

Omari struggled between absolute joy and downright suspicion.

"If you didn't want to be paid then why take the mission?" he asked.

Pomu smiled. "This mission was your test, Ngozi mtu. Eda needed to know if She could trust you."

"So you risked your lives to prove that her yoke on me was secure?" Omari's bitterness flavored his words.

Pomu shook his head. "We are Eda's children. We serve as she asks, for we know she will let no harm come to us. Now you are her child as well. You will find what you consider a yoke is truly a blessing."

"How can I consider this a blessing when I cannot live my life my way?" he retorted.

"None of us know true freedom," Pomu said. "We all are subject to the whims of others."

Omari was done talking to Pomu. He was wasting his words on a zealot. He looked at the stacks before him and a smile came to his face.

"I thank you, brothers."

They stood in unison. Omari went to each of them, pressing his chest against theirs.

Their ritual was interrupted by Narsus.

"Good, you said your goodbyes. Omari Ket, get off my ship."

There was playfulness in her voice that let Omari know her words were made in jest.

"And what of my brothers?" he asked.

"They will stay on board. Eda wishes us to spend some time

together. I believe you have a drinking house to build."

"That and a bit more," Omari replied.

Omari nodded his goodbyes to the Tyrak crew as he made his way to the gangplank, Narsus by his side. He was about to disembark when another grim thought came to him.

"There's some business I need to take care of," he said.

"Sonnai?" Narsus asked.

Omari nodded.

"Don't worry about him. He and his men were killed during the initial assault on Bashaba. There are no secrets among the Kiswala."

"Saves me the trouble," Omari said.

A clear sky ruled over the harbor city, the air warm and slightly sweet. Omari soon saw the reason why. Makadisha waited resplendent as ever, flanked by the twins Isabis and Iridisi. He could tell by her smile she was genuinely happy to see him. The twins met him halfway down the plank, showering him with hugs and kisses like a long lost brother returned. They backed away when he reached Makadisha. She gave him a subdued peck on his lips.

"You didn't die," she said.

"No I didn't."

She peeked behind him to the bags of stacks being carried by a Tyrak who placed the bag by their feet.

"It seems you have enough for your drinking house," she commented.

"And some," Omari replied.

"So you will stay for a time?" The tone in her voice was expectant.

Omari rubbed his chest wound. A feeling of contentment rushed through him.

"Until Eda calls," he replied reluctantly.

"That's all I can ask," Makadisha said. Their second kiss was more personal.

Omari lifted his bag over his shoulders then took Makadisha's hand. Together they strolled from the docks and into the wonders of Zanabar.

Into the Cleave

By Milton J. Davis

I gave eight years to the Mikijen, four more than they deserved. I made less money that I earned and killed more men than I care to remember. When my contract ended I took my settlement pay then became a farmer. It was a harder life but a safer one. So when Cheelo rode up to my house that spring day I was torn between shaking my head or putting a knife in his gut. I decided to do both. Cheelo must have perceived my intentions for he remained mounted on his horse and kept his distance.

"Good day, Mayani," he said.

"It was," I replied. If I had a throwing spear I would have sent him to his ancestors.

"I know you're not happy to see me," he said. "To be honest I tried my best not to come. But you are the only one left, and I need you."

"Look around you," I said. "What do you see?"

"I see a farm," he said.

"No," I said. "You see happiness. You see contentment. You see the reason I won't go with you."

Cheelo grinned. "You have no choice, Mayani."

I clinched my fists. "There is no contract between us. I served my time and I took my payout."

He reached into his riding pouch then took out a scroll.

"I'm not here as your debtor. I'm here as a representative of the Most High. He summons you on my recommendation."

He threw the scroll at my feet. I hesitated; once I touched it

I couldn't plead ignorance.

"What are you waiting for?" he said. "The Most High has summoned you. You can't refuse."

"How long do I have?" I said.

"Three days," he answered.

"Why me?" I asked. "I'm sure there are many more eager to follow you."

"What can I say? I know you. Besides, you are the only person capable of doing what must be done. It will be like old times."

Cheelo reined his horse then galloped away. I stood there burning in anger and helplessness. There would be no more work that day. I trudged back to my house.

Ursala lowered the crossbow as I entered.

"Who was that?" she asked.

I went to the table, pulled out a chair then sat before answering.

"Cheelo, my old Mikijen commander."

"What did he want?" she asked.

"Everything."

Ursala grasped the bowstring then unloaded the crossbow. She was strong, stronger than most men but the pregnancy made her weak. Still she could handle a crossbow better than anyone I knew. If Cheelo had made the wrong move a bolt would have cracked his wide forehead.

She sat at the table beside me. "What do you mean everything?"

I handed her the scroll then watched as she unrolled then read it. Her eyes widened as she reached the end. She looked up at me with tears in her eyes.

"Yani no!" she said.

I took the scroll then tossed it into the fire.

"He serves the Most High now. I couldn't refuse if I wanted to."

Ursala slumped in her chair. The baby was due soon.

"I'll take you to Uhuti's. We have enough trade to make it

worthwhile."

"I'm not worried about my sister," Ursala said. "I'm worried about you and I'm worried about our farm. With both of us gone someone will claim it."

"We'll buy another one when I return."

Ursala wiped the tears from her eyes. "With what?"

"With what I'll get paid from this task," I replied.

"And how much will that be?" she asked.

I hesitated before answering. "I don't know."

Ursala propped her elbows on the table then covered her eyes with hands. She always did that when she didn't want me to see her cry. It made me hate Cheelo more. There was nothing I could say to stop her except I wasn't going. So I sat beside her and held her until she was done.

When she lowered her hands her face was resolved.

"We have a lot to do," she said.

We spent the next two weeks preparing for my departure. WE slaughtered the goats then smoked the meat. We harvested what was ripe from the fields then packed what we could, selling the rest to our neighbors. After the preparations were loaded our wagon then journeyed to Uhuti's farm. She was happy to see Ursala and even happier when she learned I was leaving. She never liked me, that woman. She suspected I would leave Ursala with young ones to raise alone. I was determined to come back if only to prove her wrong.

I finally set out three weeks after Cheelo's visit. I knew he would wait; if Cheelo came for me he couldn't do what he needed to do without the talents I possessed. I was on my way to Adisesa, the city that served as a capital for Haisetti when a Ras gained enough strength to unite the land. This usually occurred after a Menu incursion. Such an incident took place ten seasons ago. It was then when I served with Cheelo and performed a service that those who knew claimed ended the war. It was something I tried not to think about. Its memory came with nightmares.

I rode north to the river then bought passage on a canoe to Adisesa. The boatman was friendly in a business-like way; though

I saw his eyes linger on my sword and knives.

Those are fine blades, master," he said. "Never seen anything like them."

"They're Kiswala blades, forged by the best smiths in Ki Khanga for the Mikijen," I said. "I learned long ago that an average fighter with superior weapons could defeat a talented man with inferior ones."

"Blades like those would fetch a good price in the Adisesa market," he said as he licked his lips.

I glared at the boatman. "Your tricks won't work on me. I swim better than most fish. Mind your oars or you might lose your head."

"I meant no offense, master," he said. "I will say nothing else.

We reached the port by nightfall then I found a nearby inn to stay the night. It was modest but adequate. The next morning I paid for my room then spent my last coin on a decent horse. My journey was uneventful, for the Most High put pride in providing safe roads for his subjects. The borders were another matter. The only time the Ras were not at war with each other was when they gathered to make war against someone else. That someone else was most likely the Menu.

After three days of riding I reached the outskirts of Adisesa. I had to admit the sight of the sprawling city brought back good memories of an exciting life, al life that was constantly in danger. A life I enjoyed until I met Cheelo.

I was barely in the city when I heard someone yell my name. I turned expecting to see Cheelo; instead I was greeted by the stern face a Wahuran, one of the Ras' personal assassins.

"Mayani Aweke, you are late," she said. I knew better not to argue with her. This was one instance where having some skill and better weapons did not apply. The Wahuran could kill me with a cotton ball.

"How do you know me?" I asked.

"Your weapons. Come, we must hurry. The others are two weeks ahead."

"We won't catch them," I said.

"We will. They are on foot. We will ride."

I almost had to run to keep pace with the wide striding Wahuran. Tethered to a post before the Ras compound were two Malian warhorses. The Ras spared no expense, which made me nervous.

We set out immediately, covering ten miles before sunset. After a quick meal we slept then awoke before dawn. The Wahuran didn't talk much; her task was to deliver me to the others and nothing more. Socializing was apparently on the agenda.

We were in sight of the Cleave peaks when we finally caught up with Cheelo's party. The temperate climate we'd enjoyed dispersed into the humid heat spilling over the Cleave's precipitous rim. Somewhere along the way the party acquired local ponies, short sturdy beasts built for the steep slopes and narrow pathways. Unlike us the locals were smart enough not to come so close to the mountains. We, however, let need overcome common sense.

Despite her hard countenance the Wahuran wanted nothing to do with the expedition. No sooner had we reached the outriders did she turn her horse about.

"May the High above the Most High protect you," she said. Her expression betrayed her true feelings. She did not expect us to return. With a snap of her reins she galloped away, leaving me with old friends and new victims.

The stragglers I didn't know. Cheelo apparently wasn't able to gather all of us so he replaced our numbers with neophytes. The familiar ones rode close with Cheelo. I frowned as I came closer; few of them were men or women I wished to see again. They turned in unison, predatory smiles splitting their faces. The meal token had arrived.

"You arrive on a ras's horse in the Ras's time, Mayani," Cheelo said.

The others laughed. One rode up to meet me, her aged face still retaining most of the beauty I once desired.

"Welcome back," Genet said. "I've missed you."

Her braids were gone, replaced by her natural hair which

rose over her head like sunrise. She smiled and I felt myself drifting into her spell. I ceased my thoughts with memories of Ursala's sweet visage. Genet was Cheelo's companion but she loved to tease me. For a brief time we'd been lovers as well.

I nudged my horse by her without answering.

"I had to put things in order," I said to Cheelo.

Cheelo chewed on a betal leaf, which was not good. Dealing with him in his right mind was difficult enough.

"I'm sure you did," he said. "You're a coward, Mayani. I bet you hid under your wife's skirt until the Ras's guards dragged you away."

I looked about at the others. "I see you were on your way without me, for whatever good that would do. And the only thing that kept my wife from putting a crossbow bolt in your head was the pile of shit we would have had to clean up afterwards."

A tense silence fell over the group which was finally shattered by a familiar laugh.

"You two never stop."

Othuke rode toward me and I couldn't help but smile. The towering Axuite appeared as if he hadn't aged a day since I last saw him. His leather armor fit tight against his lean frame. At first glance one would think him frail but Okuthe was the strongest man I knew. The axe strapped to his back weighed more that five fat Sati-Baa merchants but he wielded it like small branch.

"Good to see you, brother," I said.

"Good to see you as well," Okuthe said. "One more day with this swill and I would have jumped into the Cleave naked."

"So why are you here?" I asked.

Okuthe shrugged. "You know how I am, brother. Gold slips through my fingers like sand."

"Maybe you should eat more and fatten up those hands."

Genet rode between us.

"You two carry on like lovers," she said.

Okuthe gave her a look that withered her smirk into a worried frown. She quickly sought out Cheelo.

The others I didn't know. Time apparently had not spared

the others so Cheelo replaced them.

"Not many of us remaining," I said.

Okuthe shook his braided head. "They weren't smart like us. They stayed with Cheelo and they died."

"So how smart are we now?" I asked.

"Not very," Okuthe replied.

"Enough talk," Cheelo said. "We have a mountain to climb before sunset."

We lined up single file then began the trek up the steep path leading to the Rim. Okuthe and I straggled in the rear.

"So you are a farmer now," Okuthe said.

"Yes," I replied. "I have a wife, too. Her name is Ursala."

Okuthe grinned. "I'm happy for you, my brother. At least one of us has had good luck."

"What about you?" I asked.

"I am entertainment for the Creator," he said. "I've gained and lost three wives since I've last seen you and not one child to show for it."

"Maybe there is fourth wife waiting for you when we return."

Okuthe's smile was joyless. "Yes, I remember that about you. You were always optimistic. Tell me, can you still do what Cheelo wants you to do?"

"I don't know," I replied. "It's been a long time. But it's not like it's something I can lose. I did nothing to gain it."

We rode silent for a time. I was a boy when I discovered my ability. It was the worst day of my life. I was a boy when it manifested. I dare not call it a talent because nothing I did cause me to possess except the circumstances of my birth, of which I'm still not certain. I discovered ti by chance as I when I spied upon a strange stone by the river as I gathered sticks for the evening fire. The stone glowed blue when I picked it up; I hurried home to show it to my parents. I was not prepared for their reactions. My mother screamed then scrambled away from me; my father attacked me, pounding me with his fists while shouting at me, calling me an abomination. I fled the only home I'd ever known. I took the stone back, throwing it into the river but my fate was sealed. My parents refused to let me back into the house and the others of our village drove me away. I wandered Haiset as an orphan, surviving the best I could until I ended up in the Ras's prison for theft. It was there Cheelo found me.

The air grew colder as we climbed but I didn't don my cloak. The temperature would change once we reached the Rim and I didn't want to be overdressed. The neophytes did otherwise. Okuthe watched them then laughed.

We reached the temperate zone around nightfall. Cheelo sent the new ones to gather wood while the rest of us set up camp. The local men manage to bag two ridge goats so we ate well that night despite the less than warm company. Cheelo stared at me the entire meal as if he expected me to turn into a bat the fly away. When he continued to stare I became concerned.

"It there something you wish to say," I asked.

My question changed the mood of the camp.

"Be careful, brother," Okuthe said.

"This journey depends on you," Cheelo said.

"And?" I said.

"Can you do it? Will you do it?"

"I'm here," I said.

"Against your will," Cheelo said.

I stood. "You forced me on this mission and now you're concerned? The Ras is involved so I have no choice. I'll do what I came to do."

"You won't do this for me? For us?"

"I stop doing things for you the moment my Mikijen contract expired."

"That hurts me," Cheelo said. "After all I've done for you."

"Stop it," Genet said.

"Stay out of this," Cheelo replied. "Or do you wish it to be how it was when I was almost dying and you left my bed for his?"

There it was. I hoped he wouldn't bring it up but like Okuthe said I was optimistic.

"That was a long time ago," I said. "Let it die."

Cheelo's eyes narrowed. "You'd like that, wouldn't you?"

Cheelo stood, his right hand gripping his sword hilt.

"I'm the only person that can make this expedition successful," I said. "If you kill me you'll soothe your pride but you'll go home empty handed. Depending on the Ras's mood that would make you all as dead I would be."

Cheelo pulled his sword halfway from its sheath. I didn't move but Okuthe did. He stood, unstrapping his axe from his back then leaning on it. Cheelo was probably still skilled enough to defeat me but he didn't stand a chance against Okuthe and his massive axe. He shoved his sword back into the sheath then sat.

"You would think you'd be more grateful. After all, you owe your freedom to me."

"A debt I've paid ten times over," I said.

The captain's eyes became slits. "So you say."

"Enough of this," Genet said. She sat beside Cheelo then kissed his cheek.

"We're all tired. The morning will find us in a better mood."

Gen stood then pulled Cheelo to his feet. She led him into the darkness, flashing a grin at me before they faded away.

"She mocks you," Okuthe said.

"She wastes her time," I said. "That flame has long been spent."

"Are you sure, brother?" he asked.

"Very sure," I answered.

Okuthe grinned. "Good. That's one less thing for me to fret over. I would have a hard time killing a woman."

"Go to sleep bone man," I said. "Tomorrow we climb the Rim."

My advice was more for me than Okuthe. I was exhausted from the journey and the conversation, both which I had become unaccustomed to. It seemed I had only slept a moment when Okuthe's shouting startled me awake.

"Up! Everyone up!" he shouted. "We've been betrayed!"

I scrambled to my feet, sword in hand. I saw the others hurrying about as well as my eyes adjusted to the night. Cheelo and

Genet stumbled into the camp half dressed.

"What in the Cleave's name is going on?" Cheelo shouted.

Okuthe pointed downhill. Scores of lanterns snaked up the hill toward our position.

"The locals are gone," Okuthe said. "They slipped away while we slept."

"Who was on guard?" Cheelo asked.

"No one," I replied. "You didn't assign watch."

"And you didn't?"

"I'm not it command," I said.

"The Cleave take you!" he said.

Cheelo looked at the approaching lanterns. "We can't go back. We have to go up."

Nervous glances passed among us. Up meant further up the Rim and closer to the Cleave. That was our plan, but not at night. If we were to accidentally fall into it we might as well throw ourselves at the advancing bandits.

"It's foolish," Genet said.

"Precisely" Okuthe said.

Cheelo looked at me.

"Manyani will lead the way. But before we go, let's send them a round or two to slow them down."

We took out our crossbows, loaded them then fired. Lamps fell to the ground as wounded bandits cried out in anger and pain.

"Again," Cheelo ordered.

The second volley was less effective. I heard the familiar twang of a released bowstring. I flattened on the ground.

"Get down!" I shouted.

"What?" Genet asked, just before the arrow struck her in the chest. She was dead before she hit the ground.

"Genet!" Cheelo screamed.

I felt s brief moment of remorse for her. We had been lovers once, even though the relationship was shallow at most. But there was no time to linger.

"Come with us or die with her," I told Cheelo. I hurried up the trail toward the Rim. Okuthe caught up with me as we climbed higher, the path growing steeper with every step. Soon our way was further obscured by a thick fog. We were nearing the Rim.

Everyone slowed. Our pursuers edged closer, pushing us all to the brink of endurance. They all looked to me, desperation on their faces. Only one of us could cross over the edge and have a chance of survival; me. I had no idea if I could protect them. I'd never taken anyone else into the abyss with me. But it was either stay on the Rim and face sure death or cross into the Cleave and have a smidgen of hope.

"Follow me," I finally said.

I climbed over the Rim then lowered myself into the Cleave. I shuddered as my feet touched the soft ground. The others were not so lucky. The essence of the cursed ground forced them to their knees.

"Gather around me," I said as I drew my sword. For a moment we went undetected as we huddled together. That peace ended as the first pursuer clambered into the Cleave. I moved toward the man but was knocked aside by a blur of fur, claws and teeth. The creature tore the man apart before he could scream.

A despondent moan escaped everyone's lips. Okuthe struggle to his feet as if a massive weight rested on his shoulders. He stood beside me, his axe clutched in his hands.

"Tell me what to do, rafiki," he said. Fear was plain in his eyes.

"Be still," I said. "That's all we can do."

Two more interlopers came over the Rim, or should I say were pushed over the Rim. The creatures pounced on them just as quick as the first, splattering us with blood bone bits and entrails. The others cried out; Okuthe wiped blood from his face then managed a grin.

"It seems my luck has failed again," he said.

This time the beasts didn't fade into the mist. They lingered before us, their serpent-like snouts bloodied. Okuthe raised his axe.

"No," I said.

I stood in front of him. The creatures hissed then came closer.

"Everyone walk with me," I said. "We'll claim what we came for then leave."

"Leave to what," Cheelo said.

The listless look on his face did nothing to encourage the others.

"One challenge at a time," I said. "If you wish to live stay close."

I crept down the steep slope deeper into the Cleave. Everyone heeded my words except Okuthe. He lingered on the edge, axe in hand, his eyes locked on the trailing serpent dogs. I took my attention from him then focused on my steps. Kipande is not rare to find in the Cleave, but neither is it obvious. When I'm lucky I only have to take a few steps in its depths to find the nefarious metal. But that night the Cleave decided to be stingy with its bounty. I scanned the ground relentlessly but no stone turned up. The air grew bitter cold, a sharp wind from the Cleave Sea gutting my garments like a fisher's knife. We near the sea; we had reached the bottom of the abyss. The serpent dogs became more aggressive, darting in the group and snipping at legs and hands. Okuthe held them back as best he could. The others refused to defend themselves, so paralyzed with fear they were.

Then I saw it, a faint blue glow just under the water's surface. I wadded knee deep into the cold viscous liquid, my teeth chattering. I was reaching for the precious rock when the water exploded before me. I raised my sword to the guard position in reflex, blocking something hard that hit my sword with such force I flew out of the water then onto my back on the rocky shore.

I scrambled to my feet then into a stance before the second attack. The thing before me was as much a creature of the lake as it was of the land. Its skin was ashen like a fish's belly consisting of fine scales that shimmered in the moon glow. Its face bore no nose, only two large eyes protruding from its round head. Its mouth was a slit pregnant with numerous small jagged teeth. In its hands was a curved sword; it held a rough shield resembling the shell of the huge swimming turtles which inhabited the shallows of the Matamba Sea.

It emitted a shrill cry then attacked, possessing more fury than skill. One again I was blessed by my habits, for its sword shattered against my blade the third time they clashed. I took advantage of my fleeting future, attacking the beast man as it hid behind its shield. My blade eroded the crude guard. The creature threw the bone shield from its arm then jumped at me, a desperate tactic that almost succeeded. I lifted my sword as I fell back, plunging it into its chest. Its death cry stabbed my ears before it fell limp, dragging me down with it. As I extracted my sword the serpent canines howled. They surrounded the dead beast man, licking his wound and his face as if trying to revive it. I waded into the water while they were distracted. I plunged both hands into the frigid liquid then worked the kipande free. It was a huge piece, glowing like a piece of the moon fallen to the earth.

An ominous cry rose from the lake. It was answered by numerous other voices from beyond the fog. I shoved the kipande into my pouch then hurried to the others.

"Run!" I shouted.

We scrambled up the slope as fast as our legs would carry us, knowing the danger awaiting us beyond the Rim. It was a fate we were familiar with; we all rather take our chances with real men than battle the unknown creatures coming our way. Okuthe and I were the first over the Rim. We were halfway down the slope before the interlopers realized we were those they sought, not their disgruntled companions. The few before us fell victim to axe and sword; those behind us met far worse. The beast men tried to breach the Cleave, exacting their revenge on the interlopers. Soon those that meant to kill us ran with us, each determined to escape the terrible onslaught.

Okuthe and I ran alone, my chest pounding as I panted for air. I dare not stop; when I did it was from sheer exhaustion. Okuthe fell beside me, coughing uncontrollably. Anyone pursuing us could have killed us like trapped vermin yet no one appeared. We lay still until the sun broke free of the eastern peaks, scattering the cold and mist with its warm rays.

I sat up then clutched my stomach. I was hungrier than I'd

ever been in months. Okuthe lay on his side, his body rising and falling in synch with his shallow breathing. I was almost upon him when I noticed the arrows protruding from his back. I worked my way around his bleeding body to face him.

"It seems my bad streak continues," he said.

"Not today," I said.

I went behind him the gripped one of the arrows.

"This will hurt," I said.

I twisted the arrow and Okuthe moaned. I extracted all three arrows with as little damage as possible.

"Death may be a better choice," he said, his voice weak.

"Be quiet," I said.

I took the kipande from my pouch then placed it against a nearby rock. I struck it with my dagger hilt twice, the second blow splitting the kipande in half. I wrapped one piece in cloth then tied it to Okuthe's wound with my waist belt.

"That feels...strange," Okuthe said.

It will heal you," I replied.

Okuthe attempted to stand. He collapsed.

"We can't stay. The others are coming."

"You can't go anywhere until the kipande does its work," I said.

Okuthe reached back to touch the rock. He jerked it back when he almost touched it.

"It's hot, yet it does not burn my wound," he said.

"Leave it be," I said.

I half dragged, half carried Okuthe from the road. I set up camp in the dense thicket where we lived as Okuthe healed. As much as I was familiar with kipande I was still fascinated by its powers. That fascination was dampened by the fact that its miracle comes with a price. What price Okuthe would pay would not be known until he healed.

As soon as my friend was healthy we set out for Mali. We had to complete the task even if Cheelo and the others were dead. The Ras would be expecting our return. Okuthe and I were mostly silent during our journey. We bought horses at the first village we reached, sorry plow stock but riding was better than walking. As we left the village Okuthe looked at me with concern.

"You tainted me," he said.

"I saved your life," I replied. "I couldn't let you die. You are one of the few people I like. Besides, I've been tainted all my life. It's not so bad."

Okuthe laughed. "My luck continues. Maybe I should get married again. I could taint my wife and we'd have tainted children!

"Better find a gambling house with such luck," I said.

Okuthe's smile faded.

"Someone is coming," he said.

"What?" I said.

"Don't ask me how I know, but someone is coming," he said again.

Minutes later ten of the Ras's warriors crested the horizon before us. So there was his change, I thought. The kipande had given Okuthe the gift of foresight. At least it seemed a gift for now.

I recognized the woman who took me to Cheelo's camp among the warriors. They encircled us, their lances lowered to attack.

"Where are the others?" the woman asked.

"Dead, most likely," I replied.

The woman's eyes narrowed. "You are not certain?"

"When one is set upon by denizens of the Cleave, one's last concern is who is still alive. Your thoughts become very selfish."

She studied me for a moment before speaking again.

"Do you have what you were sent to retrieve?" she asked.

I nodded.

"Show it to me," she said.

"I'll show it to the most high."

She frowned, contempt full on her face.

"So be it."

She reined her horse then rode to join the other guards.

"Come with us."

Okuthe and I followed.

"How did I know they were coming?" he asked.

You have been healed by kipande, a piece of the Creator's Ax," I said. "It changes you."

Okuthe rubbed his chin. "This might be very useful."

"It might," I said.

"So what is your gift?" he said.

"I can hold the stone," I said.

"That is blessing enough," Okuthe said.

"Not to one born to it," I replied.

It took two weeks to reach Adissea. Our escort kept close during the day but kept their distance at night. I was used to such treatment but it bothered Okuthe. He was naturally gregarious and to be near so many without conversation was torture to him. So he sang. He always had a good voice, but at that time his voice was fuller and richer than I remembered. Another blessing from the kipande, no doubt. By the time we reached the city our escort sat closer during the night, enjoying Okuthe's vast repertoire of songs. They sang along when he happened to sing a tune familiar to them. I kept quiet; I was never one to carry a tune. I also made it about never to befriend those who might kill me.

We entered Adissea on a bright morning, the clearing sky a signal of the approaching dry season. The escort took us directly to the Ras's palace, the rampart guards scrutinizing us as we rode through the massive gates and the towering arc. Armor clad warriors met us in the courtyard then took our horses. The warriors proceeded to disarm us. Okuthe gave up his axe as he smiled. I held on to my sword.

"Give it to me," the warrior said. "No one sees the Ras with weapons."

"This sword is special to me," I said. "It stays with me."

The other warriors came closer, their weapons ready to strike.

"Give me the sword," the warrior said.

"No," I replied.

"Give it to me, then."

The leader of our escort stepped toward us.

"Stay out of this, Alemash," the warrior said.

"You're being stupid, Mehari. The Ras sent for him."

Alemash looked at me. "Give me the sword so we can move on."

I eased the sword from the scabbard then handed it her. She gave it to Mehari.

"See no harm comes to it," she said.

"I will," Mehari replied. The warriors cleared the way for us to proceed. I would never see that sword again, I thought.

We walked across the courtyard then into the palace atrium. There we waited for what seemed like hours. Finally a figure appeared at the opposite end.

As the figure approached details emerged. It was a woman, her bald head and cranial tattoos marking her a healer. She was tall, at least a head taller then Okuthe. She was most likely a Nuba healer, a prized practitioner of herbal and spiritual arts. If so, she was very expensive. The Ras was sparing no expense saving his child. Her robes swished against her voluptuous body as she approached. She halted before me then gave Okuthe a sideways glance.

"Do you have it?" she asked.

I reached for the pouch but she shook her head.

"Not here. Follow me."

We crossed the atrium into the main palace, far beyond the palace guards. To allow us beyond the Ras's protection meant his child was sick beyond protocol. I observed the healer stride before us then smiled. This woman was much more than a healer. She was a killer as well. Like recognizes like.

We entered the Ras's daughter bed chamber. The Ras and his wife sat close to the girl; they looked at us hopefully as we entered. The Ras was an unimpressive man. Dress him in cotton work pants and tunic and he would be undistinguishable from the thousands of farmers that tilled his soil. But his wife was another matter. A striking beauty with onyx skin and dimpled cheeks, the sorrow marring her face made me wish to grieve beside her if only to share her emotions. Their daughter was a beauty like her mother, her brown skin closer to her father's.

I leaned close to the healer.

"What is her sickness?"

"She wastes away," the healer said.

The brief description and the look in the healer's eyes told me this was no illness. The girl had been poisoned.

"What do you suggest, tainted one," the mother said.

"Yes, what is your remedy," the Ras said. The look in his eyes conveyed he expected a cure.

I took the bag of vipande from my hip. I extracted a small portion, an amount I knew from experience would counteract any poison.

"With your permission, I will give her a dose. After this first dose she can take the kipande on her own. No one else much touch it. It will be attuned to her."

"Will she become tainted?" the Ras asked.

"No," I replied. "As long as she has kipande in her system it will not harm her. When she is healed summon me. I will remove the remainder from your presence."

The Ras nodded and I took his place near the bed. His daughter looked at me with desperate eyes.

"Have you come to save me?" she asked.

I smiled. "Yes. Now open your mouth. The first one will be bitter."

She did as I said. I placed the first piece of kipande on her tongue and she immediately closed her mouth and shuddered.

"I told you it would be bitter," I said.

She opened her eyes. They were brighter.

"I'm ready," she said.

I gave her the other portions. As soon as she took the final piece the healer rushed us from the room, the Ras following.

"I am in your debt," he said. "But I feel you have not shared all with me."

I looked at the healer and she nodded.

"Ras, your daughter was not ill. She was poisoned."

The Ras glared at the healer.

"Why did you not tell me of this?"

"Would you have believed me?"

The Ras nodded. "Probably not," he said. "I have my suspicions about who is responsible but that is of no concern of yours."

The Ras looked upon me again then smiled.

"What of you, tainted one? You have saved my daughter. Ask what you wish and it is yours."

"I am honored, Ras," I said. "There is nothing I wish. I have my life, a good and loving wife and fertile land along a gentle river. But I do have two requests."

"As I said, ask and it is yours."

"Whatever you were prepared to bestow to me, please give to my friend Okuthe. His luck has been rather bad lately."

The Ras looked upon Okuthe then nodded. Okuthe's smile was like a rising sun.

"What do you wish?" the Ras asked.

"As many silvers I can carry, then five more," Okuthe replied.

The Ras smiled. "Now this is a man I understand. It is yours."

"And what else do you wish," he asked me.

"My sword," I said. "It's a fine blade and has saved my life many times. However it was taken from me as we entered the palace by your guards. I fear the sword that will be returned to me will not be the one I entered with."

The Ras laughed. "I offer the man unlimited treasures and all he desires is his old sword. So be it, tainted one. I guarantee your sword will be returned to you."

Okuthe and I bowed. It was time for us to depart.

"One more thing," the Ras said. "What is your name?"

"Mayani," I said.

"Mayani," he repeated. "I will remember it. I will remember you."

I forced a smile to my face. Having a ruler remember you is a double-edge sword.

The healer escorted us back to the palace entrance. The palace guards and our escorts met us.

"Bring them their items," the healer said. "All of them."

The healer's eyes lingered on the escort. She frowned then stomped away.

"My name is Hattabari. Thank you both for your help," the healer said. "I may seek your assistance again, Mayani."

"I can't guarantee you'll find me," I said. "I'm not one who wishes to be involved in the intrigues of the Stool."

"You save the Ras's daughter and exposed the foul play that instigated it. You are involved whether you wish it or not," the healer said. "Be diligent, my new friend."

"I will," I said.

The escort returned with our gear, our weapons and Okuthe's reward. The silvers came in leather satchels with straps to fasten on his back. It was as Okuthe asked; all the silvers he could carry, plus five more. His legs shook under the weight.

The guard carrying my sword glared at me as he approached. I winced as he through it at my feet then spat.

"We'll meet again, Tainted one," she said. "Make sure that sword is in your hand when we do."

"Pray that never happens," I said.

I picked up my sword then Okuthe grabbed my arm and dragged me from the palace. Two servants waited with our horses; they'd been well groomed and fed. Okuthe secured his silver bags to his horse then gave me a generous hug.

"Here is where we part ways, rafiki," he said. "This has been our best adventure yet."

"At least for you," I said.

Okuthe laughed. "Especially for me. Be safe, Mayani. And as the healer said, be diligent."

"I will Okuthe," I said.

I watched Okuthe ride away before mounting my horse and riding in the opposite direction. My commitment to the Ras was done. It was time to go home to my wife and my land.

My wife was safe with her sister but my land was another matter. I decided to ride to our abandoned farm to make sure no one else had claimed it. Three days of hard riding and my land was before me. My joy was short-lived. A familiar horse was tethered to my hitching post. I dismounted then drew my sword.

"Cheelo!" I shouted.

The door to my farmhouse creaked open and Cheelo emerged. He seemed in good health with the exception of a jagged scar that ran the length of his face.

"Mayani," he said. "I knew you would come here. I thought you would have your woman with you. As a matter of fact I was hoping you would. I so much wanted her to see you die."

I didn't answer. I took a fighting stance instead. Cheelo sauntered toward me.

"I can't blame you for leaving. I would have done the same. You assumed we were all dead. In fact the only way I survived was to play dead. It wasn't hard, actually. This scar was bleeding so much I thought I was going to die. Can you imagine feeling your life slipping from you as you listen to your cohorts being torn apart by monsters?"

I didn't reply.

"After it was over, after I knew I would live I made my way here. Your neighbors were curious but I convinced him I was your friend. They were very generous."

The captain finally unsheathed his sword.

"I'm not angry, Mayani," he said. "Just give me half of what you were paid by the Ras then I'll be on my way."

"I was paid nothing," I said. "All I asked for was the return of my sword."

Cheelo shook his head. "That won't do, Mayani. That just won't do."

Despite my preparation Cheelo almost ran me through. I barely deflected his thrust then winced as his blade cut my shoulder. A wild swing caught him off guard and he stumbled away with a cut on his chin. I attacked immediately, hoping to keep him unbalanced but his swordplay was too skillful. I was on the defensive again, barely blocking his fast slashes and thrusts.

I thought I saw an opening. The moment I raised my sword to strike I realized my mistake. Cheelo's blade burned as it entered my stomach. But Cheelo erred as well. He assumed I would drop my sword when he stabbed me. Instead I grabbed his sword hand then brought down my sword. The blade cut through his neck and his collarbone. We both fell to the ground. Cheelo lay dead. I was dying.

I grimaced as I pulled his sword free of my gut. For a moment I lay stunned, staring into Cheelo's blank face as my energy ebbed. But then something strange happened. I hear Ursala's voice as if she knelt beside me and whispered in my ear.

"Don't you die, Mayani! You promised you'd come back to me!"

Her words gave me energy. I fumbled about my belt with numb hands until I grasped my pouch. I pulled it free then undid the straps as I lay on my back. I opened the pouch then poured my remaining kipande on my wound. I screamed as the mineral burned inside me, following the swords jagged path. It was worse than being stabbed. I lingered on the edge of consciousness before the pain finally subsided. I felt my body healing, muscles and bones mending. But other things changed as well.

When I finally sat up my neighbors ran across the fallow fields shouting my name. Jorj was the first to reach me. He took an odd look on his face as he squatted beside me.

"Mayani? Is it you?"

Something was amiss.

"Yes," I said. "Have I been gone so long that you don't recognize me?"

No... No," he said. "It just that you look younger. Much younger."

The other neighbors gathered, barely noticing Cheelo's body. They asked no questions but their faces said what they would not. I had changed.

They helped me bury Cheelo's body then brought food and fresh sheets for my bed. I told them of my adventures and they smiled.

"It's said you have been tainted," Jorj said. "But you are our friend and you have always done good by us."

Everyone nodded in agreement.

"But what about Ursala?" Ghiday asked. "How will she feel having a husband young enough to be her son?"

"Grateful!" Abadeet said." I wish I had a young man in my bed. My nights would be less restful. Some of my days, too!"

We all laughed yet I worried. How would Ursala feel?

I set out the next morning healed, refreshed and laden with provisions. As I waved goodbye to my friends I focused on what lay ahead. Ursala waited for a man who would not be the same. Hattabari warned me to be diligent. The Ras's guard threatened we'd meet again. I shook my head, clearing my thoughts. A journey is made of many steps; my only concern should be for the ones I took at that moment. I nudged my horse and we trotted toward my future and whatever it held for me. May Eda continue to clear my path.

Bes

By Milton Davis

Bes broke the surface of the lake gasping for breath. He'd stayed below longer than normal, which was far longer than most. He was a good diver, one of the best. The overseers rewarded him for his skills, giving him extra meat with his meals and sometimes allowing time with the women. Though the meat was appreciated, the time among the women was not. It always reminded him of how repulsive they though he was, how even his status did not overshadow the deformities his labor had wrought. He shook his head to clear the images and the water from his mat of hair then stroked toward the shore and the awaiting collectors. The collectors, covered in their suits of woven rock fiber stepped away as he emerged from the cold water. He reached back then swung the full basket off his back, dropping it before his webbed feet. Unlike his other deliveries the basket held one large piece of kipande, the stone-like substance emitting a faint blue glow.

"By the Creator!" one of the overseers exclaimed through her mesh mask. "It's huge!"

Bes flashed his ragged smile. "More meat?"

The overseer nodded. "Much more."

Bes nodded. He turned to return to the water when he felt a clothed hand on his shoulder.

"Wait," the overseer said. "A sonchai wishes to see you."

Bes cringed. It had been a long time since a sonchai summoned him but the memory still lingered. In the beginning he saw sonchai almost every day. They beat him and constantly cursed him for his small loads of vipande and his short time underwater. But that was before the vipande changed him. Few divers lived long enough to experience the change, but those that did became valuable. Eventually even that wasn't enough. At some point they all disappeared, claimed by the water, the beasts, or the sonchai.

The collector handed him a suit. "Put this on then follow me."

Bes forced himself into the suit, knowing better not to complain of the ill fit. He followed the collector from the rocky shore up the steep slope to the observation platform. The sonchai waited, a tall broad shouldered man covered in a loose white robe, his black curled hair cut close to his head. Unlike the collector he wore no protection.

The sonchai studied him before speaking.

"Do you have any items you own?" he asked.

Bes shook his head.

"Good. You are not a diver anymore. You serve me."

The sonchai turned and walked away. Bes stood still, trying to understand what was happening. The collector shoved him.

"Go on! You belong to him now. Go!"

Bes stumbled on, following the sonchai. He glanced back in time to catch the collector disappear below the horizon then hurried after the sonchai.

The sonchai walked up to a basket like object with a round orb floating overhead. He crept up to the basket then peered inside. A large ceramic gourd filled the center, its sides lined with vipande. Blue light streamed from the gourd and into the large orb. Bes had heard much of the power of the stones he brought to the surface but he'd never actually see it used.

The sonchai climbed inside the basket. He looked at Bes then waved him forward.

"Untie the rope then get inside," he commanded.

Bes did as he was told then clambered inside, his long limbs making such a task more cumbersome than it should have been.

The sonchai waved his hand over the gourd, his lips moving. As he stepped away the blue glow became intense light, so bright Bes had to look away. To his shock the basket and the orb lifted from the ground. He threw out his arms, grasping the basket rim in terror. The sonchai smirked.

"You will become used to this," he said. "For you will feed the joka's belly."

Despair gripped Bes and he curled into a ball. So he was to be fed to a joka.

"Please, master," he said. "Do not feed me to the joka! I am a good worker. I can dive deeper than anyone. I am also very strong."

The sonchai looked puzzled then laughed.

"You misunderstand me, but I can see why. You have no idea what you are to do. You are a good worker, Bes. After transformation you will be perfect."

The sonchai's words did nothing to soothe Bes's fear. Miles and miles of jagged landscape passed under them as they ascended into the mountainous land surrounding the cold lake. The air weakened as such a height and Bes found it difficult to breathe. Just when he thought he would suffocate the craft descended. It landed with a jolt, bouncing Bes off the floor boards.

"Get out," the sonchai said.

Bes unraveled then stood. He peeked over the basket's edge to spy his new surroundings. At first he thought he was in the midst of barren peaks, but as he strained his eyes he realized the narrow grey columns were buildings, their surfaces speckled with windows, their pinnacles spouting black smoke.

He clambered out of the basket then cowered before the sonchai.

"What will you have me do?" he said.

"You are unfit as you are now," the sonchai answered. "Follow me."

The sonchai strode toward the stone and Bes followed. Others appeared as they drew near, people of various shapes and sizes, all with a look of despair and fatigue on their faces. Bes was not unused to such expressions, but the depth of the emotions in the others' faces chilled him more than the frigid air pressing against his bare flesh. The sonchai led him into a cluster of squat buildings. These streets teemed with others resembling his new master, each of them looking at him with grim, calculating eyes. He followed the sonchai into a building with tall towers. There were many sonchai inside; they all looked at Bes.

One of the sonchai, a woman with a hard face and piercing green eyes came to him.

"Another candidate for transformation?" she asked.

The sonchai nodded.

"Your timing is perfect. The chamber is empty. I'll gather the others."

The woman strode away. The sonchai grabbed Bes's arm, pulling him forward. He led him across the atrium then down a spiraling staircase. At the bottom of the staircase was a massive door flanked by two bare-chested guards holding wide blade swords. One of them stared at Bes and he turned away.

"What are you waiting for?" the sonchai said. "Open the door!"

The guards sheathed their swords then opened the door. They strained to push the door in, their massive muscles rippling with effort. A blue glow escaped from the chamber as the door opened wider.

"Take him inside then chain him," the Sonchai said.

Bes could be silent no more.

"Master, do not kill me!" he begged. "I have been a good worker."

The sonchai laughed. "Do you think I would have brought you this far to kill you? I could have done that at that cesspool where I found you. Consider yourself favored, Bes. Now go inside."

Bes let the guards take him into the chamber. As soon as he stepped across the threshold he was awed by the source of the glow. The chamber was made of vipande. Never had he seen so much. The room was bare save for the chains in the center. The room was not constructed of kipande stones for there were no mortar seams or signs of separation. It was apparently carved from a solid piece of the mineral, a feat that probably took hundreds of years and thousands of lives.

Bes was still awestruck as the guards shackled him. As they hurried from the room he gazed about, seeing a balcony circling the chamber. A door opened and sonchai filed in until they stood shoulder to shoulder. The sonchai who led him stepped forward, his staff raised.

"May the Creator guide our hands and our hearts," he said. "What we do, we do in his name. What we do, we do to fulfill his will."

The others raised their staffs in unison. They joined the master sonchai's chant, their voices melodic and strong. The muted glow of the room increased with each repetition, the light become so bright Bes shielded his eyes from the glare.

Bes jolted as tendrils of pain pierced his body. He fell to his knees then screamed. The sonchai lied to him. They were killing him, probably experiencing some sort of pleasure from his torture. Rumors of such things traveled among the workers and now in his last moments of life Bes knew them to be true.

His thoughts melted into a fire of pain. He felt he was being pulled apart as the glow became a burning glare. The pain diminished with a pulsing rhythm. Feeling and hearing returned to him as the sonchai' chants overtook his moans. He felt the coldness of the vipande floor and his trembling body. Warm hands lifted him to his knees; he sat still as a thick metal collar was fitted around his neck then bolted into place. The guards grunted as they lifted him to his feet then prodded him from the chamber.

When his eyes finally cleared he looked down upon the sonchai. The man walked around him, looking him up and down as he nodded. He ended his inspection standing before him.

"Good," he said.

The woman came to stand beside him.

"He's our best yet," she said.

"The divers were right," the sonchai said. "He's very

malleable. The vipande favors him."

He looked to the guards.

"Take him to the blacksmith," he ordered.

There was fear in the guards' eyes as they tugged on the thick chain attached to his collar. Bes didn't protest; he was happy to be alive. He strained to lift his legs, following the guards out of the chamber. He glanced at the sonchai. The man smiled, nodded his approval as he entered the atrium. He regained his strength with each step. As they left the city and approached the looming mountains he was striding. Sunlight barely penetrated the thick clouds, casting a muted light into the dark valley. The road led to a massive building resembling the mountains surrounding it. A small river flowed through it and a plume of smoke rose from the peak like a simmering volcano. The road plunged into the valley, forcing Bes and the guards to walk gingerly. Once they reached the valley floor the guards stopped.

"We must rest and eat," one of the guards said. "Are you hungry?"

"I hope not," the other guard said. "We don't have enough food for him. He's too damn big."

"I am not hungry," Bes said.

He waited patiently as the guards secured his chain around a nearby tree then built a fire. Bes inspected his new form as the men brewed a thick road stew. His arms and legs were much larger than before, his skin rippling as he flexed his hands and feet. His skin had darkened from deep umber to black. Bes look closer; he seemed to emit a faint blue glow resembling kipande. He wondered what his face looked like. Was it better, the same, or worse? The guards didn't seem to notice and the sonchai never cared. It didn't matter; he knew that once he entered the smoking building he would probably never leave.

The guards finished their meal then unchained him from the tree. The size of the building made it appear closer than it actually was. They lost what little sunlight the grey sky shared after a few hours but continued to walk through the bitter cold darkness, guided by the pulsing glow of their destination. The building became a living thing as a sound resembling a breathing beast reached their ears. Two hours later they stood before it. There was no sign of an entrance; the rhythmic sounds emitting from it almost deafening. The guards looked at each other, obviously puzzled about what to do next.

"We should leave him here," one of them said.

"No!" the other replied. "If he runs away it will be our heads."

Bes walked up to the building. He ran his hands across the surface, amazed by its smoothness. Touching the structure was like touching a living thing.

A line of light appeared on the surface and Bes stepped back. A door appeared, releasing heat and light from the building. A man stepped before him, a huge brute almost as tall as Bes and just as broad. A leather apron covered his body from chest to his ankles; his scarred face clean shaven.

"What is this?" the man said. His deep voice vibrated inside Bes's gut.

The guards bowed immediately.

"The sonchai sends you assistance," one of them said.

The man scrutinized Bes. He balled his massive hands into fist and began striking him, hitting his shoulders, arms, midsection and legs. Though Bes barely felt the blows, he could imagine that such punishment would crush a normal man. A slight smile came to the man's face after his brutal inspection.

"Zenaga has done well," he said. "Maybe too well. We will see."

His smile fled as he turned his attentions to the guards.

"You may go," he said.

The guards stepped closer. "It is dark and the cold bites like a wolf. We were hoping we could stay the night."

"No," the man said. He took Bes's chain in his hand then led him inside the building.

"I am Mhunzi," he said. "You will do as I say."

Bes nodded. "What do we do?"

Mhunzi turned to stare at Bes. "We make jokas."

Bes followed Mhunzi to the heart of the building, a massive furnace that towered to the high ceiling. The heat increased as they neared; Bes's new body became wet with sweat. Bes stopped as the heat became unbearable.

"I cannot," he said. "It's too hot."

Mhunzi smiled. "You can't now. By the time we're done you will be. The vipande in you will see to that."

Mhunzi dropped Bes's chain then continued toward the furnace. His destination was a table beside the furnace. He gathered a few items into his arms then returned to Bes.

"You will wear this when you work for now."

Mhunzi gave him an apron similar to what he wore and a pair of goggles.

"Come, I will show you the frames."

Bes followed Mhunzi into a chamber he didn't notice earlier. Rows of skeleton-like structures stretched the length of the room.

"The sonchai think I work too slowly," Mhunzi said. "They say the Creator is impatient for them to complete his work which is why they sent you. I tried to tell them that you cannot hurry perfection but they refuse to listen."

Bes stepped away from Mhunzi. To talk foul of the sonchai was to invite their wrath. He'd never done so, but he's seen what happened to those who did. Mhunzi noticed and grabbed his chain. He pulled Bes toward him.

"Do not be afraid of them," he said. "What I teach you will make you valuable beyond measure, even to the sonchai. I will share with you secrets passed down to me from my father, which were passed to him from his father, which were passed down to him from his father. We have our own nyama."

Mhunzi took him closer.

"We will bring them to life, Bes," he said. "We will build their hearts, their skin, their eyes and their wings. The joka will soar again."

"You can do such a thing?" Bes asked.

"Yes I can," Mhunzi said. "And you will too. It will take

time to teach you. You must pay attention and work hard. When you earn my approval I will remove your chain. Can you do this, Bes?"

The thought of freedom sent a surge of energy through Bes. "Yes I can," he said.

Mhunzi studied him for a moment before responding.

"We will see."

And so Bes became Mhunzi's apprentice. In the beginning he was muscle only, carrying great swaths of metal to and from the furnace while Mhunzi shaped them with his hammers. Once the metal was formed Bes held the massive sheets in place as Mhunzi fastened them to the frames. Soon the blacksmith taught Bes how to hammer the metal, his massive strength shortening the task. They worked day and night; Mhunzi needing little sleep, Bes needing none. He craved no food as well, his body feeding off the vipande fused into his being. Thirteen moons after arriving at the foundry the joka were complete. Bes looked at them with pride; never before had he built anything with his hands.

"We are finished," Mhunzi said. His voice carried the sound of melancholy.

"The sonchai will be pleased," Bes said. "They would share more food with me, if I needed it. Maybe they will give my portion to you."

"I want nothing from them," he said.

"What do we do now?" Bes asked.

"We summon the sonchai," Mhunzi said. "And they will bring the joka to life."

Bes looked puzzled. "Bring them to life? But they are metal, like wagons."

Mhunzi looked at Bes, his face bemused.

"You have no idea what we have created," he said.

Bes shook his head.

"You will soon," Mhunzi said.

The sonchai arrived a week later. They came in a procession of wagons and slaves, snaking from the mountains to the open plains. Bes watched them as they arrived, surprised at how he felt. There was no fear in him, only curiosity. Mhunzi taught him not to dread them, and the kipande within him gave him further confidence.

"Let us meet our employers," Mhunzi said.

They opened the massive doors then ambled to the sonchai. Bes remembered each one as he nodded slightly at their approach. Their reaction to him was much different than before. Most were clearly disturbed by his presence, a few actually looked apprehensive. The sonchai whom he once called master displayed no emotion as he inspected Bes. He nodded his head.

Mhunzi stood before the sonchai. The sonchai folded his arms behind his back then grinned.

"Mhunzi," he said.

"Kiros," Mhunzi said.

Bes's eyebrows rose. He'd never heard a sonchai's name before.

"Our joka are ready?" Kiros asked.

"Yes," Mhunzi replied.

"The slave was helpful I see," Kiros said.

"Bes was most helpful," Mhunzi replied, emphasizing Bes's name.

Kiro smirked. "So he was. Show us."

Bes and Mhunzi led the entourage through the foundry then into the chamber. There was a drone of approval as the sonchai saw the joka. They immediately swarmed the creations, inspecting them with the assistance of their servants.

"You've done well, Mhunzi," Kiros said. "Can they fly?"

"I have reserved that honor for the sonchai," Mhunzi replied.

"Excellent." Kiros looked at Bes.

"Come with me...Bes," he said.

Bes smiled as he followed Kiros. His work with Mhunzi had earned him some respect. He dared to wonder if all went well it would earn him his freedom. Then he could remain with Mhunzi and build more wonderful machines.

"Open the door," Kiros commanded.

Bes worked his bulk around the others then opened the door to the joka. Kiros and two sonchai entered followed by servants carrying heavy loads. Bes knew what it was as soon as it passed; vipande. They placed the bundles close to the metal heart which sat just behind the wings. Two thick metal bars attached the wings to gears within it; two smaller bars attached the heart to wheels that supported the joka. The servants evacuated the joka as Kiros and the sonchai settled into the head.

"Bes!" Kiros called out. "Fill the heart!"

Bes opened the first bundle. The enchanted stone didn't affect him like it did in the past. Instead it felt warm and familiar in his hands. He opened the small hatch to the heart, filled the chamber then closed it.

"Secure the hatch," Kiros shouted.

Bes went to the hatch. Mhunzi stood outside the door, a worried look on his face.

"What are they doing?" Bes said.

"I don't know," Mhunzi said. "I was not given instructions beyond building it."

Bes closed the door. No sooner had he done so did Kiros and the sonchai begin to chant, waving their hands over the patterned board before them. Bes dared to go to the head then saw the servants opening the massive doors he'd built to the chamber.

"Get back to your place," Kiros said. "Now."

Bes slunk back to the heart just as joka began to move. He sat as the joka rolled toward the open doors, the wings gently rising and falling.

The sonchai' chanting grew louder as the joka increased in speed, passing through the gates and rolling into the bare field. Bes braced himself against the walls. Instead of rigid wood the walls gave to his touch like flesh. He jerked his hand away.

The joka lifted from the ground. Bes tumbled away from the heart as it rose higher and higher. He crawled to the sonchai's chamber, his large body shaking with fear like a child. There he saw the hills sink below them as the grey skies filled the view. They were flying.

Kiros turned to look at him, his face stern.

"Get back to your place," he said. "The joka needs more vipande."

Bes worked his way back to the heart. As he opened it the joka shook with sound. He piled the vipande inside the closed it quickly.

Bes sat for a few more moments before working his way to the sonchai's chamber again. This time the sonchai ignored him. They flew toward the rim of the Cleave, rising higher and higher until the mountains disappeared below them. The joka angled downward and Bes saw green rolling fields bordered by forests. They were beyond the Cleave, soaring over Ki Khanga. Bes's stomach churned as pain emerged in his head. He sat, holding his head as strange images formed in his mind, images of a small city at the foothills of the Cleave. He saw short, sturdy men working the rock-filled soil with beasts and plows as women and children trailed behind them, planting seeds into the furrows. He saw merchants behind their stalls in a meager marketplace, trading their wares for food and cloth. Then he saw a boy wrapped in heavy cloth playing beside his mother, a boy he recognized as himself.

The scene in his head was shattered by the cry of a horde of grey-armored men pouring from the hills with weapons and ropes. Bes ran with his mother; pain stabbing his head as his mother fell beside him, an arrow protruding from her neck. A gray man lifted him into the air, tossing him into a wagon like a sack of feed. Then he saw himself swimming the cold waters of the Cleave Sea, a nameless slave seeking vipande for his masters.

He struggled to his feet then gazed from the joka. It circled over a large city. Bes's fear trickled away, replaced by anger and hate.

"No," he said. He stood then staggered to the belly of the joka. He opened it, the bright radiation forcing him to look away. He stuck both arms inside, grasping the warm stone the pulling it out. He dropped it at his feet.

"What are you doing?"

Bes stared into Kiros's angry face. The sonchai strode toward Bes, his face twisted in anger.

"Stopping you," Bes replied.

The sonchai gestured with his hand. Bes flinched as pain gripped his body, the sensation subsided quickly. He glared at Kiros then strode toward him. Kiros eyes went wide with fear. He gestured again, but his time Bes barely noticed the pain.

"Brothers!" Kiros shouted. "Help me!"

Kiros tried to raise his hand again but Bes caught his arms at the wrists. He twisted his hands outward and Kiros's arms snapped like twigs. The man cried out as Bes lifted him off his feet then slammed him again and again against the joka walls until he when limp. When Bes finally looked up the other sonchai glared at him.

"You control this thing," he said. "Turn it around."

"You do not control us, slave!" one of the sonchai shouted. "We answer only to the Master!"

"I will send you to him as I did this one if you do not turn this thing about!" Bes said. "No one else will suffer as I have. No one!"

The sonchai raised their arms in unison. Bes withstood Kiros's attack but he suspected he could not survive a unified attack. He leapt forward, surprised by his own speed. He punched, kicked and bit the sonchai until they lay in a pile before him moaning from their wounds. He grabbed the least injured of them then dragged him into the joka's head.

"Turn us around," he ordered.

The sonchai waved his hand over the lighted board. The joka veered away. Bes hovered over the sonchai as he flew the joka over the Rim, back into the Cleave. As they penetrated the misty clouds just beyond the Rim the joka lost altitude.

"It's weak," the sonchai said. "It needs more vipande, the vipande you took out its belly."

"Keep flying," Bes said.

"But we will crash!" the sonchai said.

Bes said nothing.

A snarl came to the sonchai's face.

"You will die, too!"

Bes did not answer.

The joka fell lower and lower. Bes looked out through its eyes, seeing what he expected. The Cleave Sea shimmered before them, its cold depths waiting.

"No!" the sonchai shouted. He jumped to his right, grapping a small knob then twisting it. A door appeared; he opened it then jumped out.

Bes grinned. He grabbed the other sonchai one by one then threw them out the door. The last was the body of Kiros. He returned to the joka's eyes, folding his arms as the joka sped toward the Sea.

The impact was stronger than he expected. He burst through the joka's face, the blow stunning him for a moment. He gasped and choked as the cold water entered his mouth and lungs but he did not panic. He knew what would happen next. His body jerked and quaked as it transformed, gills forming at his neck, webbing emerging between his fingers and toes. He swam weakly at first, gaining strength and confidence as his old experiences emerged. Soon he was speeding away, swimming faster and faster away from the wreckage and the sonchai' world.

Bes did not know how long he swam, how many days past. His new body needed no rest; the vipande seemed inexhaustible. At some point he would surface to see where his efforts had taken him, but his priority was to swim as far away from the sonchai's land as possible.

Something hard struck his side. He twisted to see when he was struck again. The blows came in rapid succession, the pain increasing with each blow. He struck out blindly, his fist meeting hard flesh. A large fish-like creature floated away from him, its large blinking eyes filled with emotion. Another creature swam to the stunned one, blocking the wounded one from Bes's view. Still others gathered around him, staring at him with intelligent eyes. He tried to swim through them but they tightened their ring. For a moment they all swam in place, and then they opened a way for him. They were forcing him to swim where they wanted him to go.

Bes obeyed. Soon he swam in shallow water, bottom rocks scraping his knees and arms. He stood then walked onto the rocky shore. He was far away from his former home, the sky still gray yet of a brighter hue. The air felt warm about him as he watched the fish beings swim into the shallows then transform into large, hulking naked men and women. The largest of them, a woman with intense brown eyes approached him first.

"What are you?" she asked.

Bes did not reply. The others surrounded him. A man stood beside the woman, a grimace on his face.

"The sonchai made him," the man said. "We should kill him now."

Bes stepped away, raising his fist.

"We can't," the woman said. "Can't you see it? He's vipande bound."

The woman turned her attention back to Bes.

"Did the sonchai of Zenaga do this to you," she asked.

Bes nodded.

"Do you serve them?" she asked.

Bes shook his head.

"He lies," the man said.

"Be quiet, Moke," the woman said.

The woman touched her palm to her head.

"I am Livanga of the Tyrak," she said. "This is my pod. We are guardians of the Cleave. We make sure that nothing enters... and nothing leaves."

Bes raised his hands higher.

"Do you serve the sonchai?" he asked.

"No," Livanga answered. "Far from it. We serve Eda."

Bes lowered his hands. He knew Eda from his former life. If this beings served her then he had no need to fear.

"Please, come with us," she said. "It is obvious that Eda sent you to us to show us what the sonchai are capable of. Events are moving faster than expected. The time of trial in near."

"Time of trial?" Bes asked.

"We will take you to our islands," she said. "All will be explained.

"This is not wise," Moke said. "He could be lying."

Livanga regarded Bes for a moment then smiled.

"No, I think not. I think he hates the sonchai. Besides, he is vipande bound. We couldn't hurt him if we tried."

Livanga tilted her head sharply and the others returned to the water, transforming as they descended. She shared an easy smile with Bes.

"Please, come with us. You are safe with us. At least for a time."

The woman turned away, wading into the deep water. Bes followed.

Livanga turned to look at him as she transformed.

"I ask you again. What is your name?" she asked.

He looked at the woman and smile.

"Bes."

-End-

You read the book, now play the game!

Ki Khanga: The Sword and Soul Role Playing Game

Available now!